SECRETS OF
HALLSTEAD
HOUSE

SECRETS OF
HALLSTEAD
HOUSE

AMY M. READE

KENSINGTON BOOKS
KENSINGTON PUBLISHING CORP.
www.kensingtonbooks.com

KENSINGTON BOOKS are published by

Kensington Publishing Corp.
119 West 40th Street
New York, NY 10018

All Kensington titles, imprints, and distributed lines are available at special quantity discounts for bulk purchases for sales promotion, premiums, fund-raising, educational, or institutional use.

Special book excerpts or customized printings can also be created to fit specific needs. For details, write or phone the office of the Kensington Special Sales Manager: Kensington Publishing Corp., 119 West 40th Street, New York, NY 10018. Attn. Special Sales Department. Phone: 1-800-221-2647.

Kensington and the K logo Reg. U.S. Pat. & TM Off.

First Electronic Edition: July 2014
eISBN-13: 978-1-60183-299-3
eISBN-10: 1-60183-299-0

First Print Edition: July 2014
ISBN-13: 978-1-60183-300-6
ISBN-10: 1-60183-300-8

Printed in the United States of America

For Papa

CHAPTER 1

My journey was almost over.

It was raining, and I looked out through the drizzle across the blue-gray water of the Saint Lawrence River. Only a few boats were out on such a raw and rainy day. From the bench where I sat on the Cape Cartier public dock, I could see several islands. Each was covered with trees—dark green pine trees and leafy maples, oaks, birches, and weeping willows. In the chilly late September air, the leaves were already tinged with the colors of fall: yellows, reds, oranges, browns. I could glimpse homes on the islands, but I didn't see any people. It was beautiful here—so different from the city I had just left behind.

Even though twenty years have come and gone since that day, I can still remember the calm that settled around me as I waited for my ride to Hallstead House in the middle of the Thousand Islands. My nerves were still ragged, but the river had an immediate and peaceful effect on me. I was only twenty then, but I had been through so much. Though I had been traveling for just a few hours, my journey to this place had begun six long weeks earlier.

As I listened to the raindrops plunk into the river, the sound of the motor from an approaching boat cut into my reverie. It was an older boat of gleaming mahogany with a large white awning covering most of it, protecting the cabin and the pilot from the rain. It puttered up to the dock slowly and in a few moments had pulled alongside, close to where I sat. The pilot moved to the stern and climbed out quickly, securing the boat to the dock with a thick rope. He turned to me with a questioning look and said, "Macy Stoddard?"

"Yes."

He shook my hand curtly. "I'm Pete McHale. I work for Alexandria Hallstead. She sent me here to pick you up. That all the luggage you brought?"

"Yes, that's it."

He shot me a disapproving look and said, "I hope you brought some warm stuff to wear. It starts getting cold up here pretty early in the fall. It's colder here than it is in the big city, you know." He smirked.

Determined to stay positive, I ignored his look of reproach and replied that I had plenty of warm clothes. Once he'd stowed my two large suitcases in the boat under the awning, he helped me on board, where I chose a seat in the front so I could see where we were going and stay dry. I had been in a boat once as a child when a furious storm blew up, and I had hated boats ever since. Still, though I was unhappy and nervous to be riding in one, there was absolutely no other way to get to my island destination. Pete untied the boat and we slowly pulled away from the dock. As he scanned the river and began turning the boat to the north, I glanced at his profile. He looked like he was in his mid-thirties—medium height, with light-brown, windblown hair, and green eyes with creases in the corners that made it look like he squinted a lot. He wore faded jeans and a Windbreaker.

When he had steered the boat out of the small, sheltered bay at Cape Cartier and into the more open channel, he glanced at me and said, "We'll be at Summerplace in about ten minutes."

"Summerplace?"

"That's the name of the house on Hallstead Island."

"Oh. I thought it was called Hallstead House."

"Its official name is Hallstead House. The people who live on the island just call it Summerplace."

We sat in silence for several moments, and finally I asked, "Why is it called Summerplace?"

Pete sighed. Evidently he didn't relish playing the role of tour guide. "It's called Summerplace because it used to be a summer retreat for the Hallstead family. Now Miss Hallstead stays there for as much of the year as she can. In early to mid-October she moves the household over to Pine Island and spends the winter there."

To keep my mind off my abject fear of being on the water, I turned my attention to the islands we were passing. Each one had a home on it, and all of the homes were beautiful. Some looked empty, since their occupants had probably left after the summer ended, but some still had boats tied to docks or housed in quaint boathouses. The homes themselves, most of which were huge and had large, welcoming porches, were surrounded by the ever-present trees. Several had bright awnings over the windows.

In the face of Pete's apparent ambivalence, I had determined not to ask any more questions. But as I sat looking around me I forgot my self-imposed rule. "Are there really a thousand islands in this area?" I blurted out.

"There are actually over eighteen hundred islands in the Thousand Islands," he replied. To my surprise, he seemed to warm to this subject and continued. "In order to be included in the count, an island has to be above water three hundred and sixty-five days a year and support at least two living trees."

I continued to draw him out, asking, "What do you do for Mrs. Hallstead?"

His attitude changed again, becoming colder. "It's *Miss* Hallstead. She never took her husband's name. But to answer your question, I'm one of the handymen. I'm also the boat captain—I maintain and pilot this and one other boat. I don't do a lot of chauffeuring. The people who live on Hallstead Island don't get out much. I just ferry the visitors."

"Who else lives on the island besides Miss Hallstead?"

"Just another handyman and a housekeeper. They're an older married couple. Leland and Valentina Byrd. They have quarters next to the main residence.

"How did you get the job as Miss Hallstead's private nurse?" Pete asked.

"My agency got a request for a private nurse for an elderly woman who had broken a hip. They knew I was looking for a change, so they offered it to me."

"Oh. Aren't you a little young for a job like that?"

"I'm almost twenty-one," I said a little indignantly. "I've been working for over a year at a hospital."

"Oh. I beg your pardon."

I turned to observe my new surroundings. Each island that we passed seemed to have its own unique personality. Some seemed dominated by magnificent homes; others were more notable for their stunning natural beauty. I prattled on with my usual tact. "Who can afford to live in these places?"

"A lot of these islands used to be owned by big businessmen. Nowadays they're mostly owned by regular people, but some of the bigger ones are still owned by the families of the original owners."

"How long have the Hallsteads been coming here?"

"Three generations now. The Hallsteads are an old oil family. They own HSH Oil Company—the 'HSH' stands for Henry S. Hallstead, the company founder and Miss Hallstead's grandfather. He bought the island originally."

"Do the Hallsteads still run the oil company?" It was none of my business and I regretted the question immediately. Pete shot me a look confirming my thoughts, but he answered my question nonetheless.

"Yes, they do. They run the day-to-day operations."

"How do you know all this?"

"I've been around for quite a while," he said dryly.

"Does Miss Hallstead get many visitors?"

Pete smirked. "Hardly. The only two people who ever stay at the house with her are her adviser and her nephew. They each have rooms in the house."

"Do you live on the island?"

"You ask a lot of questions."

"I'm just curious." *And nervous.*

"I can see that. I usually stay on the island. I have rooms over the boathouse. My family lives on Heather Island, which is not too far from Hallstead Island. I stay there every so often. Hallstead Island can get a little gloomy."

"Gloomy? What's gloomy about it?"

Pete didn't answer. He steered the boat slightly to the right and pointed to an island looming up ahead. "That's Hallstead Island. The boathouse is just around the other side, right off the channel. I'll drive you around back so you can see the island before we dock."

As the boat slowly approached, I got my first glimpse of the place that would be my new home. It was stunning. Where the island rose out of the river, a stone wall was visible above the surface of the water. The wall was about five feet high and appeared to stretch around the entire island. It had been built of gray stones of varying thickness, stacked on top of one another, and it had the effect of making the island look almost fortress-like. On the wall were long striations of colors ranging from white to dark gray to mossy green. I asked Pete what they were and he informed me that they marked past high-water levels of the river.

Rising from the stone wall were gently sloping expanses of rock, some covered with moss, some bare of any vegetation, looking dark and slick from the rain. Still other areas of the rocky surface contained large crevices choked with shaggy shrubs and wild grasses. As we continued around the considerable perimeter of the island, I saw several neighboring islands. One or two of them seemed rather large, like Hallstead Island, and one of them was tiny, with no more than a cottage and a few trees rising from the surface of the water. The boat moved slowly, barely creating a wake, and we rounded the northern end of the island. A leafy red maple tree leaned far out over the water. It was an unusual tree and looked as if a ceaseless wind had caused it to grow sideways. As we passed under, it was so near the boat that I could have reached up to touch the dancing leaves on its gently curving branches.

Trying to forget my churning nerves, I turned my attention toward the center of the island. The trees there grew in a dense stand. Some were leafy, but mostly they were evergreens, tall and dark and sturdy looking, moving in unison as the wind gently blew through their long, graceful branches. They grew thickly, reminding me of a peaceful, primeval forest. I closed my eyes and listened to the soft, low song of the wind in the trees and the tapping of the raindrops on the boat's canopy. For a moment I was even able to shut out the quiet hum of the boat's motor.

"It's beautiful," I breathed, almost afraid that talking aloud would break the spell of silence and beauty around me.

"It is," Pete agreed quietly. I glanced over at him and saw that he, too, was gazing appreciatively at the island.

"Where's the house?" I asked.

Pete looked surprised. "Don't you see it?" He pointed into the dark cluster of trees, nodding toward the middle of the island. "Summerplace—Hallstead House—is right in the middle of those trees."

I looked more closely, and this time I spied a dark-green structure rising from the forest floor. I couldn't see it very well, but as I scanned the woods I saw several dark-green turrets, each with a rich chocolate-brown roof. I would have to wait until I was closer to see the rest of Summerplace.

"The house certainly blends in well with its surroundings. I can hardly see it."

Pete nodded, saying, "Miss Hallstead likes it that way." His comment about Summerplace being gloomy came to mind, and I had to admit that the home did conjure up an image of darkness and gloom, at least from what little I could see of it.

But I wasn't ready to make any judgments yet. After all, this was to be my new job and my new home, at least for now. I forced myself to be cheerful, and asked Pete, "The boathouse is around the back of the island?"

"Yeah—it'll just take a minute." He steered the boat slowly around the side of the island facing away from the channel. The back side was just like the front: a low stone wall, rocks, grasses, wild shrubs, and lots of trees. In another moment we pulled up to the boathouse, a large, square, two-story structure painted the same shade of green as the main residence. It had a dark-brown roof, and above the roofline at each corner rose a small turret with several tall windows marching around it. A long balcony stretched around the structure's entire second story. A large cupola in the center of the peaked boathouse roof held a verdigris weathervane in the shape of a ship. In front, three large boat bays stood open, and I could see two boats moored inside.

"I love it!" I cried spontaneously.

"It's a pretty fair reproduction of Summerplace, only on a much smaller scale," Pete noted proudly. "Of course, it's not exactly like Summerplace because the front is all taken up by boat bays, but you get the idea. We keep this boat in there, plus a smaller one, plus my own boat. My rooms are upstairs, and the rest of the second story is used as storage and for maintenance equipment for the house and boats."

I nodded, absorbed in taking in the details of the boathouse and watching Pete maneuver our boat into its bay and up against the dock. He turned off the engine, jumped up onto the dock, and secured the boat with thick, heavy ropes. He hopped into the boat again to get my suitcases, and then, carrying both, he led the way out of the boathouse. I was very grateful to get onto land again.

It had started to rain a little harder, and I followed Pete away from the boathouse toward Summerplace. We made our way from a slippery, rocky surface to a well-worn path that entered the trees through a graceful arch of branches. Our shoes made almost no sound on the carpet of wet leaves and pine needles, and the trees created their own darkness, especially on this dreary day. A chill blew through me with the wind.

Neither of us spoke in the hush of the trees until Pete turned back to me and said, "Here's Summerplace."

We had reached an area where the trees were thinning and, almost out of nowhere, Summerplace appeared before me. It was dark and breathtaking. Just like its miniature double, the boathouse, Summerplace was painted a deep shade of forest green that perfectly matched the trees surrounding it. It was quite large. It had two stories, and a turret rose from each corner of the home, four in all, like those on the boathouse, but on a grander scale. Each turret was at least one full story higher than the rest of the house and wreathed in tall windows. The rich brown roof was peaked in the center, and it held an enormous cupola topped by a weathervane like the one on the boathouse, shaped like a ship and covered with the green patina of age. Around the ground floor was a wide porch covered by dark brown awnings, and around the second floor, again like that on the boathouse, was a wide balcony. Neither the porch nor the balcony held any furniture.

Pete was watching me as I got my first real look at Summerplace. "What do you think?" he finally asked.

"I don't know yet," I answered truthfully. "It could be beautiful, but it's a little forbidding."

Pete nodded. "I tried to get Miss Hallstead to choose a different color than the dark green, but this is the way she wanted it."

He led the way up the wide steps to the front porch. "It doesn't welcome me," I noted, half to myself. Pete had reached the front door, and he put my suitcases down and turned to face me.

"I don't think the front porch is the only thing you're going to find unwelcoming about this place. Don't expect all of the people here to be happy about your arrival," he said gravely.

Pete's words unnerved me, and I felt my fear rushing back. I was unsure about my new job and my new home, and I shook my head as if doing so would help me shake off my rising doubts. I forced a note of confidence into my voice that I didn't feel. "Let's go in," I told him. After all, it couldn't be any worse than what I had left behind.

If I had known then of the events that were already taking shape in the gloom of Hallstead House, I might not have had the courage to go inside.

CHAPTER 2

Pete turned the knob and the enormous front door swung open soundlessly. We stepped into a large, sparse foyer. The floor had an intriguing harlequin look, with black and white marble tiles set on point in a diamond pattern. A small bench covered in a rich red fabric sat next to the door, and a grandfather clock ticked quietly to my left. A crystal chandelier hung from the ceiling, casting a soft glow over the foyer. Straight ahead was a broad staircase leading to the second story, and next to the staircase a wide hallway stretched toward the back of the house.

It was very quiet at first. Then I heard muffled, angry voices rising from within the residence somewhere. I couldn't tell if the voices were male or female, or what they were saying. Pete threw me a quick glance and shouted, "Hello! Anyone home?" The heated voices stopped abruptly, and after a minute a tall, thin woman came into the front hall from the back of the house, wiping her hands on a dingy apron. I looked at her and was struck by how gray looking she was. Her hair, gray and shaggy, hung limply to her shoulders. She had watery gray eyes that looked slightly sunken, and even her skin had a tinge that reminded me of dirty dishwater.

She paid no attention to me as she greeted Pete, saying in a raspy voice, "Shut that door! It's cold in here." She reached past him and gave the door a shove, closing it with a thud. She inspected me through narrowed eyes and asked Pete, "Is this the new nurse?"

Pete answered her, "Yes. This is Macy Stoddard, Miss Hallstead's new nurse. Macy, this is Valentina Byrd, the housekeeper and cook at Summerplace."

I smiled and held out my hand to Valentina. She ignored me. Instead she turned to Pete and said, "You'd better go out and fix that damned awning over the porch before it starts to rain harder. It's leaking like a sieve. Miss Hallstead keeps asking me about it."

"No problem," he said, and turned to me. "Vali will show you where your room is." With that, he turned around and left, closing the door quietly behind him. I was left alone with Valentina.

She looked at me balefully and said, "Get your bags. I'll show you where you're gonna stay." I took my two suitcases and lugged them up the stairs behind her. At the top of the stairs Valentina turned to the left and walked toward a closed door. I glanced around me while she fumbled with a set of keys that she withdrew from her pocket. The second floor reminded me of a hotel, with its closed doors and dim wall sconces.

It was chilly up there and I shivered. I glanced up and saw a cavernous space rising to a point above the second-floor hallway. *That must be where the weathervane is mounted outside.* Valentina finally found the key she was looking for. She inserted the key into the door and swung it open on slightly creaky hinges. The noise made the second floor seem positively haunted. I shivered again, though not from the chill this time.

"This here is your room. Your bathroom is inside to the right. If you need something, I'll be downstairs. Miss Hallstead told me to tell you that you can look around or rest until dinnertime. She is working in her rooms and doesn't like to be bothered while she's working. Dinner's at six o'clock." With that, Valentina turned her back to me and started to close the door. Then she opened it again and glared at me, her watery eyes narrowing. "Don't get too comfortable—I don't think you're going to be here too long." Then she was gone. I listened as she clumped down the stairs. After such a reception, I felt thoroughly alone, and I was becoming increasingly apprehensive about this new job.

I looked around my room: It was huge. Opposite me was a large bank of French doors covered by thin draperies, and when I turned on the bedside lamp I was pleasantly surprised and cheered as I looked around. Unlike much of what I had seen of Summerplace so far, this room was light and airy looking. There was a second door, locked, which I assumed led to one of the turrets that I had seen earlier. A third door stood ajar, and I peered into a small dressing room.

The main room had a huge stone fireplace with a rustic wooden mantel. I couldn't wait to use it, but I would have to ask someone to show me how to build a fire. I hadn't gotten much practice building fires in my Manhattan apartment.

I brought my suitcases in from the hallway and opened them on the bed. Seeing this room had lifted my spirits a little, and I brushed Valentina's brusque words aside as I started to unpack. Luckily, I had brought several sweaters, as well as jeans and corduroys. When I had accepted this position through the nursing agency, I had been told that a nurse's uniform would not be necessary. After I had unpacked my clothes and put them into the dresser and armoire, I took my toiletries into the bathroom. When I opened the door, I saw that this was a cheerful room too.

I put my things in the medicine chest and then stood looking at myself in the mirror for a moment. My straight, shoulder-length hair was pulled back in a low ponytail and tied with a ribbon at the nape of my neck. I looked a little windblown from being in the boat. I smiled at my reflection. I wasn't going to win any beauty pageants, but I wasn't a troll either. Now, with my face slightly flushed from the boat ride and from being keyed up about my arrival on Hallstead Island, I did look nice.

Turning away from my reflection, I walked back into the bedroom. I stepped over to the French doors, flung them open, and went out onto the wet balcony. It stretched along the entire side of the house and disappeared around each corner, where the turret walls bulged. The railing was dark green with sturdy-looking spindles and the floor was a weathered brown. Standing there feeling the rain on my face, I could just glimpse the river through the trees. The only noise I could hear was the sound of raindrops falling: on the trees, on the balcony floor, on the railing, on the roof of Summerplace. I took a long, deep breath of the cool air, then turned around and went back inside and out into the dimly lit hallway. I was curious about the other doors upstairs, but I could find out more about what was behind them later. I wanted to explore the rest of the house first.

I walked quietly down the stairs to the first floor and stood for a moment in the foyer. Everything was still. Stepping through a doorway, I found myself in a cavernous living room. Despite two lamps glowing softly and a fire crackling in the fireplace, the room was dark, though I could see that it was filled with beautiful antiques that had obviously been well cared for. I walked over to the fireplace and spread my hands out before the fire to warm them.

Above the fireplace mantel hung an informal portrait of a man. He sat on a dark brown wicker chair and wore tan slacks and a short-sleeved white oxford shirt. On his feet he wore brown loafers. He bore a slight smile, and his eyes arrested the viewer with their depth. He looked completely relaxed and at ease, and it was obvious that the artist and the subject were quite familiar with each other. It was a striking painting and I liked it.

I turned around to head back into the foyer and was startled to see a man watching me from the doorway of the living room. I recovered myself quickly and walked over to him with my hand outstretched.

"Hello, I'm Macy Stoddard," I began.

"I know," said the man, shaking my hand limply. "Vali . . . Valentina—my wife—told me you were here."

The man was very tall and thin, with sparse gray hair combed over the top of his otherwise bald head. He wore jeans, work boots, and a plaid flannel shirt. We stood there awkwardly as I waited for him to introduce himself, but he didn't. "What is your name?" I finally asked.

"Leland Byrd. Miss Hallstead's handyman."

I smiled at him. "It's nice to meet you, Mr. Byrd."

His only response was to say, "It's Leland." With that, he turned and walked out the front door. I watched him go, thinking that although his welcome lacked warmth, he didn't seem quite as blatantly rude as his wife.

I walked into the room on the other side of the foyer and found myself in a small library filled with floor-to-ceiling bookshelves containing hundreds, maybe thousands, of books. A wide set of double doors stood closed at the back of the room. I turned on a lamp so I could look around. On a small table that held several small photographs was a beautiful shot of Hallstead Island, obviously taken from a boat. Another was a picture of the same man who appeared in the painting above the mantel. This time he was dressed in fishing gear and held up a pole with a small fish dangling from the end. He wore a wide smile and seemed proud of his catch. A third photo was of a young woman who smiled coquettishly for the camera, her dark eyes twinkling. She had long brown hair and a thin face and was dressed formally in a low-cut gown with a glittering necklace encircling her slender throat.

I turned to one of the bookshelves. It was lined with books of all descriptions, both fiction and nonfiction: classics, mysteries, romance novels, and books about exotic places around the world. This was definitely a room I would visit as often as I could.

I walked back into the foyer and turned toward the back of the house. The hallway led past the stairs, and I found myself in the kitchen. It was a large, farmhouse-style kitchen, but not a cheerful one. Like Valentina, everything was gray. With a little elbow grease, this kitchen could be warm and welcoming, but right now it was cold and depressing. I could easily imagine the dour housekeeper back here. A solid wooden door stood behind me, tucked under the back of the hall staircase. *Probably a cellar door.*

I walked through another doorway on the right side of the kitchen and I was in a formal dining room. There was a long table, heavy looking and stately, surrounded by twelve chairs upholstered in rich burgundy silk. A sliver of light came into the room from windows mostly concealed by long, heavy draperies. *A thoroughly dismal room.* Pete's word "gloomy" flashed through my mind again.

As I stood in the dark and still dining room, I thought I could hear voices being raised again. The words were muffled, but the vehemence behind them conveyed strong emotion. I couldn't tell where the voices were coming from and I didn't want to walk toward them unwittingly and run into the people quarreling. I stood listening for a moment as the voices got louder and louder. Instinct told me to leave quickly, so I headed for a door that led to the porch. As I crossed the dining room, the door I had seen in the kitchen, the one I had assumed led to the cellar, flung open, and Valentina and Leland stepped into the kitchen. Their voices dropped immediately. As much as I wanted to get out onto the porch, I felt compelled to stay in the dining room long enough to hear the end of the argument. Luckily I was concealed by the room's darkness. I had to strain to hear their voices now.

"Shut up, Leland. We're doing this my way," snapped Valentina.

"Vali, would you just forget it? There's nothing we can do about her," wheedled Leland.

"Just go get those rooms ready," hissed Valentina. She started banging pots and pans, and Leland turned and headed into the hallway. I could hear him trudging upstairs. I crept quickly over to the porch door and turned the knob. Fortunately, the door opened soundlessly, and I let myself out onto the porch, closing the door behind me. I didn't want to pass the kitchen, where Valentina would surely see me, so I headed around toward the front of the house. I walked slowly, my mind firing off questions I couldn't answer. Why were Valentina and Leland fighting? Were they talking about me? What had to be done Vali's way? And what made me want to hide as soon as I heard them approaching, yet compelled me to stay to eavesdrop on them? It wasn't in my nature to hide or to eavesdrop. Now I was feeling paranoid.

As I turned the corner of the porch, I saw Pete coming up the path to the front of the house, holding a box with several small tools in it. He raised his eyebrows in greeting and asked, "Leaving so soon?"

I attempted a halfhearted smile in return.

"What happened?"

I told him about Valentina's harsh words, of Leland's lukewarm welcome, and of their heated, but muffled, argument. I left out of my story the words I had heard clearly. Pete set down his tools and shook his head. "Like I said earlier, you aren't going to find a hearty welcome from some of the people around here. Try not to let Vali and Leland bother you. They've been here forever, and they're a little territorial about Alex—Miss Hallstead—and Summerplace."

I thanked him and changed the subject, talking instead about my room and my quick tour of Summerplace. I told him how happy I was to have such a cheerful room, especially after seeing that the rest of the house was so dark. I realized as I left that while I had been chattering to him nervously, Pete hadn't really said much. I was embarrassed and made a mental note to stop babbling.

As I thought about Pete's words, I doubted his excuse for Valentina and Leland's behavior. There had to be more to it than just a vague suspicion of me as a newcomer to Summerplace. It seemed almost presumptuous to think that I would be the subject of any argument between Valentina and Leland—I was a stranger to both of them—yet I had a peculiar hunch that they had been arguing about me.

I walked back into the house and went straight up to my room. I suddenly felt weary and wanted to lie down.

Once in my room I closed the thin draperies against the dank outdoors and switched on the bedside lamp. I lay down on the bed and closed my eyes. Immediately, images of my parents and Alan crowded to the front of my mind: my parents, who had lost their lives to a drunk driver only six weeks before, and Alan, my boyfriend of two years, who had left me shortly after my parents died because he couldn't handle my emotional fragility.

I thrust the mental picture of Alan aside and allowed myself to concentrate on remembering my mother and father. I missed them so very much. When I thought of my mother and father, my mother was always laughing, just as she had when she was alive. It offered me some solace to know that my mother's life, though too short, had been very happy. My father, a professor, had been a serious man, but he was always ready to lay his books and papers aside for my mother and me. My mother had brought out his fun, playful side, and together the three of us had shared many good times.

My thoughts turned suddenly to Alan. Alan Jamison, the young, handsome, successful investment banker. He and I had met at a gala fund-raiser for the hospital where I worked. I had been there as the date of a fresh-faced resident in infectious diseases, but he got called away to work and I stayed at the party since I knew so many people there. I was introduced to Alan through a mutual acquaintance, and I was immediately taken by how exciting he seemed. He drove a BMW; I took the bus everywhere. He lived in a stunning apartment that had been featured in an architecture magazine; I struggled to pay rent on my studio walk-up. He dressed stylishly too, and I guess I was a little awestruck when it seemed that he liked me, a lowly caregiver.

Of course, there were some aspects of his personality that fit the investment banker stereotype. He could be cynical and rude and rather selfish. I overlooked these, thinking that they made him seem more "human."

I should have stayed with the infectious disease resident.

After our relationship ended, I couldn't think of Alan without wallowing in self-pity, but that phase, thankfully, hadn't lasted long. Mostly what I felt now was anger: anger at myself for being so naïve and anger at him for leaving me when I needed him most. I hoped that as time went on, I would be able to think of Alan without anger and vitriol, but for this little while, I indulged myself with a little bit of resentment.

It wasn't long before I drifted off, and when I opened my eyes again, my room was growing dark and was a bit chilly, but not uncomfortable. Perhaps I would ask Leland after dinner to show me how to build a fire in my fireplace. I felt refreshed and very hungry, and I hoped Valentina cooked better than she treated houseguests. I stood up, opened the balcony doors, and stepped outside into the cool air. It was still raining, though lightly, and I listened to the peaceful sound of raindrops spattering on the trees. But as I stood listening, I was startled by another noise coming from my left, a thud followed by a scraping sound. As I turned quickly to find the source of the sound, I saw something disappear around the turret wall. I walked to the end of my balcony, where the wall bulged, and peered cautiously around the corner just in time to see another set of French doors, like the ones in my room, closing. I was baffled. Someone had been watching me outside my room. Who was it? And why hadn't they made their presence known to me? I walked swiftly to the set of French doors and peered into the glass, but I couldn't see anything inside the room—the doors were covered with heavy drapes that still swung gently from the disturbance. I made my way back to my room, pulled the balcony doors closed behind me, and locked them.

I was annoyed but not frightened. Being a newcomer to this isolated household, I would probably be a source of both interest and suspicion for a while, but I still wished that whoever had taken such pains to be avoided had made himself—or herself—known to me.

A few minutes before six I headed downstairs for dinner. In the now dimly lit dining room, Valentina was setting a place at the long table. She turned to me with a scowl on her face and said with mock formality, "Dinner will be served in a moment." I thanked her and she disappeared into the kitchen. I stepped over to admire a painting that hung above the buffet and in a minute Valentina was back, carrying a bowl of soup. As she plunked it down on the table, I asked if Miss Hallstead would be having dinner in the dining room.

"No," Valentina replied testily. "She eats in her rooms. I take a tray for her. She wants to see you in there after dinner." I smiled my thanks and Valentina left.

I sat down to eat the silky, golden butternut squash soup, and before long Valentina appeared again, this time with a plate of chicken, steamed green beans, and a basket of rolls. I praised the soup, but she ignored me. *She certainly is nasty,* I thought. I looked around the dining room, noting again the different pieces of art on the walls, and it occurred to me that the dining table looked even longer when only one person was seated there.

I finished my dinner and Valentina was at my side immediately, cleaning away my plate and unceremoniously placing before me a plate of sliced pears. After I ate the sweet, perfectly ripened fruit, Valentina came once more into the dining room, sighed, and told me, "I'll show you where Miss Hallstead's rooms are now." She strode wordlessly into the library and walked straight to the closed double doors I had noticed earlier. In response to her loud rapping, I heard a voice on the other side call faintly, "Come in."

CHAPTER 3

Valentina opened the door and stepped aside to let me in. Then, flashing me a look of utter loathing, she closed the door behind her. I looked around and found myself in what appeared to be a cozy sitting room.

A fire blazed in the fireplace, casting flickering shadows over a dainty, low table in front of it. On the table sat a silver coffee service and two cups with saucers. Like the other rooms I had seen so far, this one was lit softly and was filled with beautiful furniture. The only item that seemed out of place was a medical bag that sat on the floor next to the sofa. Nobody was in here.

I walked through the open doorway on the other side of the room into a large bedroom. A huge four-poster bed took up the middle of the room, and a fireplace stood cold several feet from the foot of the bed. Nobody was in here, either. I walked quietly to a door that stood ajar on the opposite side of the room and slowly pushed it open.

"Hello? Miss Hallstead?" I asked.

I stood in the doorway looking into a richly appointed office. The focal point of the room was a huge desk with a smart leather chair behind it.

Behind the massive desk, engulfed in the chair, sat Alexandria Hallstead, looking slightly younger than her seventy-eight years and emanating professionalism. She had bright, alert eyes and a ready smile, and her white hair was coiffed stylishly atop her head. Capping the pen she'd been using, she stood up slowly, placing her hands on the desk for support, then walked around the desk and came toward me, limping slightly and using a cane. She held out her free hand to me as I walked toward her, and her clasp was warm and strong when she took my hand in hers.

"You must be Macy," she said, smiling. "I hope you're settling in comfortably and that you are enjoying your first hours on Hallstead Island. You've no idea how much I've looked forward to meeting you."

I returned the greeting, and then Miss Hallstead suggested that we have coffee and talk a bit in her sitting room. I followed as she led the way, walking stiffly.

In the den, Miss Hallstead gestured for me to be seated on the sofa in front of the fireplace, and she slowly eased herself down next to me.

"Can I help you?" I asked, but Miss Hallstead shook her head resolutely.

"I am so glad you're here," she said, settling herself. "Now, you must tell me all about yourself."

"Well," I began, "I'll be twenty-one years old in three months and I've worked for the past year at Empire Hospital in New York City. I—"

"Oh, I know all about your work. I've seen your credentials. I want to know about *you*. We have to get acquainted if you're going to be living here!"

"My work is pretty much who I am; at least, it's been that way for the past year. But I also like to run and hike and ride my bike. And I like to paint, although it's been quite a while since I've had the time to do that."

Miss Hallstead's eyes lit up. "Paint! I love to paint! Some of my paintings are hung up around Summerplace. I used to be quite good, actually." Miss Hallstead's voice trailed off and she stared into the fire. Then she blinked and turned toward me again. "Maybe you can do some painting while you're here. I still have my painting supplies and you're welcome to use them."

I thanked her and she continued. "Tell me what you think of your rooms."

"They're beautiful . . . so light and cheerful."

"Those rooms used to be mine. I decorated them myself. This old house hasn't always been as gloomy as it is now." She sighed and pointed to her hip. "It's been a while since I was up in those rooms."

"We'll get you up there again," I assured her. "It just may take some time." Miss Hallstead smiled weakly, as though she doubted what I said. She then changed the subject to her doctor's orders and her recent medical history. I reviewed several notes that the doctors had left for me, and Miss Hallstead and I discussed a possible schedule for rehabilitative therapy that would allow her to continue working as she had been.

As our lengthy conversation drew to a close, I offered to help her prepare for bed.

"Oh, good heavens, no," she replied. "I'm a tough old bird, you'll see." She laughed and I bid her good night.

CHAPTER 4

I wasn't yet ready to go to sleep, so I lingered in the library after I left Miss Hallstead. There were hundreds of titles and countless genres to choose from. I came across several shelves of books devoted to the Saint Lawrence River, and I chose one written by Paul Malo. If the Saint Lawrence River region was to be my temporary home, I should learn more about it.

I took the book to my room and got undressed quickly since by now it was very cold. Before getting into bed, I peered between the drapes and saw that the sky had cleared, leaving a perfect half-moon shining brightly. It had been a long time since I had seen anything in the sky so clearly! The lights of Manhattan had a way of obscuring the moon and stars at night. With my book in hand, I climbed between the covers. Before I started reading, however, I made the mistake of reaching for a small photo album I had placed inside the nightstand. It contained photos of me and my parents, as well as a few shots of Alan. I paged slowly through the album, remembering, and tears began to well up in my eyes. I blinked them away and placed the album back in the nightstand. Determined not to upset myself on my first night in this unfamiliar place, I began to read the book, with its fascinating stories of life on the Saint Lawrence River in days gone by.

Despite my interest in the book, my eyelids soon began to get heavy. It had been a long day. I turned out the light, thinking again of how nice it would be to use the fireplace in my room.

I slept well that night, despite the cold. When I awoke, a little after five o'clock, I showered quickly and got dressed, then slipped downstairs and out the heavy front door for a walk.

It was cold outside. My breath hung in the air, frosty white. I walked quickly to stay warm, staying for a short distance on the flagstone path around the front of Summerplace, but then setting off through the trees toward the dock, in the direction I had come from the day before.

As I emerged from the stand of trees, I could hear the plaintive sounds of a flock of geese flying low overhead. It was still too dark to see them, but I knew there were a lot of them. Their honking had a lonely sound. As I approached the dock, I saw Pete on his knees, looking at the boat I had ridden in yesterday. I went down to say hello.

"Morning," he grunted as he straightened up next to the boat.

"Good morning," I replied. "Checking out the boat?"

"Yeah. I'll be taking her out of the water in another month or so. Trying to get away from Summerplace already?"

I smiled ruefully. "I think it's going to take me some time to get adjusted here."

"Well, I guess you'll get used to it soon enough."

We exchanged strained small talk for a couple of minutes, but after Pete checked his watch for the third time during our brief conversation, I said good-bye and continued walking. I headed back toward the house and walked briskly around it several times. I saw a set of steps leading to a door that I hadn't noticed on my self-guided tour the previous day; I presumed it opened into Miss Hallstead's office. As I rounded the back of the house for the third time, I saw Vali leaving the cottage she shared with Leland. She hadn't seen me, so I slowed my steps to avoid speaking to her. Once she'd plodded along the flagstones and let herself in the kitchen door, I quickened my pace again and entered quietly through the front.

It was close to six a.m., so I went to the kitchen to find out about breakfast. Miss Hallstead had told me that Vali always brought her a breakfast tray before six thirty, so I thought I should probably eat breakfast around the same time.

Vali was in the kitchen, banging a skillet and a butter dish down on the stove. I greeted her from the doorway. "Good morning, Mrs. Byrd."

She turned to me with a sour expression and replied, "If you're looking for breakfast, you'll have to make it yourself. I'm fixing Miss Hallstead's tray."

Somewhat taken aback but determined to stay cheerful, I eventually found a few ingredients to make myself breakfast. While the water for my tea heated, I offered to take Miss Hallstead's tray to her. Valentina grunted that that was *her* job and she would do it. As she walked off carrying a tray laden with coffee, eggs, fresh fruit, and a muffin, I sat down in the dining room to tea, toast, and a banana.

She returned to the kitchen shortly but didn't stay long. She ignored me and went out the back door. I ate quickly and washed my own dishes, not wishing to give her any more reason to resent my presence, and then set off for Miss Hallstead's rooms, anxious to get started with my new patient.

I knocked on Miss Hallstead's sitting room door and she answered immediately, calling out, "Come in, Macy." When I entered, she was standing by the sofa in a long light-blue nightgown, her hair flowing down her back—I wouldn't have guessed it was so long! She greeted me cheerfully and suggested that I wait while she dressed. I offered to help her, but as she had done the night before, she refused.

I had her physicians' orders and her medical file, so I took those and waited for her in the library. Having already read them the night before, I began browsing again through all the books. After several minutes, I came to the section on the Saint Lawrence River, from which I had taken the Paul Malo work. This morning I was quickly drawn to a beautiful book of photographs of the Saint Lawrence River and the Thousand Islands. Leafing through the book, I started to become more acutely aware of the astounding beauty of this region of North America. There were pictures of every season, of people and landscapes, wildlife and waterscapes. I drank in the beauty of every photo slowly and, after quite some time, was interrupted by Miss Hallstead, leaning slightly on her cane in the library doorway.

"Aren't Ian Coristine's photographs amazing?" she asked, nodding at the book I was holding.

"They're breathtaking," I agreed. "I'd love to actually visit some of these places sometime."

"You will. You passed several of the islands featured in that book on your trip here from Cape Cartier.

"As a matter of fact," she continued, "Summerplace is in there, too." She came toward me and reached for the book, then flipped several pages and pointed to a picture of Summerplace taken from a low-flying airplane. It was a gorgeous photograph. It had been taken on a brilliantly sunny day and I could see the entire island rising starkly from the still, slate-blue water. Only the rooftop of the home, crowned by its magnificent weathervane, was visible through the thick forest of trees encompassing every shade of green. Seeing this photo gave me a better perspective of the size and shape of Hallstead Island.

I placed the book of photographs back on its shelf and turned to Miss Hallstead. "Shall we walk outside a bit? It's a good, easy way for you to start warming up your muscles, plus it feels great out there—I've already had a walk this morning."

Miss Hallstead agreed to accompany me. "If you're going to walk outside, you should probably change your shoes," I noted, pointing to the stylish, low-heeled pumps she wore with her pantsuit.

"No," she answered flatly. "I'm wearing these."

"Okay," I acquiesced reluctantly. "We'll just take it nice and slow. Will you at least put on a coat?"

"That I'll do, my dear." Miss Hallstead smiled back, and after she donned a warm fall jacket, we set out. She held my arm as we slowly descended the stone front steps, but after that she used only her cane for support. We walked slowly, staying on the flagstone path close to the house, and as we progressed, Miss Hallstead told me a little more about the Thousand Islands.

"The Europeans—actually, the French—'discovered' the river in 1535," Miss Hallstead began. "Jacques Cartier was a French explorer looking for a northern passage to Asia when he happened upon the river. Until the French appeared, this entire area was largely under the control of the Confederacy of the Iroquois.

"When my husband, Forrest, was alive, he took a great interest in the history of this area. He had a wonderful collection of Native American artifacts that were found all throughout this region," Miss Hallstead stated proudly. She was quiet for a moment before adding, "After Forrest died, I gave the entire collection to a museum in Canada that he used to love visiting."

Miss Hallstead slowed her pace and looked off into the trees. I slowed with her and then asked, "What was Forrest like?"

She smiled and kept walking but didn't answer right away. As I began to think she had simply ignored the question, she spoke again. Her voice was quiet and wistful.

"Forrest was wonderful. He was tall and handsome, and he was the love of my life. I met him when he came to work for HSH Oil. He was in charge of research and development, so he was in my father's office quite often. All the secretaries used to fawn over him, but I mostly ignored him at first. I was too busy with my work. At that time, not many women held positions in business, plus I was the daughter of the company's owner and the granddaughter of the company's founder, so I felt constant pressure to prove to myself and everyone else that I deserved the position I held. Anyway, I think he viewed me as a challenge at first, but it wasn't long before we were both in love. Madly. We were married within eighteen months, but our only child, Diana, was not born until many years later. She was the best surprise I ever had! Forrest's work, at which he always excelled, took him away from me and Diana more often than any of us liked, but he loved his job. It was important to him and he wanted to do it well."

She laughed softly, almost to herself, and then continued. "Forrest loved to read and dance and go out on his boat. He was never happier than when he was on this island."

She looked at me suddenly with tears in her eyes. "You know, sometimes I'm absolutely lost without him. He died here at Summerplace four years ago. I miss him so very much."

I felt so sorry for her that I put my arm around her shoulders. "I'm sorry," I said. "I didn't mean to bring back painful memories."

She smiled again and sniffled. "Nonsense—they're very happy memories! Though they make me miss him even more."

At that moment Pete came striding along the path. He smiled at Miss Hallstead and started to say something, but he stopped immediately when he saw her tears.

"What's the matter, Alex?" he asked as he took her arm. He glared at me. "What happened?" he asked me angrily.

"Pete, dear, I'm fine. I was just telling Macy about Forrest and, just like a silly old lady, I got all choked up. I'm really fine."

"Okay, if you say so. I have some things to do, but I'll come see you later," he promised. She gave him an affectionate smile and continued walking. Pete held me back for a moment.

"That didn't take you long. Why'd you upset her like that?" I opened my mouth to protest, but he continued. "She doesn't deserve it. Don't do it again." Then he turned on his heel and stalked off. I was left feeling angry and embarrassed. My cheeks felt hot.

"You coming, Macy?" Miss Hallstead asked. "Shall we head back in? I have work to do." She must have noticed that I was flushed, and she added, "Pete looks out for me and he's suspicious of anyone new. Just give him a little time and he'll come to trust you, I'm sure."

I wasn't so sure, but I smiled at her and we turned around and walked back toward Summerplace.

Miss Hallstead changed the subject. "Tell me about your family, Macy."

"Well," I answered, taking a deep breath, "I recently lost my parents. They were killed by a drunk driver in Connecticut, not far from where they lived." It was my turn to become pensive. After a few moments, during which Miss Hallstead said nothing, I went on. "I miss them very much. In fact, they're part of the reason I decided to come here to work. I needed a change of scenery. I felt like I had to get out of the city for a while."

Miss Hallstead nodded knowingly. "So we've each lost two people close to us. Diana passed away eleven years ago, and not an hour goes by that I don't think of both her and Forrest."

I was shocked. I didn't know Diana had passed away. I couldn't imagine the pain of losing one's only child, and I wondered how Miss Hallstead was able to stay focused and strong. But she didn't linger on her own sorrow. She took my hand in hers and patted it. "I hope Hallstead Island can be the peaceful place you need and deserve, my

dear." Just like that, she was concentrating on my feelings. I smiled
my thanks. I hoped Hallstead Island could be that place for me too.

We walked slowly back to the house, each lost in our own thoughts.
Once in the foyer, Miss Hallstead took off her coat and took my hand
again. "Come in here, Macy. There's something I'd like to show you."
She led me to the living room and over to the fireplace. Today there
was no fire in the grate and the room was chilly. She looked up over
the mantel and pointed at the portrait I had seen and admired yesterday. "This is Forrest," she said. "Wasn't he distinguished?" I smiled
and nodded. I stared at the painting for a long moment, admiring the
man in the wicker chair. I found myself wishing that I had been able
to meet him.

"It's a wonderful painting," I remarked.

"Do you like it?" Miss Hallstead seemed pleased. "I painted that
myself."

I was struck by her talent. "That's amazing," I marveled. "I wish I
were as good as you are."

Miss Hallstead laughed. "Well, I may have been good at one time,
but I don't think I could ever paint another portrait quite as well as
that one." Her eyes lingered on the painting for a moment, and then
she turned away briskly. "I need to head back to my office and get
some work done or the day will be gone," she said.

I walked to her rooms with her, and as I turned to go, Miss Hallstead said, "Wait, Macy. You mentioned last night that you enjoy running and biking. There is a YMCA in Cape Cartier and I have a
lifetime membership there because Forrest used to be on its board of
directors. Of course, I never go over there, but you're more than welcome to use my membership anytime. I'm not sure exactly what fa-
cilities they have, but I know there's a pool and treadmills and
stationary bikes. Just ask Pete to take you over in the boat."

I smiled inwardly, imagining Pete's dismay if I asked him to taxi
me over to Cape Cartier so I could use a treadmill. But I thanked
Miss Hallstead, saying, "I may take you up on that if Pete is ever
going to Cape Cartier on an errand. It would feel good to run or bike.
I never learned how to swim, though."

Miss Hallstead suddenly turned ashen and gripped her door handle for support.

"Miss Hallstead!" I cried, running to her. I put my arm around her waist in case she should fall, and helped her into her sitting room. She lay down on the sofa and looked up at me wildly, her hands fluttering nervously. I held her hands in mine—they were like ice. I grabbed the stethoscope from the medical bag and used it to listen to her heart.

Normal.

I took her blood pressure.

Normal.

I was getting up to yell for Vali or Leland, thinking we should call for a doctor, when she finally spoke.

"I'm sorry to have scared you, Macy. I just didn't know that you can't swim." I sat down again.

"All that because I can't swim?" I asked, incredulous. "I told the nursing agency that I can't swim before I accepted this position. They said I didn't need to know how."

Miss Hallstead closed her eyes and moved her lips silently. I sat, waiting. She remained quiet for a few moments, then opened her eyes again and looked at me sadly.

"Diana died by drowning," she said quietly.

Suddenly I understood. "I'm sorry. I didn't know," I murmured. Naturally Miss Hallstead would be upset by anyone not knowing how to swim.

She sat up slowly and patted my hand. "I overreacted," she stated. "The agency people were obviously right; of course you don't need to know how to swim for this job. I was just taken aback for a minute."

You were more than just taken aback, I thought. Aloud I asked, "Are you all right, then?"

"Yes, dear. I'm fine now. I'll work for a few hours; then you come and see me, okay?" She smiled.

I promised to return, then went back to my room, where I sat down at the desk and wrote a quick note to my best friend in New York, Simone. She had asked me to update her when I got settled. Ever since my parents died and Alan left, I hadn't been interested in spending time with my girlfriends, or even my aunts in Connecticut. I had withdrawn into myself, preferring to be alone; I wasn't ready to get back into the world I knew. It probably would have been better if

I had spent time with other people, but my friends had been good about giving me the space I needed. They were concerned, though. I knew Simone would be anxious to hear how I was doing. I would ask Pete to mail the letter for me the next time he went to Cape Cartier.

I fixed my own lunch and ate alone again in the dining room. Vali had taken a tray to Miss Hallstead and I made a mental note to try to encourage Miss Hallstead to take her meals in the dining room. It would be good for her to venture out of her rooms for a change of scenery a few times a day.

After lunch, I peeked in on Miss Hallstead. She was working busily, so I took a notepad and systematically went through the rooms downstairs, making notes of the changes that would have to be made in order for Miss Hallstead to move through the rooms with ease. In most of the rooms there were area rugs that would have to be secured with double-sided tape so that she wouldn't trip on them. In addition, I would have to rearrange the furniture in some of the rooms to facilitate her movement through them. I went in search of Leland to ask for help in completing these tasks. I found him in the kitchen getting instructions from Vali for airing out and cleaning two rooms upstairs.

When I entered the kitchen, both Vali and Leland turned around and waited impatiently for me to speak.

"Leland, if you get some extra time this afternoon, could you give me a hand moving some furniture around and taping down some of the rugs downstairs? I'm trying to make it a little easier for Miss Hallstead to move around on this level of the house."

Leland nodded and mumbled, "I'll help you later, when I'm done helping Vali."

Vali looked at me malevolently and snapped, "I'm going to need him for quite a while. Stephan and Will are coming late this afternoon and their rooms have to be ready."

I had no idea who Stephan and Will were, although I remembered that Pete had mentioned something about Miss Hallstead's adviser and nephew. Before going upstairs, I thanked Leland and said he could find me in my room or with Miss Hallstead. It was becoming clear that I was going to have a significant amount of downtime in this new job. I located the camera I had brought and I headed outdoors to try my hand at some river shots.

It had warmed up since morning and was beautiful outside, so I left the flagstone path almost immediately and set off through the woods. The trees swayed in the gentle breeze, and I could hear again the music made by the wind in the branches. I could also hear other sounds: a boat, several birds, and a low rumble that I couldn't identify. I kept walking, figuring that I would eventually find the water, and came out of the woods on the channel side of the island. I immediately saw that the strange noise I had heard was coming from a ship moving slowly through the channel. I snapped several pictures of the gigantic boat as it churned past Hallstead Island. It was a behemoth of red and black steel, longer than one football field in length, with a small bridge and a large gray smokestack. It passed within a few dozen yards of the island, and I felt like I could almost reach out and touch its massive bulk. I watched in fascination until the stern of the boat passed by. A flag I didn't recognize, presumably the flag of the nation under which the ship sailed, flapped in the wind from the back of the boat, and several men stood on the deck, watching the scenery go by. They all wore peacoats and wool caps, and they waved at me from their perch high above where I stood. Delighted, I enthusiastically waved back and then watched the boat until it was well down the channel and the waves from its huge wake had stopped slapping against the low stone wall that surrounded the island.

After the ship had continued on its way, I looked around at the other nearby islands. Now that the ship was gone, the waves lapped softly against the shore again, gentle and rhythmic. The water surrounding the island sparkled in the bright autumn sunshine, like an ever-shifting blanket of diamonds. The islands I could see from where I stood were of varying sizes, and the homes on them displayed different architectural styles. On the island closest to me was a large white Victorian-style home surrounded by beautifully manicured formal lawns and gardens. Across the channel, I could see a large island with an old, rambling red house on it. There were lots of trees on that island, as there were on Hallstead Island, but unlike Summerplace, the red house commanded a sweeping view of the river.

I continued walking along the river's edge, keeping far enough away from the water that I wouldn't have to worry about losing my footing and falling in. I took quite a few pictures of the neighboring islands and of my surroundings. Eventually, I came upon the unique-looking tree that I had seen yesterday from the boat. It was a rather small tree; its trunk grew straight out of the ground for about three feet and then arched over the river, where its slender branches grew both up toward the sky and down toward the surface of the water. Red leaves tinged with saffron swayed in the breeze. I took several photos; then, turning to go back to Summerplace, I noticed a path leading into the denser woods away from the leaning tree, so I followed it, hoping it led back to the house. After several minutes of walking through the cathedral of trees, I emerged at the back of the cottage used by Vali and Leland.

As I walked back toward Summerplace, Leland came around the corner of the house. When he saw me, he slowed his pace and looked away. Undeterred by his obvious desire to avoid talking to me, I walked up to him and said, "I'm glad I ran into you, Leland. Would you mind coming up to my room and showing me how to build a fire in the fireplace?"

"All right," he agreed. "I'll be up in a few minutes." I went upstairs and put my camera away, and in just a few moments I heard a knock at the door. I opened it and Leland was standing there glumly, holding a box of long matches, some sticks, and several newspapers. He said, "All right, let's get this over with."

I followed him into the room. He knelt in front of the fireplace and asked over his shoulder, "Do you just want me to light it now, or do you want to do it yourself later?"

"I'll light it myself tonight," I answered.

Leland proceeded to crumple up several sheets of newspaper and throw them onto the grate inside the fireplace. Then he stacked the small, spindly branches and twigs on the paper. Finally, he took two logs from the small pile next to the fireplace and placed them on the grate, on top of and slightly behind the papers and the kindling.

"Just strike a match and throw it on the bottom of the pile when you're ready," Leland stated.

I thanked him and he left without another word.

After a moment, I also went downstairs, hoping to get some of Miss Hallstead's exercise therapy started this afternoon. I knocked on her sitting room door and, just like the night before, heard her answer faintly, "Yes?"

"It's Macy, Miss Hallstead. Are you ready to start your exercises now?"

"Almost, dear. Come on in," Miss Hallstead called. I walked through the sitting room and bedroom to the office, where I knocked softly again before opening the door.

"Have a seat anywhere, Macy. I'm almost done here. And for heaven's sake, please call me Alex." She finished looking over a sheaf of papers and made several notations on the pages. Then she stood up slowly, tidied her desk, and smiled at me. "I'm ready," she said.

We decided to work on her exercises in her sitting room. Alex had changed out of her pantsuit and into more comfortable clothes, suitable for exercising. For the next hour, we discussed and worked on several of the exercises that she had begun during her recent stay at a rehabilitation center following her hip surgery. As I had suspected, Alex proved to be an eager and determined patient. At the end of an hour, I advised her to rest for a bit, but she wanted to continue. I was about to insist that she rest when we were interrupted by a knock on the sitting room door. Vali poked her head into the room and informed Alex that Pete had just left for Cape Cartier to pick up Mr. Marks and Mr. Harper.

"Thank you, Vali," Alex answered. Vali left, closing the door behind her, and Alex turned to me with a broad grin. "Stephan and Will will be here soon—I'm anxious for you to meet them."

"Who are Stephan and Will?" I asked.

"Stephan Marks and Will Harper. Stephan is a dear old friend of mine and Forrest's, and Will is my nephew. They both work for HSH Oil. Stephan is what you would call my right-hand man, and Will works in finance. They're visiting now because we need to meet to discuss some negotiations that HSH has initiated. They'll probably be coming and going between Summerplace and New York several times over the next few weeks.

"Macy, I need to change out of these clothes and into my suit again. I know I'm vain, but they don't need to see me in these awful things. Could you just help me out of these sneakers? I had a terrible time getting them on." She laughed.

I helped her with her sneakers, but she refused any additional help, so I returned to my room after promising that I would be back down in thirty minutes to meet Stephan and Will.

A short while later I was reading the Paul Malo book when I heard muted voices in the hallway outside my room. *Stephan and Will must be here*, I thought. My thirty minutes were almost up, so I checked my reflection in the bathroom mirror and went downstairs to Alex's rooms.

She had indeed changed into her suit and looked every bit the consummate professional. She was at her desk again, this time talking on the phone. She motioned for me to be seated, and I sat down across the room at a small conference table so that she could have some privacy for her call.

I was still sitting there a few minutes later when there was a knock on the office door that led to the porch outside. Alex hung up the phone hastily and walked over slowly, without her cane, to open the door to the two men who stood outside.

"Stephan! Will! I'm so happy to see you both!" she greeted them. They stepped into the room and I got my first look at two men who would come to play an important role in my life very soon.

CHAPTER 5

Stephan embraced Alex, then held her away from him, looking at her with affection. "Alex, you never cease to amaze me," he said, smiling. "Hip surgery, then rehab, and look at you! Working like a Trojan as always, and in a suit, no less! I'm very impressed!"

She turned to me and winked. "Stephan, I'd like you to meet my new nurse, Macy Stoddard. She's wonderful," Alex said.

I blushed and held out my hand to Stephan. "It's a pleasure to meet you, Mr. Marks."

He shook my hand warmly. "It's Stephan, please. And I'm very glad to know you. It seems Alex here is in very capable hands."

I liked Stephan immediately. He was about sixty-five years old, tall, with white hair and blue eyes behind rimless glasses. He was dressed casually but impeccably—the collar of an oxford shirt peeked out from underneath his sweater.

Next Alex turned to Will and held out her hands to him. He took them in his and kissed her cheek. "Hi, Aunt Alex," he said. "You look great."

"Thank you, dear. This is Macy Stoddard, my new nurse. You two have a lot in common. She's from New York City too."

He smiled at me and held out his manicured hand. "It's nice to meet you, Macy," he said.

Will was one of the most handsome men I'd ever seen. Dressed like a model in jeans and a black turtleneck, he was well over six feet tall and had wavy dark brown hair. His eyes were a piercing black and his chin was strong and square. He looked like he was in his late thirties.

"Alex," I said, "if you don't need me for anything right now, I'll leave you three to talk."

"That's fine, Macy. I don't need anything. I'm sure you'll have a chance to become better acquainted with Stephan and Will later on. Vali is planning dinner at seven."

I hoped that meant that Alex would be joining us in the dining room, but I found out when I went downstairs for dinner that Vali had already taken Alex a tray. I would definitely mention to Alex the following day that it might do her good to eat in the dining room with other people.

Dinner was slightly more formal than it had been the night before. Candles were lit on the table and very soft jazz music played in the background. When I walked into the dining room, Stephan and Will were seated at the table, talking in low voices. I hesitated to sit down and interrupt them, but Stephan stood up to pull out my chair and invited me to have a drink from a bar that stood in the corner. I had just accepted a glass of white wine when Vali appeared to serve the first course, a crisp green salad topped with pears and candied walnuts. It was delicious. As we ate, Will asked me about New York.

"Where do you live in the city?" he began.

"I have an apartment on the Upper West Side," I answered. "Near Columbus Circle. And you?"

"I have a place in Gramercy Park, not too far from our offices. It's a four-story brownstone," he remarked.

Bit of a braggart, I thought.

"Gramercy Park is a beautiful neighborhood," I said.

"Yes, it is. Many of the homes have important historical significance. In fact, the building next to mine houses an art society that's over two hundred years old."

I turned to Stephan. "Do you live in Manhattan, too, Stephan?" I asked him.

"Yes, I do," he replied. "I live right in midtown, in a small, quiet neighborhood called Tudor City. It's right across the street from the United Nations."

"Stephan could live anywhere he chose, couldn't you, Stephan?" Will laughed. "But he picked some quiet little street that no one's ever heard of." He shook his head in apparent disbelief.

"Actually, Tudor City is an area that many people are familiar with. We just don't like to advertise ourselves," Stephan replied, looking pointedly at Will. "People don't move there because they want an address that everyone recognizes. They move there for peace and quiet. It's like an oasis in the middle of New York City."

"It sounds very nice," I said blandly, then changed the subject. "How often do the two of you get up here to Hallstead Island?"

"A bit too often for my taste," Will stated.

"Not often enough," Stephan said simultaneously.

Just then, Vali appeared with small bowls of soup. As she cleared away the salad plates, Will looked up at her. "Vali, my love, you're looking beautiful this evening." She rolled her eyes at him and smiled, shaking her head.

"Always the flirt," she answered.

When she returned to the kitchen, Will turned to me.

"So, living on the West Side, you're probably familiar with the clubs in that area," he said.

"Not really," I acknowledged. "I don't go to any clubs."

"How about that wine bar right on Columbus Circle?" he probed.

I knew the place he meant. Exclusive, expensive. "No, I've never been there either," I replied with a politeness I did not feel.

"No? Did you get to see any of the new shows on Broadway before you came up here?" he continued. This was getting tiresome.

"One doesn't go to those places on a nurse's salary," I informed him. Will seemed finally to get the point and stopped talking.

We ate our soup in silence for several moments and then I told them, "I'd like to get Alex to start taking her meals in the dining room. She's eaten all her meals on a tray in her room, and I think it would do her good to eat with other people."

" 'Alex'? Awfully familiar, aren't we?" Will asked me.

"She asked me to call her Alex," I replied.

"I think it would be wonderful if you could get her to start eating meals with other human beings again," said Stephan. "It's been quite a long time since I've seen her eat anywhere but her own rooms."

"I'll mention it to her tomorrow," I promised.

Over the rest of dinner, which was a magnificent beef tenderloin, the three of us, led by Stephan, made small talk about the very lively history of Cape Cartier. Stephan seemed to know a great deal about the area, and he was a captivating storyteller. Thankfully, Will did not have much of an opportunity to quiz me further about my social life in Manhattan.

After dessert I excused myself, leaving the two men alone to discuss business. Before going upstairs, I checked in on Alex to make sure that she didn't need anything further from me.

I found her reading a book in her sitting room, still dressed in her suit. She said she'd be fine for the rest of the evening, so I went upstairs.

Before changing into my pajamas, I was anxious to try my hand at building my first fire. Feeling a little silly, I took the kindling and logs and crumpled newspapers out of the fireplace and laid them on the hearthrug next to me. I then repeated the steps I had watched Leland take. I struck one of the long matches Leland had left for me and cautiously reached into the fireplace and touched the flame to the paper and kindling. Ever so slowly, the flames began to spread and get bigger. I was delighted at this small victory, and I sat back on my heels to enjoy the fire unfolding before my eyes.

Not wanting to miss any of this beautiful show, I hurried into the bathroom to wash and put on my pajamas. It took me only a few short moments.

When I stepped out of the bathroom I knew immediately that something had gone wrong. The room was quickly filling with a thick, choking smoke, and for just a split second, I stood there, my mind paralyzed with fear. An image of my parents' car engulfed in flames following their accident flashed through my mind, and it seemed to jolt me into action. I sprang across the room and in a few seconds was dashing down the stairs, yelling "Fire! Everyone out!" at the top of my lungs. I bolted into Alex's rooms, where she was still reading in front of her own gaily crackling fire.

"Alex," I panted, "there's a fire. We have to get you out."

"What!?" she exclaimed. She looked up at me with horror and confusion. "But how—"

I grabbed her book and tossed it aside, then took her hands and, as gently and quickly as I could, helped her stand up. I put my arms around her quaking shoulders and led her toward the door I had seen Stephan and Will use earlier in her office. I was helping her quickly through the bedroom when Stephan burst in.

"What's going on?" he asked quickly, taking Alex's hand and pulling her along.

"There's a fire," I said grimly. "Upstairs."

Alex walked as quickly as she could through her bedroom and office, and Stephan and I helped her onto the porch. Stephan looked at me and asked, "Can you get her down the steps by yourself? I'm going back in to put the fire out."

"You can't go back in there, Stephan!" Alex yelled.

"Alex, just go with Macy. It will take firefighters too long to get here. I won't do anything stupid, I promise." And Stephan disappeared through Alex's door.

I helped Alex down the stairs near her porch door and we stood well away from the house. Will ran up to us from the front of Summerplace, calling out, "Are you okay, Aunt Alex?"

"Yes, Will, I'm fine. But Stephan went back inside." Her voice was filled with dread, her face looking white even in the darkness.

"What the hell for?" Will demanded.

"He wants to try to put the fire out because it takes time for firefighters to get to the islands," she replied tearfully.

Then Vali and Leland came jogging around the back of Summerplace and Vali demanded, "What happened?"

I answered her. "There's a fire upstairs." She fell silent and we all looked upward into the windows of the second floor.

At that moment, Stephan appeared again at Alex's porch door. He opened it and stepped outside. "It's all right, everyone. False alarm—there's no fire."

"Are you sure?" I cried. "Where did all the smoke come from?"

Stephan came to stand with the rest of us. Just then, Pete came running up and joined us. "What's going on? I heard shouting and couldn't find anyone downstairs."

Stephan answered him. "It's okay, Pete. Macy thought there was a fire upstairs, but it turned out to be just some smoke from her fireplace. As soon as I opened the flue, the smoke started drawing up the chimney."

All eyes turned on me. Will and Pete looked incredulous. Vali and Leland both shook their heads in disgust. Alex and Stephan looked at me sympathetically.

"You've got to be kidding me," Will said. He glared at me. "Don't tell me you forgot to open the flue." He stared at me for a minute, then tilted his head back and started laughing. I had never been so embarrassed.

"I'm ... I'm sorry," I stammered, looking around at everyone standing there in the cold. "I didn't realize that I forgot to open the flue." Leland hadn't said a word about a flue—that much I was sure of—but I didn't want to make a scene and start pointing fingers. I had created enough of a scene already.

Vali and Leland turned to leave, and I saw Leland give me one last malevolent look, but I ignored him. Pete left too, but not before he shook his head at me, chuckling. I felt my face grow hot and I knew I looked as flustered as I felt. I hastily apologized again to Alex for causing her anguish, but she smiled at me. "It could happen to anyone," she said. "Now, let's get inside before we all freeze."

Stephan and I walked up the steps on either side of Alex, and Will followed us into her office. She invited us to join her in her sitting room for tea, but she looked so weary that we all declined. Stephan walked to the sitting room door and turned to me. "Macy, don't let this get you down. I know you're embarrassed, but don't dwell on it. It's over and you did the right thing by getting Alex out of here when you thought there was danger. I thank you personally for that." He looked fondly at Alex and bid us good night. Will followed Stephan out, kissing Alex and raising his eyebrows at me. I sighed deeply and apologized one last time to Alex.

"I can't tell you how sorry I am."

"Macy, it's already forgotten. Now, I want you to go up and get some sleep, and that's what I'm going to do, too. And by the way, what Stephan said is right. I think you were very brave coming in to save me when you thought Summerplace was on fire, and I thank you." I smiled at her and left.

When I got back to my room, the fire was burning brightly and my room was warm, but it smelled terrible and smoke still hung in the air. I now noticed a small handle above the fireplace grate that I hadn't seen before. *That must be the flue handle*, I thought ruefully. I sat down in front of the fireplace for quite some time, thinking of nothing in particular, but feeling very sorry for myself. I was exhausted but I didn't want to get into bed yet. When the fire died down, I crawled into bed, but it was a long time before I was able to fall asleep. When I finally did, in the early hours of the morning, I was tormented by a nightmare I had had so many times in the past six weeks.

I stood on a hillside watching a horrifying scene unfold before me, but I was powerless to help. My leaden legs prevented me from running to rescue the occupants from the burning wreckage of their car. The only noises my throat could muster were choked, feeble sobs, and my vision was blurred by the tears streaming from my eyes. Suddenly the wailing sirens were piercing my ears, and within moments several state trooper cars had converged on the scene, their lights swirling red and blue around me. Then came the fire trucks and three ambulances. Other motorists had pulled over to watch or to try vainly to help, but there was nothing anyone could do. My parents were dead. I turned to Alan, but he was walking away.

After waking from the horror, it always took me some time to calm down. This night was no different, but I eventually was able to get back to sleep.

I woke up early the next morning and was glad that I had a patient to care for, to keep me focused on work instead of on my nightmare or my lingering humiliation and embarrassment. When I went in to see Alex, she said nothing of the "fire," and for that I was grateful. I didn't mention it either. I did mention, however, that it might be good for her to start eating with other people in the dining room rather than by herself in her sitting room. She didn't agree with me, but she didn't exactly disagree either. I told her how much I personally would like to eat meals with her and she said she would think about it. Then she changed the subject and asked, "Do you think we could postpone our exercises a little today so that I can meet with Stephan and Will?"

I reluctantly agreed. I wanted her to stick to a schedule to optimize her recovery time, but I realized that she also had a job to do and that I would have to be a little flexible. There was something I needed to do while Alex worked anyway.

I went in search of Leland, and I soon found him, on the porch around the rear of Summerplace, replacing a broken floorboard. As I approached him, he looked over his shoulder and saw me but turned away and kept working. I stood next to him silently for a while, waiting for him to acknowledge me.

Finally, he grunted, "What do you want?"

"I think you know the answer to that, Leland. Yesterday, when you showed me how to build a fire in the fireplace, you deliberately left out the part about the flue," I accused. "You knew exactly what was going to happen when I built that fire."

He swung around to face me. "If you can't remember a simple thing like using the flue, which I *did* tell you about, then you're going to have an even harder time living on this island than I thought you would," he snarled before stalking off.

I stood there looking after him, wondering how Alex could have tolerated this man and his wretched wife under the same roof for so many years.

I continued around to the front door of Summerplace and met Pete as he was leaving. He saw me immediately, so I couldn't turn around and head in the opposite direction. I would have to face him. He put his hands in his pockets and waited for me to get to the door. "That was some show you put on last night," he said.

"Thanks," I retorted, wincing inwardly.

"How'd you forget a simple thing like opening the flue?" he asked.

I resisted the urge to tell Pete that Leland had left out the part about the flue, because blaming someone else would undoubtedly make me look even worse. Instead I said hotly, "I said I was sorry. And I still am. What do you want from me?"

"Nothing, nothing. Sorry I brought it up. I guess someone from the big city shouldn't be expected to know how to use a flue." With that he left.

Defensively, I called after him, "You know, people in New York City have fireplaces too! I just never used one!" I immediately heard the petulance in my own voice and was embarrassed all over again.

I decided to go indoors and start moving furniture around to make Alex's paths around the house a little easier to navigate. Although I had asked Leland for help yesterday, I figured I would be better off just doing the work myself. I started by looking around for double-sided tape. Luckily, Valentina wasn't around and I found some in a drawer in the kitchen. I went first to the living room. I moved several small occasional and end tables back toward the walls and placed the tape along the edges of the rugs. Once that was done, I rolled up the hearthrug and placed it by the doorway. It was so thick and fluffy that it could still trip Alex even if I taped it down. Leland would have to put it somewhere else. The room didn't look as nice as it had before I started, but at least it was safer now, and it would have to stay like this only temporarily. I walked over to the fireplace again and looked at the portrait of Forrest Harper above the mantel. He had indeed been a handsome man. I wished again that I had been able to meet him. His eyes looked so kind.

Next I went into the library. The room was practically a minefield of obstructions for Alex, and I spent a good deal of time securing rugs and moving furniture and reshelving the stacks of books that lay about on the floor and tables. I didn't know whether there was a system for replacing the books, so I put them where I thought they belonged. It was an interesting job, actually, and I pored over many titles that I hadn't seen before.

After I finished in the library, I checked on Alex. She hadn't mentioned what time she wanted to start her exercises, nor had she said how long her meeting with Stephan and Will was expected to take. I knocked softly on her door and heard her call to me to enter.

When I walked into her sitting room, I was surprised to see Alex sitting on the sofa with a man I hadn't seen before. A woman sat in the leather wing chair near the sofa. Stephan and Will were nowhere to be seen. I stopped short and started to apologize for interrupting, but Alex held out her hand to me and beckoned. "Macy, I'd like you to meet Brandt Davis and Giselle Smythe. I've known them both for a very long time."

"It's a pleasure to meet you, Mr. Davis," I said, holding out my hand.

He stood up and smiled, saying, "It's very nice to meet you, Miss Stoddard."

"Please, call me Macy," I replied.

"I will if you call me Brandt." He smiled again, a very wide, contagious grin. He was of medium height, probably in his mid-forties, with wide, dark eyes and very short-cropped, graying hair. He was trim, and wore blue slacks and a white oxford shirt.

Next I turned to the woman, who remained seated, eyeing me warily. "It's nice to meet you, Macy. Please call me Giselle," she said in a clear, cultured tone.

"It's nice to meet you, Giselle," I said.

Up close, Giselle appeared to be about forty years old, but it was clear she had made an effort to appear younger. It worked, at least from a distance. She had blond hair that hung to her shoulder blades and light-blue eyes. Even seated, I could tell that she had a very good figure, and her clothes suggested that she knew she did too. She was dressed in a tight sweater with a low scoop neckline and slim capris. She made a very striking appearance.

"Brandt and Giselle sometimes come to visit me when Brandt isn't working," Alex explained. "He works for the Coast Guard, so his hours can be unpredictable. I never know when he's going to show up, but he's always welcome. And Pete just loves Brandt's boat," she added. "I'll bet he's down at the dock admiring it right now." Alex looked at Brandt fondly and smiled.

"Would you excuse me, please?" Giselle asked. "I promised I'd stop in to see Aunt Vali and Uncle Leland."

I was surprised to hear that this woman was related to Vali and Leland but said nothing. She smiled thinly at me as she walked by, then squeezed Brandt's hand and said, "I'll meet up with you soon, darling." She kissed him quickly and disappeared.

Brandt looked at Alex with concern and asked, "So how have you been feeling? I'm sorry I haven't been able to stop by in several days, but things have been very busy at work."

"That's fine, Brandt. You know I always appreciate it anytime you can visit. And I've been feeling fine, thank you. Macy has been a big help and we have even started some special exercises so that I can get back to normal."

Brandt looked at me and chuckled. "It sounds like you're a good influence on Alex, Macy. It's not everyone who can get her to stop working and exercise!"

I liked Brandt right away. His was an easy laughter, and he seemed solicitous of Alex. For her part, she clearly had a great affection for him.

After some small talk about local events and the weather, Brandt excused himself, saying that he had to go find Giselle. He promised to return as often as he could and gave Alex a gentle hug as he left.

As he closed the door behind him, Alex said to me, "That Brandt is a dear. You know, he used to be married to my daughter. He was heartbroken when she died." She sighed. "Giselle is not my favorite person, but Brandt loves her, plus she's related to Vali and Leland, so I put up with her. She grew up in Cape Cartier, but this was kind of her second home. She was always here visiting Vali and Leland, and she and Diana became very close friends. She's a morning news anchor for the local TV station. She doesn't like to have Brandt out of her sight for a moment, but he doesn't seem to mind. I think she's too clingy."

She put her hands on the sofa and rose slowly. "Shall we do those exercises now?" she asked.

We worked on exercises for an hour and then I suggested that she take a rest and a warm shower before lunch. She declined to rest again, as she had yesterday, but she did agree to a shower.

I ate lunch alone in the dining room. Alex had decided to work through lunch with Stephan and Will, so Vali took three trays to Alex's office.

After lunch, I knocked on Alex's door to see if she was ready to go for a walk. Stephan and Will were gone so she was by herself working again. She noted that Stephan and Will each had a "satellite office" in their rooms upstairs, and they had gone to confer and make some phone calls up there for a while. As she had done in the morning, she asked whether we could postpone a walk outdoors until later in the afternoon so that she could get some work done. "You know,

Macy, I've been thinking," Alex said. "You mentioned that you love to paint, and there are still some of my painting supplies in the turret above your room. How would you like to go up there and have a look around? You're welcome to use any supplies that you find."

My eyes must have lit up, because Alex laughed. "Here," she said, taking a key from one of her desk drawers. "This will unlock the turret door from the balcony. You can't get up there from inside your room because that door is locked from inside the turret stairway."

"Why is that?"

"It's really a very interesting story. Long ago, when many of these large homes were built in the Thousand Islands, their owners had listening and spying posts built into many of their rooms, but particularly the guest rooms. The owners of the homes were successful businessmen and entrepreneurs, and I suppose they wanted to know what guests may have been saying about them. So they had secret spots built into the homes to allow them to see and hear without being seen or heard. The turret doors in Summerplace are examples of those spying places. With a key one can enter a turret stairway from the balcony and listen to a guest's conversation or even enter the guest's room without the guest knowing anyone is there. It's something about this house that has always fascinated me."

"What intrigue!" I exclaimed. "Guests could have gotten themselves into real trouble if they didn't watch what they were saying." I laughed.

I took the key to the balcony door and went up to my room excitedly. I let myself out onto the balcony and unlocked the turret door. The stairway was dark and smelled musty, and the stone walls were clammy to the touch. I shivered when my shoulder brushed against them as I looked and felt around briefly for a light switch. I could not find one, so I slowly made my way up the winding staircase inside the dank turret.

When I emerged from the gloom at the top, I stepped out into a large, bright room with tall windows inviting sunlight from every direction. There were shades on each window, but they were rolled up at the top. I couldn't imagine ever wanting to pull them down! The wooden floors were planks painted a pale blue-gray. The walls were taken up mostly by the glorious windows, but in between the windows the walls were completely covered by paintings and pencil drawings. More paintings stood stacked against one another under the windows and against the walls. A large wooden table on one side of the turret held a wealth of art supplies, including oil paints, acrylics, watercolors, brushes, pencils, charcoals, chalk, jars, and rags—an artist's dream! A pile of blank canvases stood waiting for inspiration in a large basket under the table. It looked like Vali had been up here to clean, because there wasn't a speck of dust anywhere. Beyond the table were an easel and a stool. I walked over to the easel and looked at the painting that hung there.

It was a beautiful, but unfinished, watercolor of two Canada geese flying low over the surface of the river in what looked like a narrow cove between two wooded islands. A gray, overcast sky was reflected in water that looked blue-black. A lone figure in a rowboat drifted nearby, fishing peacefully. The islands, which were only sketched in pencil, were covered with dark fir trees that reached loftily to the sky. Looking at the painting, which showed a great deal of talent, I could almost hear the geese calling starkly over the silent water.

I turned from the easel and walked around the perimeter of the large room, drinking in the breathtaking views on all sides. I could see all of Hallstead Island from this room, as well as the trees and homes on the neighboring islands. The river stretched away on either side of the island, and I could see other islands dotting the surface of the water far into the distance. As I walked around I peeked at some of the paintings that were stacked against the walls. There were some lovely waterscapes, as well as a few amateurish paintings of wildlife. There was even a charcoal sketch, signed by Alex, of that strange tree I had seen leaning over the water on the other side of the island.

This was such a tranquil room. I hoped I would be able to visit it often. The art books on the coffee table looked very interesting, and I sat down and began to look through them. I leafed first through the pages of a landscape book and had just turned my attention to a beautiful volume on watercolor painting when I heard a noise. I looked up, expecting to see a visitor emerge from the turret stairway, but no one appeared. I had probably heard something from outside. I got up to look out one of the windows and I could see Pete on the balcony below, just outside my room, using some sort of tool on one of the railing slats. I must have been so engrossed in the books that I hadn't heard him working.

I needed to check on Alex and see if she was ready to go for that walk, so I put the books back the way I had found them and started downstairs. I had already decided that I would try to peer inside my room, as though I were an Industrial Age entrepreneur spying on one of my guests. At the bottom, though, I gave a start when I saw that the door to my room was already ajar.

I cautiously opened the door further and looked around for whoever had been here while I was upstairs. The person must have entered the turret from the balcony—that must have been the noise I had heard. Nothing seemed to be amiss, but I took a quick look around anyway. I noticed with dismay that the nightstand drawer was partially open and I knew before I looked inside what was missing.

My album was gone. Why? Who would have taken it? It was of interest only to me, for I was the only person who knew any of the people in the pictures. Thinking of all the pictures of me and my parents that had been in the album, I grew very upset. Then I got angry. I wanted that album back. I didn't know where to start looking, though. Then I remembered that I had seen Pete on the balcony while I was up in the turret. But why would Pete call attention to himself if he were going into my room? And why would he take an album full of pictures of strangers? It didn't make any sense. Of course, maybe it hadn't been Pete. It could have been anyone else on the island: Stephan or Will or Vali or Leland. Not Alex, since she couldn't have gotten up to the balcony. I was getting more confused. I checked my room quickly to see if anything else had been taken, but everything else seemed to be untouched. I let myself back into the turret stairway, locked my bedroom door from inside the stairway, then went out onto the balcony, locking that door behind me, too.

I went back into my room, then headed downstairs to talk to Alex. On the way, I met Vali dusting in the library. She scowled at me. "If I were you, I wouldn't go disturbing Miss Hallstead constantly like you've been," she said. "She likes to be left alone while she works."

I was already flustered by the loss of my album, and I had no patience right now for Vali's insolence. "I'll let Alex tell me that herself, thank you." And I left her glowering after me.

I found Alex still at work in her office. Stephan was with her. I asked her if she was ready to take a break and go walking with me, and she smiled and agreed. Stephan excused himself from the room and Alex and I set out. Though it was a beautiful day outside, I was preoccupied by my missing album and Vali's admonition in the library. I broached the subject of Vali's warning.

"Alex," I began, "would you prefer that I not disturb you when you're working? I thought that perhaps you would rather summon me than have me just show up unannounced."

"No, Macy. I want you to feel comfortable coming to get me at any time—and for any reason. Anyone is welcome to pop in without giving me advance notice. Why do you ask?"

"No particular reason," I answered, deciding not to reveal my brief conversation with Vali. "I was just wondering."

We walked in silence for a few minutes, enjoying the beautiful afternoon. The sunlight slanted through the trees, dappling the flagstones where we walked. The breeze carried a slight chill, reminding us that colder weather would be here soon.

Finally Alex spoke. "This weather reminds me so much of Forrest. This was his favorite time of year. He didn't like really hot weather, so he was happiest when it started getting cooler outside."

I thought of the portrait of the man above the living room mantel and smiled. "I think I know just how he felt," I told her. "Fall is my favorite season. Summer, especially in New York City, can be uncomfortably hot. When fall comes I feel like I get my energy back."

"That's exactly what Forrest used to say." Alex laughed. She looked wistful, as if she were remembering happy autumns past, and fell silent again.

When she next spoke, she changed the subject. "Did you visit the turret?"

"Yes, I did. Oh, and here's the key." I reached into my pocket for the key and handed it to her.

"What did you think?" Alex asked.

"I loved it! It's so bright and peaceful up there. And the views are gorgeous!"

"I knew you'd like it. That room used to be my haven. I could spend hours up there painting and drawing. Sometimes I would go up there to take a break from my work. To me, it is a place of refuge, and I wanted to keep it separate from all the things that used to take up my time. Now, of course, my work takes up even more time than it used to and I haven't been up there in quite a while." She pointed to her hip. "Plus, this keeps me pretty well confined to the first floor of Summerplace and this path we're walking on now."

"There was an unfinished painting on the easel up there. It's beautiful," I said.

"Yes, I remember that," Alex mused. "I had only to finish the islands and the trees around the edges of the picture."

"Why don't you finish it?" I urged. "I could bring your supplies downstairs and you could start working on it again."

"No, dear, I don't think I could paint anywhere but in that turret, and of course it's impossible for me to get up there."

"Then that will be one of our goals for your recovery process, for you to get back up into that turret and start painting again."

Alex's eyes shone and she turned to me excitedly. "Do you think we could do that?" she asked hopefully.

"Absolutely!"

"Oh, I hope so." She sounded almost girlish in her enthusiasm. It made me happy to watch her.

We had reached the front of Summerplace again and Alex said she was a bit tired and wanted to rest for a little while. "I think that's a good idea," I agreed. "We need to make sure that you're not working too hard."

I had been trying to think of a casual way to ask whether anyone knew I had been up in the turret earlier but could think of nothing to say that wouldn't arouse Alex's suspicion, so I remained silent.

I saw that Alex was resting comfortably in her bedroom before heading outside again. It was too nice a day to stay indoors. Aimlessly, I wandered down to the boathouse. Pete was walking up one of the docks toward me. Despite his behavior since I arrived on the island, I felt a sudden determination to win his trust.

"Hi," I called out to him. "Is there anything I can do to help you down here?"

He came to stand near me and asked, "What exactly did you have in mind?"

I shrugged. "I don't know. It's just such a nice day and Alex is resting right now. I thought maybe you could use a hand with something."

"Is Alex all right?" Pete asked quickly.

"She's fine," I assured him. "We went for a walk and she's just a little tired. She spent most of the morning working in her office."

"There's really nothing you can do down here," Pete said shortly. He chuckled. "I don't know what you thought you could possibly help me with, especially after that fireplace episode last night."

My anger flared up at him again. Why bother trying to gain his trust, anyway? I was getting sick and tired of his snide comments. "You know, just because I'm a woman and from New York doesn't make me a useless half-wit," I said hotly. "I may not have been brought up around here, but I'm willing to learn what I need to know to help out." I turned on my heel and started to stalk away, but Pete called me back, laughing.

"Whoa!"

I was infuriated, and his laughter made matters worse. "What do you want?" I snapped.

"I'm sorry if I underestimated you," he said with mock formality. "Maybe I can find something for you to do after all." He smiled, and I softened a little bit, in spite of myself. I followed him into the boathouse and stood watching while he took down several ropes from a large cabinet. "It's busywork, but you can start by getting all of the knots out of these lines," he said. "When you're done, if you're still looking for something to do, come and find me and I'll get you started on another job."

"Thanks." I smiled. Pete picked up a wrench and walked toward the mahogany boat I had ridden to the island. I turned and put the twisted pile of ropes on a large workbench in the rear of the boathouse. The ropes were damp and it took me quite a while to get all the knots out. When I finished, I coiled the ropes on the workbench and called out to Pete, who was still working on the boat.

"I'm done with these ropes, but I think I should go check on Alex. Could I start a different project on another day?"

"Sure. And thanks for helping—I appreciate it. Tell Alex I said hi." He smiled at me and went back to his work.

I found Alex working in her office again.

"HSH Oil must be a great success, since the lady in charge so rarely takes a break," I teased.

Alex laughed. "I love my job," she said happily.

"It's almost time for dinner," I noted. "Are you going to join us in the dining room tonight?"

Alex's smile faded. "No, Macy, not tonight."

"I wish you would. It would be good for you."

"I know. I like eating in my sitting room, though. Sometimes I talk to Forrest while I have dinner. I can't do that in a room full of people."

I felt a stab of pity for Alex. I could imagine her sitting on her beautiful gold sofa, alone, talking to a ghost. "You're right. But you might enjoy conversation with Stephan and Will and me too. I'm not trying to force you. Just think about it," I said softly. After seeing this glimpse of Alex's pain and vulnerability, I felt somehow closer to her. We shared the ache of loss, and I thought again of my own parents. Alex sensed my thoughts.

"Do you ever talk to your parents, Macy?"

I thought for a moment. "I think about them all the time, and I feel like they're with me, but I don't actually speak to them aloud. Maybe I talk to them silently, without even realizing it," I said slowly.

Alex nodded. "I'll bet you do." She opened her mouth as if to say more, then apparently changed her mind. She brightened and asked, "Have you been in the boathouse? I smell grease."

I smiled. "Yes, I helped Pete while you were resting and working this afternoon. I didn't realize that I stink! I should shower before dinner."

I left her with a promise to see her later, and I went up to my room quickly to shower. When I went to the dining room for dinner, Stephan and Will were already there, talking. Stephan pulled out my chair and we all sat down together.

Dinner was quiet. We talked benignly of stories from the newspaper. A couple of times Will tried to steer the conversation to New York City, but that was a topic I was bored of discussing with him, since his main interests tended to be high-end places I did not frequent. *How like Alan he is*, I thought, surprising myself. I had not thought consciously before of the similarities between Will and Alan, but there were several. They were both handsome and knew it; they both enjoyed patronizing trendy hot spots. Just thinking of Will's similarities to Alan was enough to make me find him disagreeable.

Alex did not join us for dinner. I thought of her talking to Forrest in the soft lamplight. It must be very comforting for her.

After dinner I went to check on her and found her reading in her sitting room. She seemed tired and said she might go to bed early. I was concerned, since Alex didn't seem the type to tire easily, but when I checked her pulse, blood pressure, and heartbeat, everything was normal. She didn't need me for anything else that evening, so I went up to my room, built a fire—correctly this time—and read until I was ready to go to sleep. I was thoroughly absorbed by Paul Malo's book. How interesting it must have been to live on the river all those years ago!

I had the nightmare again that night, no doubt because of the conversation with Alex about my parents. I awoke in the middle of the night trembling, with tears streaming down my face. I got up and pushed open the doors to the balcony. The cold assailed me when I stepped outside, but it felt good. I needed a few moments away from the bedroom, to allow the nightmare to fade again from my mind. I stood with my hands on the railing, looking out over the trees on Hallstead Island. The moon shone with a bright white light, and now and then clouds scudding across the sky would throw shadows onto the ground. It was tranquil and I could feel my heart slowing down, calming the pounding that had begun while I slept.

After a few minutes, I became acutely aware of the cold again, and shivering, I turned to go inside. As I turned, though, I thought I saw a movement out of the corner of my eye. It was down among the trees, and I stood very still, waiting to see it again. But though I stood there for several moments, there was no more movement. I must have been imagining things, my mind still restless from my dream. As I went back inside, I pulled the doors closed behind me, grateful for the locks.

CHAPTER 6

I must have slept well the rest of the night, because I awoke in the morning feeling refreshed. The memory of the nightmare remained with me, but I didn't feel exhausted and drained, as I so often did after the dream. The clouds I had seen in the night had evidently thickened, because it was raining hard. I peered between the drapes covering the doors and saw the raindrops falling heavily from the tree branches. *It's beautiful here even when it's pouring*, I thought. I dressed and went downstairs for breakfast.

By now I was getting used to making my own breakfast. Vali cooked breakfast for Stephan and Will, but I wasn't about to ask her to make mine too. Besides, I was sure she would refuse. She always seemed to have me fixed with a look of loathing, and I talked to her as little as I could. I ate alone but as I was finishing, Will walked into the dining room. He nodded in greeting and sat down to look through some papers while he waited for Vali to bring him his food. I gathered up the plates and silverware I had used and started to walk out of the room. Will called me back as I left.

"Macy, I know this is going to sound very lord-of-the-manor-ish, but I am wondering if it's a good idea for you to be bursting in on Alex whenever the mood strikes you. She seems to be distracted and I think it's because she's been unable to concentrate on her work. As

I'm sure you're aware, her work is very important to her." He went on reading as if he expected me to submit to his suggestion without comment.

I looked at him evenly. "It's interesting that you should say that, because Vali told me the same thing yesterday. I did, in fact, discuss it with Alex, and she told me that I, as well as everyone else in Summerplace, am welcome to see her at any time. And I'd hardly call the work that I do 'bursting in' on her. I am here to do a job and I'm responsible for Alex's health as long as I'm here. But thanks for the suggestion," I added sarcastically. He raised his eyebrows at me and said nothing as I left the room.

It rained most of that day. A couple of times I went to Alex's sitting room to work on her physical therapy exercises, but most of the day I spent in my room reading some books and articles on recovering from hip surgery. Alex's doctors had left them and I was grateful to be able to do some extra reading on the subject. I also looked in vain for my photo album. It had to be somewhere around Summerplace. Who could have taken it?

I asked Vali and Leland about it when I went down to the kitchen for lunch. "What would either of us want with something like that?" was Vali's reply.

Late in the afternoon, I went to Alex's rooms to check on her. I had expected to find her working in her office, but to my surprise she was in her sitting room before the fire. Brandt and Giselle were chatting with her.

"Alex, are you all right? I expected to find you working," I said with concern.

"I'm feeling just a little run-down right now, dear. Brandt and Giselle called to say they were coming over to the island, so I decided to take a break to visit with them for a little while." She smiled at Brandt, who was seated next to her on the sofa. He patted her hand.

"Giselle and I are going to be leaving soon. She wants to visit Vali and Leland, and there's a book I'd like to borrow from you if that's okay, Alex," said Brandt.

"Of course." Alex smiled weakly.

As he stood up, Giselle came over and linked her arm in his. "See you soon, Alex," she said. They left and I took Brandt's place next to Alex. She looked rather wan.

"I want you to lie down right here for a little while. I think you've been working too hard and you need some rest," I told her firmly.

She didn't resist. I helped her to lie down on the sofa and I covered her with a light blanket. Once she was comfortable, I went into the library. I wanted to be nearby if Alex should need anything. Brandt was there, leafing through a book. He looked up when I came in.

"Hi, Macy."

"Hi, Brandt. I hope I'm not disturbing you."

"Not at all. I knew I'd be able to find this book in here. It's a maritime history of these islands. I need it for a project at work. Alex and Forrest acquired lots of great books that are hard to find anywhere else in this area. Alex has mentioned before that she'd like to donate some of these books to a local library, but she just hasn't had the time recently to go through everything."

"I think that would be wonderful," I told him.

"Is she resting?" he asked.

"Yes, for now. She's a tough lady, though. I expect she's not going to lie down for long. I hope I'm wrong—she's been working too hard and she needs some rest."

"I think it's good for you to be here with her," Brandt said. "She needs somebody whose only responsibility is to take care of her. It may be a little boring for you at times, but she needs this arrangement. When Vali was looking after her, she couldn't do a good job simply because she had too much work to do."

"Well, I'm enjoying Alex and my job here very much," I said warmly. "Would you excuse me while I look in on her again?"

I left him and tiptoed softly into Alex's sitting room. She was still lying on the sofa, but I was glad to see that her eyes were closed and her breathing was light and regular. She would be asleep soon. I turned off the lamp so the room was illuminated only by the flames dancing and crackling in the fireplace. Alex's eyes fluttered open for a moment and she murmured, "I was going to join you in the dining room tonight."

I smiled at her and whispered, "You rest now. You can eat with us in there tomorrow." She nodded faintly and I went back to the library. Brandt was gone so I curled up in a chair for a few minutes. I wanted to wait until I was sure that Alex was sleeping before going upstairs to change my clothes for dinner. I looked around the room contentedly. Brandt was right; this arrangement did seem to suit Alex, and the quiet time that I was able to spend alone was just what I needed, too. I was growing quite fond of Alex, and she seemed to like and trust me as well.

When I was sure Alex was asleep, I started upstairs to change. I smiled inwardly—it was nice to hear that Alex had changed her mind about eating dinner in the dining room with the rest of us. As I mounted the stairs, the big front door flew open and Brandt stumbled in, thoroughly soaked. Rain ran in rivulets into his eyes and ears, and water puddled around his feet on the foyer floor.

"This is unbelievable!" he exclaimed. I ran to the kitchen in search of some towels for him. As I looked through a drawer under one of the kitchen windows, I could see the rain slamming against the glass. Suddenly there was a flash of light that lacerated the sky, followed by a terrific boom that made the house shudder. I found several towels and ran back to Brandt. As he mopped his face and head, he said in wonder, "I haven't seen anything like this in a long time. There's no way Giselle and I can get back to Cape Cartier while there's thunder and lightning out there."

I agreed and winced when lightning rent the darkness again and the thunder bellowed just beyond the front door. "You and Giselle need to stay here until the storm blows away."

Brandt went off to change, explaining that he always kept a set of clothes at Summerplace. I went in search of Vali to tell her that Brandt and Giselle would be having dinner with us.

I found her and Giselle coming in the back door under cover of a big umbrella.

"Vali, would you mind setting a couple extra spots for dinner? Brandt and Giselle are staying for a while, until the storm lets up."

Vali glared at me. "Giving orders now? Didn't take you long to settle right in, did it?" she sneered.

"Aunt Vali, I'm sure Macy is just trying to be thoughtful." Giselle looked as if the rain hadn't touched her. Her clothes were dry, her makeup was perfect, and every hair was in place. She was again wearing a form-fitting top with tight jeans and stilettos. She looked a little out of place.

Vali rolled her eyes. I ignored her and went upstairs to change my clothes. When I came down again, I went into the dining room to find Stephan and Will as usual. Stephan offered me a hot buttered rum from a tray on the sideboard and I accepted gratefully. It tasted wonderful and seemed to ward off some of the chill from outdoors. Brandt and Giselle made their appearance just a few moments later. Brandt had changed his clothes and looked comfortable and dry. As they entered the dining room, Giselle took Brandt's hand possessively and looked at me with a slight smile, almost triumphant. *She certainly seems insecure*, I thought.

Dinner was an uncomfortable affair. Vali served a creamy onion soup, followed by a fabulous roast of pork with autumn vegetables and homemade applesauce. During the meal, we talked lightly about the storm, which seemed to be letting up a bit; then Stephan regaled us with an unsettling story of being caught in a storm on a cruise ship. I was unpleasantly reminded of my own experience aboard a boat during a storm. After we were done with our main course, Vali came to clear the dishes. As she left the room Will looked at me and pointedly asked, "Speaking of stories about water, Macy, have you ever heard the story of our local pirate, William Johnston?"

"No," I answered slowly. Something vaguely malicious in Will's tone made me fear that another unnerving story was coming.

"No? Well, it's a famous tale around here, and you can't go home without hearing it. William Johnston was originally from Canada and a self-described patriot. He lived a good part of his life in northern New York and was a tavern keeper there. During the Canadian rebellion of 1838, there was a British ship called the *Sir Robert Peel* that was docked at Wellesley Island. You may have seen Wellesley Island on your way here.

"Anyway, under the cover of darkness one night, Johnston led a group of other patriots onto the *Peel*. They plundered the boat and forced all of her passengers ashore. Then they cut the boat loose from her moorings and set her on fire. The boat drifted down the river and finally ran aground at Rock Island, which is not too far from here.

This had all been done in retaliation for a similar event that had taken place on the Niagara River sometime before.

"Both the U.S. and the British condemned Johnston and branded him an outlaw. He went into hiding. They put a bounty on him and they arrested several of the men that had been in his party on that fateful night. Prosecutors weren't able to convict them, though.

"But here's where it gets interesting. During the time that he was on the lam, legend has it that he hid in a cave underneath an island right near the scene of the crime. He had a faithful daughter who used to take a rowboat to visit him and bring him food. The place where he hid later came to be known as Devil's Oven. I've seen it. It's a small, rocky island with a fairly small opening above the waterline.

"I wonder what it must have been like for him to live in that cave for so long. So cold and dark and wet. Can you imagine what he must have felt as the water level rose and fell? Or when a storm blew up and the waves came crashing in around him?" Will looked at me with malice in his eyes. "Can't you almost feel the water rising?" I felt the room growing smaller, as though the walls were pressing on me. I must have looked uncomfortable, because Will chuckled softly.

"To get on with it, Bill Johnston eventually tired of living in an underwater cave of sorts, so he arranged to have his son arrest him to get the five-hundred-dollar reward. He was tried and acquitted, and then rearrested. He escaped but gave himself up several months later. After spending six months in jail, he escaped again. A year or so later, with a petition for pardon in hand, he went to Washington and presented the petition to President Van Buren. Van Buren said no, so Johnston just waited ten days. By then President Harrison was in office, and he signed the pardon. Johnston returned to the Thousand Islands and spent a good deal of the rest of his life as the lighthouse keeper on Rock Island, where the *Peel* had run ashore."

He looked at me again. "We'll have to take you over to Rock Island to see where the old pirate spent much of his later life. And we'll have to show you Devil's Oven. I think you'll be interested." He smiled at me over the rim of his water glass as he raised it to his lips.

I shivered involuntarily. Why was he doing this? He seemed to be enjoying my discomfort. I didn't want him to know he had unnerved me, so I looked at him squarely in the eyes and answered him. "I think you're right. A trip to Rock Island and Devil's Oven would be very interesting."

"I heard Aunt Alex telling Stephan that you can't swim. Is that true?" Will asked.

I stared at him for a moment. "Yes, that's true. I never did learn how to swim."

Giselle glanced at me, her eyes bright. "Oh? You don't know how to swim, Macy? Then you must let me teach you. I used to swim competitively and I was quite good." She smiled brightly. I was at a loss for words. The prospect of learning to swim under Giselle's tutelage was unappealing, to say the least.

Stephan looked sternly from Will to Giselle and changed the subject. "Anyone for coffee? Vali makes magnificent coffee."

I looked at Stephan gratefully. "Actually, I must go and check on Alex now," I said, excusing myself. I left the room hastily.

When I tiptoed into Alex's sitting room, she was sitting up on the sofa. She smiled at me wearily and waved me over to where she sat. I asked how she was feeling.

"I'm just tired, Macy," she replied. "I think I'll go to bed now, and I'm sure I'll feel more like myself in the morning." Surprisingly, she allowed me to help her into her nightgown. She got into bed and looked at me gratefully as she leaned back against her pillows. She sighed. "Macy, I'm so glad you're here to help me. I don't know what I'd do without you." She patted my hand.

I was touched. "Thank you, Alex." I smiled. On impulse, I leaned over and kissed her quickly on her soft, papery cheek. She closed her eyes and I turned off the light and left the room quietly.

When I went back into the foyer, I could hear the low murmur of voices from the dining room. I had no wish to return there, so I went up to my room, put on a jacket, and let myself quietly out the front door. The storm had passed, so there was no rain to contend with tonight. Keeping to the flagstone path, I walked slowly around the outside of Summerplace, listening contentedly to the night sounds of the island and the Saint Lawrence River. I could hear the low throb of humming insects against the soft background sound of the night breeze blowing through the tree branches. The water of the river moving slowly on its course to the Atlantic Ocean made a comforting sound, almost mesmerizing, and I loved it. It was so different from the noise of the neighborhood I had just left a few days before. On this peaceful island there were no wailing ambulances, no rumbling street cleaners, no cars honking incessantly. Here one lived in the company of nature and its soothing rhythms. In the short time I had been on the island I was already feeling some of my stress draining away. I felt I could now allow the memory of my parents to surface without having to thrust the grief aside. It helped knowing that Alex had experienced grief too.

As I walked around Summerplace, I saw a glimmer of light shining through the closed dining room drapes. Brandt and Giselle would probably be leaving soon since it wasn't raining anymore. Giselle undoubtedly had to get up early in the morning for work and would want to be in bed at a decent hour. It was also getting chilly, so I pulled my jacket tighter around me and headed for the front door.

I went up to my room without meeting anyone. I was getting tired, so I didn't bother to build a fire. I just crawled between the covers and was almost asleep when I heard a faint knock at my door. Concerned that Alex was ill, I jumped out of bed and went quickly to open the door.

Will was standing there, still dressed in his dinner attire. As usual, he looked debonair and handsome. "I'm sorry to bother you so late, Macy, but I wanted to talk to you alone. May I come in?" he asked politely.

Still thinking that he might be here with information about Alex, I let him in. He sat down in one of the chairs before the cold fireplace and motioned for me to sit down too. I was getting impatient. "Is Alex all right? Is that why you're here?"

He sighed and passed his hand over his eyes. I noticed for the first time the ever-so-slight graying at his temples. "As a matter of fact, Macy, Alex is the reason that I'm here. Oh, she's probably sleeping peacefully right now, so there's no need for you to worry about her tonight. But I must tell you that I am starting to get a little concerned that your presence here is perhaps not in Aunt Alex's best interests. I have noticed that she seems to be a little preoccupied while she's trying to work and now there's this illness that seems to be affecting her.

I am of the opinion that your notions of a quick recovery and exhausting physical therapy are doing Aunt Alex more harm than good."

I was speechless. I certainly had not expected this kind of opposition from Alex's nephew. I stared at him for a moment.

"Will, I am sorry to hear that you feel this way. I'm here because Alex hired me to be her nurse. My job is to see that her doctor's orders are carried out. As for my 'notions' of a quick recovery, don't you agree that it's best for her to begin her normal activities again so that she can get back to her life? I'm not rushing her into anything. This is standard procedure for a patient of her age recovering from hip surgery. Furthermore, the illness that you feel she is currently suffering from seems to be no more than fatigue. It is common among surgery patients, particularly those who are almost eighty years old."

Will did not waver from his position. "But can you explain why she doesn't seem to be able to concentrate on her work? I think I know why. It's because you arrived here with your sad stories about your parents and you've dredged up all the unpleasantness about her own family—about Diana and Forrest and their deaths. It's impossible for her to concentrate when she can't get her own grief out of her head."

"I happen to think that she's dealing with her sadness in a very healthy manner. She doesn't seem to be dwelling on the past, and she seems generally happy and content."

Will stared at me steadily. I met his gaze evenly, refusing to let him know that he was making me uncomfortable. Finally he spoke.

"I can see that you're determined to stay here despite Aunt Alex's best interests. Fine. There are other ways to persuade you to go." He stood up. Relieved, I rose as well. He stepped closer to me and put his face very near mine. His dark eyes flashed anger. His lips curled and he hissed at me, "You are not wanted here. Go away from Hallstead Island or you will be very sorry you stayed."

Then he left, closing the door softly behind him. I found that my knees were trembling and I sat down on the bed with my face in my hands, feeling alone and thoroughly unnerved. What was behind Will's animosity? I didn't believe that his actions were caused by a deep concern for Alex's well-being. I wished there was someone I could talk to. I didn't want to discuss this incident with Alex since Will was her nephew and I didn't want to upset or alarm her. I could perhaps speak with Stephan, but that seemed too much like tattling. I needed to know what was driving Will to speak to me in this way. I certainly wouldn't ask either Vali or Leland, and I didn't really feel comfortable asking Giselle. That left only Brandt and Pete. Since Pete spent so much time on the island, he seemed the better choice. Perhaps I could talk to him, make some inquiries about Will, tomorrow.

Rest was what I needed. I pulled the covers up and closed my eyes, expecting sleep to elude me for a long time. But thankfully I was wrong and I fell asleep almost instantly.

It was not to last.

CHAPTER 7

I don't know what time I was jarred awake by the sound of crashing glass. My heart pounding, I jumped out of bed and switched on the bedside lamp. Looking around, I saw in dismay that a pane of glass in one of the French doors leading to the balcony had been shattered. Glass lay strewn across the floor in a million tiny shards. My mind still foggy from sleep, I could only stand there for a few moments, staring dumbly at the mess. What had happened? Was the wind really blowing that hard? Maybe a branch had been sent flying through the glass. But as I stood still and listened to the night breeze sighing, it seemed unlikely that a sudden gust of wind had caused this damage. I recovered myself enough to put on a pair of slippers, then walked toward the glass slowly, wondering how I was going to clean it up.

Then I saw something under one of the armchairs near the fireplace, and I froze with shock. I knew with sudden clarity what had happened. There sat a large rock. Someone had thrown it through the door.

Now I was afraid. Will must have done this. He had been so angry earlier, and he had promised that I would be sorry for staying here. Had he been standing on the ground below my balcony and tossed it up? Or had he been standing outside my door and thrown it from nearby? Somehow the thought of someone standing right outside my door in the middle of the night sent chills down my spine; it was even more disturbing than the rock throwing itself.

I needed to go downstairs to the kitchen to find a broom and dustpan. Before I went into the kitchen, though, I went to check on Alex, who was sleeping peacefully. I moved quietly, in part not to awaken anyone and in part because I was so frightened. I didn't want to notify anyone who might be lurking around that I was up and alone, but the house was dark and silent. Whoever had thrown the rock didn't seem to be around.

I swept the glass from the floor and disposed of it in my bathroom. I didn't want to venture around the house again to get rid of it. It had become very cold in my room; I was shivering, and my teeth were chattering by the time the floor was free of all the glass. I didn't know what would happen if I tried to build a fire in the fireplace with a draft coming in through the broken French door, so I opted not to try. The last thing I wanted right now was another fireplace incident.

I didn't know what to do with the rock I had found, so I put it in the back of the armoire. I would decide what to do with it later.

There would be no sleep for me now. I went into my dressing room and curled up in an armchair with a blanket. It was slightly warmer in there, since the dressing room door had been closed when the rock was thrown. I had the book with me containing stories of the history of the Saint Lawrence River and I tried reading that for a while.

But my mind was elsewhere. Maybe I should be taking Will's threats more seriously. Maybe I should think about going home. Was it possible that my presence here was upsetting Alex? I didn't think so, but this incident had unraveled me enough that I was beginning to doubt myself. Perhaps I should talk to Alex, but I didn't want to upset her. It was possible that she would even send me home after this incident. What if that rock had landed on the bed? I could have been seriously hurt. I shuddered. I didn't want to think about that. I had to get control of myself. I needed to organize my thoughts and stop thinking about what might have happened. I had known from my first few moments at Summerplace that I was not welcomed by everyone here. Pete had told me that Vali and Leland disapproved of my presence here, and Will had made very clear to me that he didn't want me here either. I shouldn't be surprised that someone was trying to scare me off the island.

My thoughts reeled round and round until morning. I tried to rest but couldn't. Several hours after going into the dressing room, I stepped into my frigid bedroom and saw that a beautiful, sunny morning had dawned. As was common, morning brought with it a renewed purpose and a sense of courage. I had a job to do and I was not going to be scared off. Whoever had thrown that rock into my room would see that the attack hadn't succeeded and that I couldn't be intimidated in such a cowardly way.

The first thing I would do today would be to find Leland and ask him to repair my balcony door. Next, I would see Alex and find out directly from her whether she truly wanted me here. If she did, I would stay.

I felt a little better when I went downstairs. Vali had made Alex a tray and taken it to her already, so I made myself a quick breakfast that included lots of strong coffee, then went in search of Leland before I went to see Alex.

I found him working outside the house where he and Vali lived. He was kneeling on the ground and didn't hear me as I approached, so I startled him when I spoke.

"Leland, pardon me for bothering you, but I was wondering if you could do something for me."

He twisted around to look up at me and said nothing, waiting for me to continue.

"The glass in one of my balcony doors broke and I need a new pane of glass installed."

"I'll see what I can do," he said noncommittally. He straightened up and stood next to me. "How'd that happen?" he asked.

"Someone threw a rock through it," I answered. Then I turned and left him there. I didn't wait to see his expression. I didn't think he had thrown the rock, but in case he had, I wanted him to see that I wasn't afraid.

I went to see Alex next. She was already in her office working, surrounded by sheaves of papers. The phone was ringing, and she looked like she was back in her element. She waved me in, smiling, and I sat down to wait for her to get off the phone.

When she hung up, I waved my hand toward her desk and grinned. "It looks like you're feeling better this morning!"

"Oh, Macy, I slept so well last night. I feel much better today. You know, you were right. I think all I needed was some rest. I *have* been working too hard lately."

"Well," I cautioned her, "it's easy to overdo it. Please take it slowly."

"I will, dear. I promise." She winked.

I had been trying to decide on the best way to broach the subject of my presence, and I had finally concluded that I should just come right out and ask her what I needed to know.

"Do you have a minute to talk?"

She looked at me with concern and laid her papers aside. "Of course, Macy. What is it?"

"I've been wondering whether my presence here is helping you or making things harder."

"Macy! How could you say such a thing? Now that you're here, I can't imagine what I did without you. You have been a great help and comfort to me; you must know that."

"Thank you, Alex. I was just wondering; that's all."

She looked at me suspiciously. "What made you ask such a question?"

"I don't know. I guess I just wanted to make sure that you feel I'm doing my job." I didn't want to tell her about my conversation with Will or about the rock-throwing incident last night. Apparently she knew nothing about it or she would have mentioned it to me by now.

"Macy, please don't think that. I love having you here. I know that Vali and Leland can be a little rough around the edges, but try to ignore them. They feel a little territorial about me and Summerplace."

Vali and Leland weren't the ones I was concerned about at the moment, but I let that go. I got up and thanked her, promising to return to do exercises with her later.

Before I left the office, Alex called me back. "Macy, why don't you go up to the turret today and try your hand at some painting? Isn't that something you'd enjoy?"

My face must have betrayed my excitement, because Alex laughed and added, "I'll bet you've been dying to get your hands on a paintbrush again." She once again handed me the key to the turret door. "You enjoy yourself, and I'll see you later."

I was thrilled to be able to go up into that marvelous turret room and paint. It had been so long since I had created anything with my hands; I was anxious to get started. Upstairs I was welcomed into the turret room again by the clear blue sky and an enveloping sunshine that brightened everything it touched.

The first thing I did was to turn on a large space heater I had seen on my previous visit. I would need extra heat so that my hands would stay warm. Cold, stiff fingers were the bane of a painter's existence.

The heater worked well and soon the room was cozy and comfortable. I looked around for a sketchbook and found one in a large drawer in the artist's table. As I walked slowly around the perimeter of the room, I tried to empty my mind and let the gorgeous scenery inspire me. Then, sketchbook in hand, I sat down on the sofa with several pencils and closed my eyes, breathing deeply. I began to feel myself relaxing and I opened the sketchbook.

I started drawing the first thing that came into my mind: a small pinecone hanging from a bough. I wasn't satisfied with it, and I drew the same pinecone several times on the same piece of paper. Finally, after a number of tries, I finished one that I liked, so I picked up some chalk pastels and experimented for a bit with different hues. Then, holding the sketch pad away from me to look at the picture, I decided I needed watercolors to bring it alive, but I could do that later. Right now, I wanted to draw something else. I began with a picture of a rowboat. It wasn't in the water, since I had always had trouble with outdoor scenes; the light playing off the water was difficult for me to catch on paper. So I drew just a rowboat, old and well used. Pleased with my efforts, I added some muted color to that picture too.

I must have been so engrossed in my drawing that I didn't hear Vali come up into the turret room. When I looked up, she was standing at the top of the stairs, watching me. I gave a start and her lips curled in a crocodilian smile.

"Yes?" I inquired tersely. I was not pleased that she had come up here and I wanted her to go away. She had broken the turret room's spell and I was feeling a little peevish.

"I came up here to see if I could clean. But I see you've taken it over. You have a habit of doing that."

"Vali, I don't know what you're talking about. I haven't taken anything over. If you're still upset about my asking you to set two extra places at dinner last night, then I apologize. But we couldn't send Brandt and Giselle out into that storm."

"What I mean is that you've inserted yourself into this household rather nicely. You walk around here like you own the place. I'd advise you to remember that everyone at this house was here long before you were."

I didn't know what to say in the face of this tirade. I was starting to feel a little nervous up here alone with this woman. I tried to talk to her calmly.

"Vali, I am here to do a job, just like you. And of course I'm aware that I have the low spot on the totem pole here. I can assure you that I have no delusions about my position on Hallstead Island."

"You aren't even wanted here. Why don't you just go back where you came from?"

Not this again, I thought. "Vali," I responded evenly, "I was hired to be Alex's nurse. I am not leaving until she asks me to. Besides," I added, "I spoke to her just this morning and she assured me that she wants me to stay."

She said nothing but stared at me venomously. I met her stare and tried not to flinch. *She's a bit unstable*, I thought. I waited for her to say or do something. Finally she spun around on her heel and left. I listened until she slammed the turret door behind her, and then sank back onto the sofa. *What am I doing here?* I wondered.

I was at a loss to explain why Vali and Will disliked me so. Pete had warned me on my first day at Summerplace that I wouldn't find a warm welcome here, but I had no idea that the feelings against me would be so strong. I laid my head against the back of the sofa and closed my eyes, sighing deeply. How could I convince Vali and Will that I meant no harm to anyone and that my only purpose at Summerplace was to be a good nurse to Alex?

I didn't have long to think, because I heard footfalls on the turret steps again. My body tensed, waiting for another uncomfortable encounter with Vali, but to my surprise it was Stephan's head that poked into the turret room. He looked around and saw me on the sofa.

"Mind if I come up?" he asked genially.

"Not at all; please do," I invited.

He sank down in one of the low armchairs opposite the sofa and looked around the room. "I haven't been up here in quite a while."

"Have you come up here to tell me to go home too?" I couldn't help asking.

Stephan looked at me, confused. "Of course not, Macy. Why do you ask that?"

I smiled at him ruefully. "I'm sorry. I just had a confrontation with Vali and I'm a little ruffled by it."

"What kind of confrontation?"

"Oh, she was just up here suggesting that I go home," I explained. "I told her that I'm not going away until Alex sends me away."

"Good for you," Stephan encouraged me. "Actually, I suppose that's part of the reason I came up here looking for you." He crossed his legs and settled into his chair more comfortably. "You and I haven't had much of an opportunity to talk since I got here, and I just wanted to know how things are going for you at Summerplace. And how Alex is doing, of course."

"Well, let me start with Alex. I think she's doing quite well. Hip surgery is very painful and recovery can be a long, drawn-out process. But she is a remarkably determined woman with a great deal of stamina. Her physical therapy exercises are going well, and she and I walk outdoors every day if it isn't raining."

"She's mentioned several times that she likes to go on walks with you around the house."

"I must say that I'm glad that flagstone path is there for her. Without it, I think walking around Summerplace would be much more difficult. Particularly as she refuses to wear more sensible shoes for walking," I added with a grin.

Stephan laughed. "She does not like to make concessions to her hip," he agreed. "If she doesn't want to wear sensible shoes, no one's going to be able to convince her to do so."

After a moment's pause, Stephan looked at me and said, "And what about you? How are you doing at Summerplace?"

I had been trying to think of an answer to his question, and since he already knew I was having a problem with Vali, I decided to broach that subject.

"Summerplace is breathtaking, and working here is a once-in-a-lifetime opportunity. But, as I mentioned when you came upstairs, not everyone is thrilled to have me here. Vali seems determined that I leave as soon as possible, and she has told me that in no uncertain terms on more than one occasion. And I don't know quite what to make of Leland. He's not as openly rude as Vali is, but he seems to want me gone too. Do you know why they want so much to be rid of me?"

Stephan was silent for a moment before answering. "Vali and Leland have been with Alex for many, many years," he began. "Neither one of them is terribly easy to get along with, as you've discovered, but they have always been loyal to Alex. And she appreciates that. I think she also knows that, because of their ages, they might have a hard time finding other employment if she were to let them go. So they stay on and we more or less put up with them."

"Yes, but that doesn't explain why they want me to leave."

"Before you came here Vali was Alex's nurse in addition to being the cook and the housekeeper for this big place. It got to be too much for her. If you think she's cranky now, you should have seen her a month ago! Anyway, Alex decided it would be for the best if she got another nurse and let Vali go back to the housekeeping and the cooking. Vali is good at those things, as I'm sure you've noticed."

"She is," I admitted.

"Here's what I think is going on: Vali thinks she's going to become less and less important to Alex the longer you're here."

"In other words, she's jealous of me," I said.

"That's exactly it. She thinks that the closer you become to Alex, the more of a confidante you'll become and the more she'll be pushed to the sidelines. Don't forget—Vali has held an important post at Summerplace for a long time now without much interference from anyone. I think she views you as a great threat to her position in the household."

"But that's ridiculous. I'm the last person who could usurp Vali's position here," I protested. "I'm no cook, and I'm not much of a housekeeper, either."

"You know it and I know it, but Vali is looking at this less objectively than we are. I know this sounds pat, but try to ignore her. And as for Leland, he's a good handyman, but he lacks personality. I'm sure that hasn't escaped your notice, either. He more or less does Vali's bidding. So ignore him too. He's harmless."

I wasn't sure how harmless Leland was, but I didn't say anything. I thought briefly about discussing Will's behavior with Stephan but decided against it. After all, Will and Stephan worked together on a daily basis and I didn't know the extent of their relationship.

Stephan seemed to sense that I was mulling over something, and he looked at me intently. "Is there anything else you'd like to discuss, Macy?"

"No, I'm fine. Thank you for telling me about Vali and Leland. It helps me to know a little of their background with Alex."

Stephan went back downstairs then, and I tried sketching again. But my mind wasn't on the page and I knew I was done for the day. I paced around the room for several minutes, trying to find that calm feeling I had had before Vali's visit. I could see Pete down on the dock, working on one of the boats. *It must be nice to work outdoors in solitude*, I thought. Problems start when you have to deal with people. I sighed and went downstairs, locking the turret door behind me when I reached the balcony. I went through my room again, noticing that Leland hadn't replaced the glass yet. The room had warmed up a little but was still quite cold. Then I headed downstairs to make lunch and to check on Alex and return the turret key.

I found her eating lunch from a tray at her desk. She said she would be ready to go for a short walk afterward, so I waited for her in her sitting room.

It was indeed a short walk. We went around Summerplace once and then she said she had to go back to her office to prepare for a conference call with people in New York in just a little while. I helped her up the stairs, and after she went into her office alone I went upstairs for my camera then back outdoors. I wasn't ready to stay inside just yet.

I walked briskly around Summerplace a couple of more times just for some exercise. When I came to Vali and Leland's house a third time, something compelled me to step off the flagstone walkway and set off through the woods on the path to the leaning tree I had found earlier.

I walked slowly, enjoying the peace of the outdoors. *This is how Pete must feel when he's working outside*, I thought a little enviously. I could tell that this place was quickly starting to grow on me, and I wondered how I would feel leaving it to go back to the big city. I snapped lots of pictures to remind me of days like this when I eventually returned to New York.

When I came to the leaning tree I walked up to it carefully, lest I get too close to the edge of the water and slip in. I felt its rough bark under my fingertips, and I stood for some time looking up into its leafy branches. Then I saw something on the trunk of the tree that I hadn't seen before. There were initials carved into the bark: "AH + FH." *That must be Alex Hallstead and Forrest Harper*, I thought. How sweet! I took a picture of the initials to frame as a gift for Alex. My sense of happiness at seeing those initials was inexplicable. It was as if I was getting an intimate glimpse into a happy time in Alex's past. I examined the tree trunk carefully for other initials but found none. That somehow made me happy, too. This tree seemed to belong just to Alex and Forrest. I noticed that the vegetation around the base of the tree was slightly tamped down, as though someone had been visiting it. Probably Pete or even Will, who perhaps missed his uncle and felt close to him in this spot. I must bring Alex here sometime, once her hip allowed the trip through the woods.

I headed back to Summerplace with lifted spirits. I felt somehow closer to Alex, and the feeling gave me the strength I would need to face Vali. Once back at the house, I spent the afternoon tidying up the library and starting a rudimentary system for categorizing the books in there.

At dinnertime, I went downstairs still feeling lighthearted over my small discovery at the leaning tree. I went in to see Alex before dinner and was very happy to learn that she planned to join us in the dining room. As always, she was dressed becomingly, complete with jewelry and low-heeled pumps.

I admired her outfit, and, looking pleased, she replied, "I didn't want to dress up too much and feel foolish, but this is a special occasion, so I wanted to look nice. After all, that dining room hasn't seen me in quite a long time!"

We walked into the dining room together. Stephan and Will were already there, as usual, talking. They came over to us immediately.

Stephan wore a wide smile as he pulled out the chair at the head of the table. "The seat of honor, madam," he said laughingly. Will hooked Alex's arm through his and walked slowly with her to her seat, a handsome picture of gallantry. And clearly Alex was enjoying the attention. A place had already been set for her at the dining room table, so Vali must have known that Alex would be dining with us.

And Vali outdid herself for the occasion. There were fruited Cornish game hens with sautéed vegetables, a mesclun salad with herbs and white wine vinaigrette, and a sublime pumpkin mousse. The four of us enjoyed the dinner thoroughly, and Alex's presence seemed to bring out the conversationalists in Stephan and Will. They both talked animatedly throughout the meal, and I could almost forget— almost—Will's previous behavior toward me.

I didn't say much during the meal because I was so interested in listening to the conversation, but I did pipe up during dessert.

"I went for a lovely walk this afternoon in the woods behind Vali and Leland's house," I began. "The path ended at that really interesting tree that leans out over the water."

I continued, taking only brief notice of the looks being exchanged among my fellow diners. "Alex, I found the initials 'AH + FH' carved into the trunk of the tree—I think that's enchanting!" I gushed.

An uncomfortable silence settled over the table like a wet blanket. I groaned inwardly. I had obviously said something wrong, but I had no idea what it was.

I was seated next to Stephan, who put his hand over mine on the table. "Macy," he said quietly, his eyes on Alex, "the leaning tree is where the ashes of both Diana and Forrest were scattered after their deaths. So it's a place of bittersweet memories for Alex."

I gasped and turned to Alex. "I'm so sorry, Alex. Please forgive me. I had no idea . . ." I trailed off.

"Macy dear, there's nothing to forgive. How could you have known the significance of that tree? You know, finding those initials must have been fun. That tree didn't always represent sadness, you know." She smiled, but her thoughts seemed far away. Now I understood why the ground beneath the tree was lightly worn; one or more people must visit that place to mourn Diana and Forrest.

I had ruined the dinner conversation with my faux pas, and Stephan tactfully brought the meal to a close. "Alex, I hate to bring up work, but would you mind terribly meeting with me for a few moments? There are some finer points in one of the negotiation documents that I'd like to discuss with you before tomorrow. Will, would you run upstairs and bring us the file, please?"

"Of course I don't mind, Stephan," Alex replied. She stood up and asked, "Macy, you'll be in later to see me?"

I nodded mutely and she left with Stephan.

Will stood up to go after Stephan and Alex were gone. "Nice going. What did I tell you? You're nothing but a reminder of her pain," he said, shaking his head. I didn't answer him and he left the room.

I didn't go upstairs because I didn't want to run into Will up there. I sat before the fire that was crackling in the living room, feeling sorry for myself once again. Leland poked his head in at one point, saw me, and left again. I was starting to feel totally alone here. How I wished I could talk to my parents.

Maybe I could. I could follow Alex's lead and talk to them. Not out loud here in the living room, but in my head. I closed my eyes and concentrated on the comforting hisses and crackles coming from the fireplace.

In my mind, I went back to my childhood. It was nighttime, and my mother and father had come into my room to tuck me in. It had been a miserable day at school because I had inadvertently hurt my best friend's feelings and she was upset. I remembered asking my parents what I should do to make her feel better. "It was an accident," they had soothed. "You didn't know you hurt her. You need to explain to her what happened, ask for her forgiveness, and then forgive yourself. Everyone makes mistakes, and very often forgiving yourself is the hardest thing to do. Even harder than asking forgiveness from someone else." I remembered that night as if it were yesterday. I could recall how my mother smelled of violets, how my father's face was scratchy as he leaned down to kiss me good night. Their words had been true that night, for I fell asleep peacefully and spoke with my friend the following day. She forgave me as soon as she heard my story, and all was well. I had learned an important lesson that night about allowing myself to make mistakes, and I was amazed that the scene had replayed so vividly in my mind just now when I needed it most. I had already asked Alex for forgiveness, and now I needed to work on forgiving myself. This experience had indeed been like talking to my parents, and I was filled with a sense of peace and stillness. I breathed a prayer of thanks for their wisdom and understanding, even these many weeks after their deaths. I was especially grateful to Alex for sharing with me her practice of talking to Forrest when she was alone.

I opened my eyes again to the fire blazing before me. I stood up, feeling better, and went to see Alex as I had promised. She was alone in her sitting room; Stephan and Will had left. I sat down next to her and we sat together in silence for quite some time. It didn't seem awkward or uncomfortable, but I did break the silence after a while to speak to her.

"Alex, I had no idea that the leaning tree held such important significance to your family, and if I had known I certainly would have respected that."

Alex remained silent for several more moments before she answered me. "This is the second time that you've felt like you've done something to upset me, but what you've really done is to bring back for me memories that are more precious than anything else. I can't thank you enough. I am so grateful that you came here to remind me of these things."

We talked companionably of insignificant things for a while longer before Alex went in to bed. I went upstairs, relieved that the evening had ended so well, but when I went into my room, I was met again with the shock of cold from the icy wind that blew through the broken window. I suppose I wasn't really surprised that Leland hadn't fixed the window. I ran downstairs, where I found a flimsy piece of cardboard and tape, then returned to my room and fashioned a makeshift window where the glass had been. It would do to keep out the worst of the wind, but it was still very cold. I vowed not to sleep again in the chair in the dressing room, so I undressed quickly, grabbed a heavy quilt from the bottom of the armoire, and jumped between the covers, pulling them up to my chin. If the space heater in the turret hadn't been so heavy, I would have brought it down earlier in the day to use overnight.

I had the nightmare again that night—the sirens wailing, the police officers walking around the wreckage of the cars, and me sitting helpless on the hillside nearby. I woke up with my heart pounding but without tears this time. Thinking back to my "conversation" with my mother and father just a few hours earlier, I was strangely comforted. Perhaps the nightmare was losing its hold on me. I was able to calm my pounding heart, but it took me a long while to fall asleep again because of the frigid air still swirling around me. I finally dropped off, but not before promising myself that if the door didn't get fixed tomorrow I would sleep somewhere else.

When I went downstairs for breakfast the next morning, Vali informed me that I would be alone in the dining room since Stephan and Will had left for New York an hour earlier. I hadn't known they were leaving, but I was pleased that Alex might have some extra time now to spend on her exercises and rehabilitation. I went in to see her after I had washed my breakfast dishes, and she was indeed relaxing, enjoying a news magazine in her sitting room.

"No work this morning?" I asked.

"Oh, I always have work to do, but Stephan and Will left early today. They have a meeting to attend, and they'll be back in a couple of days. Since they're gone I thought I would catch up on some reading before going into my office."

"Would you like to work on some exercises before you get dressed?" I suggested.

"That would be fine, Macy. Then I can shower and dress afterward."

We worked on her exercises for less than an hour. I didn't want her to tire, especially because she had been worn out earlier in the week and because she had taken a short break from the exercises. She did well, though, and didn't seem too tired when we finished. I told her I thought she should go outdoors later for a walk around Summerplace. She agreed and I left her to her shower.

When I walked into the foyer, Leland was clumping out the front door. I didn't want to bother him any more than necessary, but I felt I could not spend another night in that icebox of a room.

"Leland," I called after him, "were you able to find glass to replace that broken door in my room?"

He didn't turn around. "Nope. Gotta go all the way to Cape Cartier to buy glass to replace what broke. Don't know when I'll get to it." And he left.

I was feeling frustrated. I had to do something about that door. I could think of only one person to ask for help, so I walked down to the boathouse to look for him.

I found Pete wiping paint from his hands with rags that reeked of turpentine. The odor mingled with the smell of diesel from the boat engines and the tangy and unmistakable scent of the river water, which I was learning to recognize. It was not unpleasant.

"Morning," Pete said when he saw me.

"Good morning. It looks like another beautiful day!" I responded.

"Enjoy the nice days while you can, because once it starts to get cold, it doesn't stop. There'll be snow on these islands before you know it."

"Pete, I was wondering if you could help me with something," I said tentatively.

"Sure, if I can," he replied. "What do you need?"

"Well, the glass in one of the doors in my bedroom is broken, and Leland doesn't seem to have the time to fix it. I wouldn't pester you, but it's so cold in there at night and . . ."

"And you want me to replace the glass," he finished.

"Yes, if it's not too much trouble."

"That shouldn't be a problem. I think there's some replacement glass in the storage rooms above the boathouse. Let's go have a look, and if there's some there, I can replace that for you this morning."

I thanked him, relieved and hopeful that I might be sleeping in a warm room again tonight.

He led the way up the stairs inside the boathouse to the upper level, where his rooms and several storage rooms were located.

"Let me just run into the kitchen and wash this turpentine smell off my hands," he said. He opened an old, thin wooden door and entered his apartment, waving me in behind him, and I stepped inside and found myself in a sparsely furnished, masculine apartment. The walls were all off-white, and an old, comfortable-looking sofa sat in the middle of the large open room. Pete had walked into the next room and he called to me from there, "Make yourself comfortable— I'll just be a minute."

I wandered over to the large windows, which gave the room a beautifully tranquil and ever-changing view of the water. After staring out the windows for a moment, I continued my self-guided tour around the room, walking over to have a look at some pictures I noticed grouped on one wall. They were all outdoor shots, and Pete was in most of them with other people whom I didn't recognize: Pete with several men about the same age, each holding a fishing rod; a picture of a woman who looked to be in her sixties, probably Pete's mother; a photo of a large group of people in graduation robes, Pete in the top row with a wide grin. There was also a picture of Pete with his arm around an attractive woman who appeared to be several years younger than him. The one photo without any people in it was a picture of one of the boats that was housed downstairs. I remembered that Pete had mentioned that he kept his own boat at Hallstead Island.

I sat down on the sofa to wait for him. He came out of the kitchen a moment later holding a cup of coffee. "Coffee?" he offered.

"Yes, thanks."

He disappeared into the kitchen and then came to the doorway again. "Why don't you come in here and get your own cream and sugar? I don't know how you like it."

I followed him into the small, neat kitchen. The walls were blue and everything else was white, from the appliances to the towels to the small table and chairs that stood in the middle of the room. I helped myself to the cream and sugar that he had placed on the table, and then he gestured toward my mug and said to me, "If you want to bring that along, we'll go into one of the storerooms to look for that glass."

I followed him out of the apartment and down a short, dimly lit hallway that ended in a huge room filled with all kinds of boating equipment and various unidentifiable pieces of small machinery, likely for use on boats or around the island. There were several smaller rooms off the big one, and I followed him into one that was filled with cans of paint, outdoor painting supplies, and cleaning equipment. "Not in here," Pete mused aloud. He went into another small room, and there we found several pieces of glass leaning against one another in a metal contraption. Each pane of glass was buffered by a large chamois cloth. He went to a cupboard that hung on the wall and took down a sheet of paper. After scanning the paper for a few moments, he turned to me and said, "We've got one that'll fit in your door. It's right over here." He quickly found the pane of glass we needed, and, very carefully, he eased it out from between two other panes. He slid the glass, still covered with its protective cloth, over to a bare wall and leaned it there. Then he said, "If you can carry my tools up to the house, I can put it in your door today. Otherwise, I can get Leland to do it."

"I can help," I said eagerly. I didn't want this job left up to Leland or it might never get done. I put my coffee cup down and joined Pete. He disappeared for just a moment and came back with a pair of gloves.

He gingerly picked up the glass and headed downstairs. I followed with his toolbox. Once downstairs, we made our way carefully out of the boathouse and up through the trees to Summerplace. In my room, Pete set the glass against the wall, I handed him the toolbox, and he went to work. I stayed in case he needed any help.

As it turned out, he needed my help only to maneuver the glass into the correct position to install. I mostly watched him. He worked intently, stopping only now and then to stand back and look at his work. When he was satisfied, he put his tools away and said to me, "There you go. You ought to be a lot warmer in here tonight. Why did you stay in here last night?"

"I don't think I even realized that it would get as cold as it did. And with the air seeping in around the cardboard, I wasn't sure I could build a fire in the fireplace. Plus, I felt a little uncomfortable sleeping in the living room."

"How did the glass break in the first place?" he asked.

I had been waiting for this question. "Someone threw a rock through the glass a couple of nights ago," I explained lightly.

Pete looked shocked. "Who would have done that?"

"I have no idea."

"Have you told Alex?"

"No," I replied quickly. "I don't want Alex to know. I don't want to upset her."

He was silent for a minute and I continued, "She's been very busy, and earlier in the week she was under the weather, and I know she has a lot on her mind with her work. I don't think this incident needs to be on her radar just now. After all, my job here is to make her life easier, not more complicated." I smiled. "Besides, now that the glass is fixed, the whole thing is over." *But not forgotten*, I thought.

"I hope so," Pete agreed.

"Thank you for helping me," I said. "Leland thought he had to go to Cape Cartier to get new glass, and he didn't have the time to do that. He must not have known that there was glass stored above the boathouse."

Pete looked grim. "He knew. He just didn't want to do it. Remember I told you to expect some hassle from Vali and Leland? That's exactly the sort of thing I was talking about."

"Oh, I've experienced some of that," I told him. "You were right; they don't seem to want me here. But I've explained to Vali that I have a job to do and I intend to do it."

"That's the spirit." Pete nodded approvingly. "As hard as it is to do, just try to ignore them."

I laughed. "I've heard that before."

Pete picked up his tools and looked around my room. "Anything else need fixing?"

"No, thanks. Just the door. I'll definitely sleep better tonight," I said gratefully.

"You get a great view from this room," Pete noted, looking out the French doors. He certainly was more talkative, even friendly, today.

"It's beautiful," I agreed warmly. "Looking out over those trees is calming and energizing at the same time."

Pete seemed to know exactly what I meant. "The water has the same effect on me," he said.

Our conversation stalled then, and he headed toward the bedroom door. I was walking over to the door to open it for him when something on the small table in front of the fireplace caught my eye. I gave an involuntary exclamation.

"My album!"

"What album?"

I went over to the album and leafed through it quickly. All the pictures were there and intact. "It's a photo album that I brought with me when I came here," I explained. "After my first day here, it disappeared. I looked everywhere for it, but I couldn't find it. I was beginning to doubt I'd ever see it again."

"I'm glad it turned up," Pete said. "I wonder where it's been." He cocked his eyebrows and looked at me intently.

"I have no idea. The only thing I can think of is that someone took it out of idle curiosity and gave it back when their curiosity was satisfied."

"And you're sure it was really missing?"

"Of course I'm sure!" I exclaimed in exasperation. "Why would I say it had been missing if it's been on that table the whole time? I'm not crazy!"

"I didn't imply that you're crazy," Pete answered softly. "I was merely wondering if it's possible that you misplaced it temporarily."

"It is not possible," I replied shortly.

"Okay, okay. May I see it?" he asked.

Reluctantly, I handed him the album. He set down his tools and looked at the pictures slowly, occasionally pausing to ask a question.

"Are these your parents?" he asked, pointing to a shot that had been taken earlier in the summer at a restaurant in Connecticut.

"Yes," I answered quietly.

"Where do they live?"

"They lived in Connecticut, but they were both killed in a car accident almost two months ago," I answered, staring at the photo with tears welling up in the corners of my eyes. I blinked them away quickly.

"I'm sorry," Pete replied. "I had no idea."

"That's okay."

He continued looking through the album. "I recognize a lot of famous New York City places in these pictures," he noted. "You must miss the big city."

"New York is exciting, but I wouldn't say I miss it that much," I said.

"Well, I'd better get back to work," Pete said. "See you later."

I opened the door for him and thanked him again for helping me, then turned back to my room and sat down in front of the fireplace. Picking up my album again, I turned to the page Pete had asked about. My mother and father smiled at me from a photo taken just a few months ago. The tears started falling onto the protective covering of the photo before I even realized I was crying. Mom and Dad had been visiting me the night they died. I wished I had kept them in New York City for just a few more minutes that August night. Then they would have missed that drunk driver and they would still be alive.

I suddenly found that I couldn't stop crying. I put the album down, bowed my head, and let the tears come. I had been resisting this moment for weeks, and now that I was alone in this room on this island, I could mourn the two people who had been so important to me. I wept for a long time, and it felt good.

After a while, as sometimes happens, I was all cried out. I found that I was hungry for lunch, and I needed to look in on Alex. I checked my reflection in the bathroom mirror; my eyes and nose were predictably puffy and red, so I ran some cold water and splashed my face several times, then applied some concealer under my eyes. The effect was certainly not glamorous, but it was passable.

Rather than going downstairs right away, I stepped out onto the balcony for a few deep breaths of fresh air. I stood with my hands on the railing, thinking about my conversation with Pete. These trees were indeed calming, and their flowing movements and soft sounds soothed me.

But the calm didn't last for long. As I stood looking into the distance at nothing in particular, a sound interrupted the peace. I looked quickly in the direction the noise had come from and saw Vali standing at the corner where the balcony disappeared around the turret wall. I said nothing while I waited for her to speak, and finally she walked up to me.

"Miss Hallstead is asking for you," she said simply.

"Thank you. I'll go see her right now," I answered. I didn't want to be up on this balcony with Vali for long, so I started walking away from her. But she wasn't finished speaking.

"Come with me. I want to show you something."

I had no desire to accompany Vali anywhere, but something in her voice compelled me to turn and walk with her around the balcony to the opposite side of Summerplace, where a long, gracefully curving staircase led to the ground. I could see nothing, so I turned to her questioningly.

"I thought you might like to have a look at the place where Mr. Harper died," Vali said in a low voice.

"Why would you think that?" I asked, becoming a little alarmed at her strange behavior.

She shrugged and pointed to the staircase. "He fell down those stairs. Broke his neck."

I started down the stairs, hoping Vali wouldn't follow me. "It wasn't necessary to show me this place," I informed her over my shoulder. "I have to go see what Alex needs." I continued down the stairs and looked back only when I reached the bottom. Vali still stood on the balcony, staring at me. *She gives me the creeps*, I thought. *I need to be more careful about finding myself alone with her*.

Not wanting Vali to see that I was disconcerted by our encounter, I walked slowly until I reached the front of Summerplace. Then I hurried inside to Alex's rooms and found her waiting for me in her office.

"Macy, let's have lunch outdoors on the porch," she suggested. "It's such a lovely day outside, and I want to tell you about a project I have in mind for you tomorrow."

"That sounds great," I responded, intrigued. "Shall I get us something to eat?"

"I've already asked Vali to bring us something on a tray, and Leland has put some chairs and a small table outside my office. It's just a little cool, but I don't think it will be uncomfortable."

I was looking forward to having lunch with Alex. Her initiative in inviting me to join her in a meal outdoors was an encouraging step in her recovery.

We went outside to sit and in a few minutes Vali appeared carrying a large tray containing chicken salad sandwiches, sliced melon, lemon cookies, and hot tea. She looked at me archly as she set the tray down on the table, and I ignored her. I poured tea for Alex and for me and Vali left, taking the tray with her.

I enjoyed my lunch with Alex very much. We talked of art and books and the weather and trivial things. Afterward we went for a walk around Summerplace and Alex told me about her winter home. The house, called Solstice, was apparently much smaller than Summerplace and was located on Pine Island, not far from Hallstead Island. Because the winters here in upstate New York were harsh and long, many of the houses lacked the capability to operate year-round. Summerplace was one of these. So every fall Alex directed the household's move to Solstice, where everyone would remain until spring was in the air. Alex said she hated to leave Summerplace but she had no choice. Even if she were to enable it to remain habitable all winter, the snow and ice made it very difficult for people, particularly Stephan and Will, to get to and from Summerplace during the winter months. The homes on Pine Island had amenities that made winters more bearable in this region, and there were bridges connecting Pine Island to the mainland of both the United States and Canada. She informed me that she kept two cars at her home on Pine Island and that the household used them over the winter for everyday needs and short trips.

Alex's project for me was to accompany Pete to Pine Island the next day to have a look around Solstice. She wanted me to begin rearranging furniture and carpets, just as I had done in Summerplace, to enable her to move around her winter home more easily. Pete's job was to check the cars and the outside of the house for any work that would need to be completed before the household moved there for the winter. I was eager to go. I was interested in seeing Solstice.

After our walk, I gave Alex a short break and then joined her for a brief period of physical therapy. She did quite well and seemed pleased with her progress. She said she hoped to be able to get up to that turret room before the move to Pine Island.

The rest of the day passed quietly. Alex and I ate dinner together in the dining room, a simple meal. After dinner we sat in front of her fire and she showed me several art books that she kept in her sitting room, antiques that she had bought on a trip through Italy many years ago, and I felt privileged to look through them with her.

When she was ready for bed, I left her and went upstairs to my room. After building a small fire in the fireplace, I sat up in bed for a long time reading the Paul Malo book, eventually finishing it and then falling asleep quickly. I didn't have the nightmare that night, and I think it was because I had been able to openly grieve for my parents earlier that day for the very first time.

CHAPTER 8

In the morning, I was surprised when I walked into the dining room to find Will sitting at the long table alone. He raised his glass of orange juice toward me in greeting and I sat down at the table with him.

"I didn't expect you back so soon," I remarked.

The smirk on his handsome face did not become him. "I'll bet you enjoyed my absence."

I chose not to answer him, and we ate breakfast in silence, though he turned his dark gaze on me several times as we sat there. Uncomfortable, I ate quickly so I could leave the room. When I had finished washing my dishes, I noticed that he had also left, leaving much of his food untouched.

I hurried through the living room on my way to check on Alex but paused for a moment as I glanced up at the portrait of Forrest Harper. I shivered as I visualized the winding staircase on which he had died. I wished Vali hadn't shown me where the tragedy occurred.

When I reached Alex's sitting room, I knocked on the door and poked my head in. Alex was already there, pacing slowly up and down in front of her sofa. She was still dressed in her nightgown and seemed not to have noticed my presence. Her hands were fluttering nervously and she was talking softly to herself.

I was alarmed. This was not the Alex I expected to find this morning, especially after the good day she had had yesterday. I walked to her quickly and took her cold hands in mine. She looked at me, confused, and I gently helped her to sit down.

"Alex, are you feeling all right?"

"Macy, I'm glad you're here." She was silent for several moments. I didn't probe, feeling sure she would tell me the problem when she was ready. At length she spoke again.

"We had a good day yesterday, didn't we, Macy? It felt good to walk around outdoors, and it felt good to do the physical therapy exercises. And I especially enjoyed our luncheon outdoors." She stopped.

I nodded in agreement, waiting for her to continue.

"You know, I was glad to start the process of moving the household to Pine Island. Are you still going over there today with Pete?"

"Not if I'm needed here." I looked at her pointedly.

"Well, we need to be organized about the move. It's a long process and we need to get started. The weather will be getting very cold soon. It will probably even snow before too long. We need to get started," she repeated.

I tried to soothe her. "Alex, I think you're very organized about the move. And we'll get started today. But you seem to have the move to Pine Island down to a science—I can't believe that's what has you upset this morning." Again, I waited for her to tell me what was bothering her.

"Macy, you've been here barely a week. And I don't know what I would do without you anymore. Have you seen the picture of my daughter, Diana, in the living room?"

"I don't think so," I answered, not sure where this conversation was headed.

"Come with me. I want to show it to you."

She led the way out of her rooms and into the living room, where she made a beeline for a portrait that sat on an antique console table behind a sofa. Somehow I hadn't noticed the portrait before now. She picked it up and stared lovingly at it. It was, in fact, a portrait of the same woman who appeared in the photo I had seen on my first day here, the photo in the library of the smiling young woman wearing a formal gown and a sparkling necklace. Not only was it the same woman, but she was wearing the same dress and the same necklace, too.

"I saw a picture of her on my first day here. In the library," I added. "I didn't know that was Diana. It's a lovely portrait."

"Thank you. I painted it. I painted it from a photo that was taken on Diana's eighteenth birthday."

I stood next to Alex, unsure of what to do next. She was still staring fixedly at the photo and seemed oblivious to anything else. Suddenly she turned to me with tears in her eyes.

"Diana died eleven years ago today," she stated flatly.

My heart swelled with sympathy for her and, impulsively, I reached out and hugged her. She clung to me for a moment before holding herself away from me, tears trickling down her cheeks.

"I wasn't the best mother in the world. God knows I made mistakes. But I miss her very much."

"Of course you do. And I'm sure you were a very good mother to Diana. You know, we always seem to dwell on the things that we did wrong once it's too late to fix them. But a couple of wise people once taught me that you have to learn to forgive yourself. Maybe you should think about forgiving yourself."

Alex smiled. "That's good advice, Macy. I will try to forgive myself. But our relationship *could* have been better. She could be very tempestuous, and Forrest and I spoiled her, I'm afraid. We were always working and we wanted to make up for the time we weren't able to spend with her, I guess. She and I fought a lot, and I will always wish that we had been closer." She sighed.

"On this date every year, I get distraught thinking about her. Yesterday I thought that, with starting to plan for the move to Pine Island and with my work and my rehabilitation, I would be able to keep myself busy so that the pain wouldn't touch me. But obviously it has. Talking to you has helped. Thank you."

"You're welcome. Would you like to talk some more?"

"No, I think I'd like to get dressed now, and then I'd like to do some exercises. Could we do that for a while?"

"Of course. I'll meet you in your sitting room after you get some clothes on."

Alex and I spent the rest of the morning walking and doing her physical therapy. While she bathed and dressed, I wrote a report for her doctors. My job required that I report weekly to her team of doctors and this was already my seventh day here. Happily, I was able to note that Alex was making significant progress in her rehabilitation and seemed to both enjoy and look forward to her exercises. Her primary doctor was nearby on the mainland, so I could mail the report from Pine Island later that afternoon.

While I wrote my report, Will came looking for Alex and the two of them disappeared into her office to work. I had a short time before I had to start getting ready to go to Pine Island, so I slipped into the library to work on my new categorization system. After a quick lunch I ran upstairs to change my clothes. I knew it would be a chilly boat ride and I wanted to be sure I would be warm enough. I was already dressed warmly, but I added a thick wool sweater and a shearling coat. I pulled my hair back into a ponytail, checked my makeup, and went in search of Pete down by the boathouse.

I found him loading some tools into one of the boats. It was smaller and more modern than the mahogany one he had brought to pick me up from Cape Cartier. It looked sportier and faster and I found myself getting apprehensive about making the short trip to Pine Island. I must have given myself away somehow, because Pete noticed.

"What's the matter?"

"It's nothing, really," I answered, not wanting him to know how nervous I was. "I—"

"Hmm?"

"I just—I guess I'm not used to being in boats. They make me a little nervous; that's all."

"You didn't seem this nervous when I picked you up in Cape Cartier last week."

"I think that was because I had a lot of other things on my mind."

"Oh. There's nothing to be afraid of. They're perfectly safe. And this is a state-of-the-art craft. Besides," he added, grinning, "you know how to swim, right?"

I winced. "Actually, I don't," I said almost apologetically.

He looked at me sharply. "You can't swim?" he asked in surprise.

"No."

"That's okay. Just make sure you learn at some point. But don't worry about the boat ride. I'll get us there in one piece. Could you give me a hand with these tools?"

I started handing him several boxes of tools that sat on the dock and was grateful for the diversion. Before long we were ready to board the boat.

"Hop on," Pete directed me. I stepped gingerly into the boat and chose a seat near the front, a little out of the wind.

"It's a nice day, but it'll be pretty chilly once we start moving," Pete told me. "There are a couple of extra Windbreakers under that seat," he said, pointing to the seat behind me. I nodded. He looked sideways at me from the driver's seat. "Do you want a life jacket?" he asked. "Maybe that would make you a little more comfortable."

I was undecided. The nurse part of me knew wearing a lifejacket was the smart thing to do, but the woman part of me didn't want to look foolish. Vanity lost out and I opted for the life jacket. Before we pulled away from the dock I was outfitted in a bulky orange vest. With my sweater, coat, and lifejacket, I must have looked puffy and ridiculous, but I didn't care. I felt less panicky and that was worth the embarrassment.

Pete eased out into the channel, where there was hardly any other boat traffic. I must have been gripping the sides of my seat, because he looked at me and laughed.

"You can let go now. Why don't you relax and enjoy the view? You won't find scenery like this anywhere else in the world."

After that, I tried to take his advice. I loosened my grip on the seat and sat up straighter to look around. Luckily, he wasn't going too fast and before long I found myself forgetting my fear somewhat and actually enjoying the trip. As we motored along, Pete talked amiably about the islands we were passing, ones he hadn't mentioned on my first trip to Hallstead Island.

"That one over there is called the Isle of Caprice. And that one on the port side is called Fuller's Folly. The story goes that a Mr. Fuller, from New York City, bought the island in order to build a getaway home for his wife, but when she found out she hated the idea. She was a city person, through and through. He visited only once in a while after that and built a small fishing lodge on the island instead of a big, fancy home. He left the island to his children, who are apparently still alive and never set foot on it. I guess they got their love of the river from their mother."

I nodded and smiled absently.

"That right up ahead is actually called Snake Island. No one really knows how it got its name, but the locals have some ideas. One story tells of a young girl who was a passenger on a boat that capsized nearby. It was getting dark and she couldn't swim. She was found the next morning, perfectly fine, on the island. She swore that a huge snake had passed her in the water, encircled her with his tail, and pulled her to safety."

"If a snake had wrapped itself around me, I think I would have had a heart attack," I noted.

"Nobody knows how she made it to the island, so it *is* a little strange. Another tale is of an old man who was marooned there one summer night. He was rescued the next morning by a fisherman. When the old man got on the fisherman's boat, he acted like a madman, screaming and ranting about the snakes slithering all over the island." Pete shook his head. "Personally, I think someone made that story up to scare local kids off the island. If you look at Snake Island from the air, it's thin and long and shaped vaguely like an 'S.' It looks like a snake; that's probably why it's called Snake Island."

I shivered. Wasn't it enough that I had to be on a boat? Did I have to be subjected to stories about snakes, too?

We were both silent for several minutes after that, looking around at the autumn river scenery. It *was* beautiful. The leaves were a rainbow of warm colors and the air was crisp and clear. The waves danced across the channel, their small whitecaps rising and then disappearing. Though the breeze on the boat was a little chilly, one could easily forget the cold and sit mesmerized by the idyllic surroundings.

Before long, Pete pointed out Pine Island looming ahead of us. As its name suggested, the first things I noticed were the abundant pine trees. They were tall and slender and grew thickly, their stands parting every so often to allow boaters glimpses of the island's stately homes, mostly Victorians. Many were white, but I also saw yellow, blue, pink, and even lavender homes. Most had quaint boathouses at the water's edge.

"Alex's house is around the other side of the island, away from the channel," Pete informed me. "There's a lot less boat traffic over there. I thought I'd show you the rest of Pine Island first."

I thanked him and watched the attractive homes slip past. When we rounded the end of the island we were in a shady narrows between Pine Island and a smaller one that was just a stone's throw away. Pete nodded toward the smaller island and said, "That's Bella Island. Alex's place is coming up." I turned my attention back to Pine Island and saw a hunter-green boathouse about a hundred feet ahead. As we drew closer, I could see tan Victorian gingerbread on the boathouse. It looked dark, much like Summerplace and its matching boathouse, but it was charming. A long, narrow flight of steps led from the boathouse to the main house, which was perched high above the water on a hill of rock and scrub grass. I immediately recognized the stairs as a dangerous hazard for Alex and mentioned my concern to Pete.

"Alex hasn't used those stairs in a long time," Pete replied. "When the household is on Pine Island, Alex has two cars that she uses if she has to go anywhere. Vali and Leland use the cars to run errands, too. So whenever Alex leaves the house, she goes out the front and never has to go up or down these stairs. And if she does want to go out in the boat for some reason, Vali or Leland drives her in the car to the public dock and I pick her up there in the boat. In fact, that's how we'll take her over when she closes up Summerplace this fall. I'll take her to the dock and Vali or Leland will pick her up in her car. We make it as easy as we can for her. Besides that, going on a boat isn't going to be an option too much longer on the river. We put the boats in storage over the winter."

When Pete had docked the boat, I finally took off my life jacket and placed it on my seat.

"That wasn't so bad, was it?" he asked, grabbing two large wooden boxes from the floor of the boat.

I grinned. "It was okay. I'm glad I wore it, even if it did make me look like a big orange marshmallow." I picked up a small toolbox that

Pete had placed on the dock and followed him up the stone steps, some of which were a little wobbly and unstable.

"I'm going to have to shore up some of these steps," he remarked as we climbed. "These are worse now than they were in the spring when Alex moved back to Hallstead Island."

I counted forty-two steps, turning this way and that up the hill and around boulders and trees. When we got to the top I was a little out of breath. Pete laughed good-naturedly. "Maybe you'll want to use the car too, whenever Alex does." I laughed with him and we continued walking to the front of the house.

Solstice was a very pretty Victorian house. It had a wide double front door of dark oak with a large brass door knocker on each side. Pete took a huge key out of his coat pocket and inserted it into one of the locks. It turned hesitantly, making metallic scraping sounds. He grimaced and noted, "I'll need to oil these locks, too. It looks like I'm going to have to start making a list of the projects I'll have to get done before everyone moves here for the winter."

I was anxious to see the inside of the house. Pete opened the door and let me step in front of him into a small, rather dark foyer with several pieces of antique furniture. Pete told me he was going to the garage to start working on a couple of projects, and I started wandering around the rooms on the first floor. The first room I came to was a small but cozy and inviting living room decorated mostly in chocolate-brown leather furniture. On the walls, as in Summerplace, were drawings and paintings that appeared to all have been done by Alex. Next I came to a library, done in reds and browns and home to thousands of books.

Besides the living room and the library, I found the dining room, the kitchen, a small formal parlor, and a large suite of two rooms that I supposed to be Alex's office and bedroom. She didn't appear to have her own sitting room in this house, so she probably used the living room when she wanted to relax. The rooms on the first floor contained many obstacles to Alex's easy movement, and as I walked through the rooms I noted on a pad what I would need to do to make the house safe for her.

After I had looked around downstairs, I took a look at the second-floor rooms, three bedrooms and a small sitting room. I took a peek in the bedrooms, one of which would be mine, and found that they were identical. The two extra bedrooms, I assumed, belonged to Will and Stephan.

I didn't bother to look around the third floor, since Alex had told me that those rooms belonged to Vali and Leland and Pete.

I made my way back down to the first floor and started working in the living room. Several occasional tables had to be moved, and I eventually succeeded in moving one of the heavy sofas several inches as well. After rifling through some of the kitchen drawers to find tape, I secured all of the electrical cords that could potentially cause Alex any trouble. I needed double-sided tape to anchor the area rugs, but that would have to wait since I couldn't find any in the house.

I continued through each room downstairs, systematically removing any obstacles to Alex's easy movement through her house. I didn't move any furniture or items upstairs, since Alex probably would not go there very often. If she wanted to, I could move that furniture quickly at a later date.

When I was finished I went in search of Pete. I found him in the garage, tapping on something with a small hammer. He looked up at me in surprise and glanced at his watch.

"Are you done already?"

"Yes. I was able to go through the rooms downstairs and finish what I needed to do."

"Good. I didn't realize it was getting so late. We'll have to be heading back before too long." He turned his attention back to the machine he was tapping and gave it two more quick whacks.

"There. That's it for today. Are you hungry?"

"I guess so," I answered.

"That's good, because I'm starved. What do you say we grab a bite to eat at the only restaurant on this island and then hightail it back to Summerplace?"

"Sounds good to me."

After making sure all the doors were locked and the lights off, we made our way down the stairs to the boat. Going down was easier than going up.

When we got in the boat, the first thing I did was don the life jacket. Pete chuckled. "We're not going very far, you know. It's just around the island."

"I know," I admitted sheepishly. "I just feel better with it on, that's all."

He steered the boat around Pine Island and put in at a small, rickety dock that looked like it hadn't been painted in years.

"This restaurant is our island version of the haute cuisine you're probably used to in the big city." He smirked.

"I guess we'll see if it measures up," I replied good-naturedly.

He looked at me out of the corner of his eye and grinned.

I liked the restaurant immediately for its rustic interior. There were pine plank floors, and a big brass chandelier lit up the room. We sat down at one of the many vacant tables and looked at the menu, which was well used and stained.

We both ordered the trout, which came with a cheesy polenta and squash. When the waitress disappeared with our orders, Pete looked at me intently and said, "So. Tell me what you really think of Summerplace and its inhabitants so far."

I thought about my answer before speaking up. "Well," I began, "Alex is a wonderful lady. I hope that I can help her get to a point where she can walk without pain. I want her to be able to climb stairs and take a boat ride and do whatever else she wants to do. She certainly is determined to get back on track and heal herself."

I paused, and Pete said nothing. He raised his eyebrows, obviously waiting for me to continue. I looked outside at the scenery and thought again how beautiful these surroundings were. Just then, the waitress brought our food.

"That was quick," I observed.

"They probably had some ready. We're the beginning of the dinner crowd, if you can call it that. There will be a few people trickling in while we're here. In the summer, this place is jam-packed. But I don't believe you were done discussing Summerplace and its residents. And part-time residents."

"You don't give up, do you?" I asked. "I wish Vali and Leland liked me better. They don't seem to have gotten used to me being around."

"And they won't," Pete put in.

"And as for Stephan and Will, I find Stephan to be a charming man and I find Will to be bored and dissatisfied with everything. He doesn't act his age. They both seem to dote on Alex, though, which I think is wonderful. She needs that."

"Bored and dissatisfied, huh? I never thought about Will that way." Pete was quiet for a moment. "But you're right that they both dote on Alex. And you're right that she needs that."

We ate the rest of our meal, which was delectable, in comfortable silence. We had to eat quickly because the sky was already starting to turn a pink-yellow color. It wouldn't be long before the sun disappeared.

When the check came, I tried to take it, but Pete was too quick for me. "You can pay next time."

We left hurriedly and got into the boat. Pete had already pulled away from the dock before I got my life jacket on, and the ride back was much quicker than the ride to Pine Island earlier in the day. In a way I was almost disappointed, despite my apprehension over being in the boat. I would have liked talking with Pete a little longer. He seemed pretty down-to-earth, and, despite our rocky start, he was the closest thing to a friend that I had around.

When I got back to Summerplace, I went in to check on Alex. I found her slowly pacing the floor of her office. She had been unable to work all afternoon, she told me. She was just as agitated as she had been when I had left her earlier, and my heart ached for her. Losing her child must have been an unbearable experience, and it was no wonder she was upset on the anniversary of her daughter's death.

I went to the kitchen and made her a mug of warm milk with cinnamon and nutmeg to flavor it a bit. Back in her sitting room, where Leland had built a fire, she had taken off her shoes, and I massaged her feet and lower legs while she drank the milk. She also took a mild sedative that the doctor had left for her, and we talked, mostly about Diana. Alex seemed to need to talk about her daughter, and she was happy to have a willing and interested listener. She told me stories of Diana's childhood and of her somewhat wilder and rebellious teen years. I got a glimpse of what it must have been like for Diana to grow up in a very affluent household where the parents had lots of love but not much time to give their child. I came away from the conversation feeling rather sorry for the girl, who had obviously tried so hard to get her parents' attention.

After a while Alex began to get sleepy. I helped her into bed, knowing that she would sleep soundly through the night.

I wish *I* had. But I wasn't to sleep again for a while.

CHAPTER 9

The familiar nightmare came again just a few hours later, with its terrifying sounds and lights and images. I woke up with tears streaming down my cheeks, my pajamas clinging to me with cold sweat. I could take little comfort in the lessening frequency of the dream, because when I finally fell into a fitful sleep, I had yet another nightmare. In this one, I was caught in a swirling eddy of water, reaching out wildly to a hand that I couldn't quite grasp as the water closed over my head again and again. I woke up this time gasping for breath, my heart pounding violently.

I didn't sleep the rest of the night and got up in the morning feeling groggy and cross. I also had a throbbing headache.

I made myself a cup of coffee and sat down at the dining room table, grateful to be alone. But my solitude didn't last, as after several minutes, Stephan came in, to my surprise. He explained that he had come back from New York very early that morning and Pete had picked him up in Cape Cartier.

Then I went to look in on Alex. I found her standing in her office holding a sheaf of papers, still as agitated as she had been the evening before. I was a little startled to see her in a velour exercise suit with her hair up in a braid, since she was always coiffed and dressed in business attire by the time I got to her rooms in the morning. She was pale.

"Alex, are you all right?" I asked with concern.

"I don't know, Macy," she replied shakily. "Here."

She thrust the papers at me and I looked at her, bewildered. "What do you want me to do with these?"

"Read them."

I looked at her warily as I opened the top folder. What help could I possibly be with the work that she did?

I leafed quickly through the first several pages, not understanding what I was reading. I was becoming confused, and my headache combined with the lack of sleep was beginning to make me a little irritated.

"This looks like a copy of a birth certificate. For a baby named Lily. Who's Lily?"

Alex said nothing, and I read on.

That's when I saw it.

Mother's name: Diana Hallstead.

"Diana had a baby." It came out of my mouth as more of a statement than a question.

Alex nodded.

"How old was she when the baby was born?"

"Fifteen."

"What happened to the baby?"

"She was given up for adoption."

I kept reading, but there wasn't much I understood. There were copies of tests that had been taken at the time of the baby's birth, showing that everything was normal. There were short notes from Diana to her mother, written, it appeared, during the several months leading up to the birth of the baby.

"Weren't you with Diana when she was pregnant?" I asked.

"No. She went to stay with family in Canada."

"Why didn't she stay here?"

"I didn't want a pregnant teenager in my home," Alex answered simply.

Then there were other pages of correspondence and legalese between an attorney and the Hallstead family.

I almost missed what I was supposed to see. I had quickly scanned one page and turned to the next one when I saw a name I recognized out of the corner of my eye. I flipped back nervously and sent papers scattering to the floor. I focused in like a laser on the sheet I had been reading and snatched it up, leaving the rest of the papers jumbled on the floor. This time I examined the words more carefully, and suddenly I understood. It felt like someone had punched me in the gut.

Child's adoptive parents: Fred and Marianne Stoddard. My parents.

Slowly I looked up at Alex. She was staring at me with a pallid face and thin white lips. She swallowed hard and I heard her grind her teeth.

"What is this?" I heard myself say.

"Macy, dear, I—"

"Please don't call me dear," I interrupted her.

"Macy, I'm sorry. I needed you to know. I need to explain everything to you."

"Don't explain anything. Don't say a word. Just leave me alone." I gathered up the papers I had dropped and put them under my arm. Then I turned on my heel and walked out without looking at her again.

I don't remember how I got my feet to move. I needed to get as far away from Alex as I could. I was feeling sick to my stomach and my head was pounding like a jackhammer.

I found myself sitting at the base of the leaning tree.

The place where the ashes of my biological mother—and my grandfather—were scattered.

I didn't know what to feel. I had always known I was adopted as an infant. I had even tried looking for my biological family once, but I'd gotten nowhere.

I'd never expected *them* to find *me*.

So many emotions were reeling inside my head. I felt angry, confused, sad, and deceived. How could I have been duped like this? I sat dumbly staring at the water, at its ceaseless undulations, my over-whelmed thoughts taking no particular direction.

What to do now? Go back to New York? Stick it out here until my job with Alex was completed? Should I go somewhere else? Where? I supposed I could move in with Simone. I had two elderly aunts in Connecticut, but I didn't want to move in with them. There was no one else. No other family. I wished I could talk to my parents. My *real* parents, the ones I grew up with, Fred and Marianne Stoddard. Even talking to Alan would be better than bearing this alone.

I don't know how long I sat at the leaning tree before I looked up and saw Stephan standing beside me. Lost in my own gloomy thoughts, I hadn't even heard him approach.

"Can we talk a minute?" he asked quietly.

"What do you want to talk about?"

"I think you know."

I swept my arm toward the ground, indicating that he was wel-come to sit down. He looked around, picked out a large stone, and sat on it. He said nothing, and I merely waited for him to speak. I cer-tainly didn't intend to say anything.

But he just sat there, looking at me. Finally, in spite of myself, I asked in exasperation, "Did Alex send you to look for me?"

"No. She didn't have to."

I stared at him in stony silence.

"Macy," he began, "I can't imagine how you must be feeling right now."

My expression remained unyielding.

"I spoke to Alex shortly after she spoke to you this morning. She's very upset."

"*She's* upset?" I asked a little too hysterically.

"Yes, she is. I suppose some of this is my fault. I mean, I am the one that facilitated this entire saga."

That got my attention. "What are you talking about?"

"You can't picture the . . . how shall I say this? . . . the unpleasant-ness around this place when Diana announced that she was pregnant. Alex and Forrest were devastated, as most parents would be. The histrionics and drama were constant and exhausting. From all three of them.

"Diana had spent her young life longing for attention from her parents, and they had spent her young life trying to make up for all the time they had to spend away from her," he continued. "It was a situation that was bound to explode at some point.

"When she became pregnant, they sent her away. Far away. She went to stay with extended family in Nova Scotia, which is quite secluded and which they knew would be like a prison for her."

"So what happened when the baby—when I—was born?"

"There was never any question that the baby would be given up for adoption. Diana certainly wasn't mature enough to raise a baby, and—"

"What about the father?" I interrupted.

He waved his hand in the air in a gesture of dismissal. "No one ever even knew who he was. Including Diana."

"Go on," I directed him.

"As I was saying, Diana couldn't have kept the baby. And Alex and Forrest had careers that prevented them from raising the child. Not only that, but they had social reasons for not keeping the baby. The fact that Diana had a baby as a young teenager would have been in all the social papers in New York, and the family had to keep up appearances. They had no choice but to send her away and hide her pregnancy."

I made a scoffing sound. "Keep up appearances?" I asked incredulously.

"Things were different then, Macy. It was scandalous when a teenage girl became pregnant. It reflected badly on her parents. It's still not exactly accepted, but it's a lot more common.

"Alex had a reputation to uphold. She represented, and still does, a successful international company. She didn't need negative publicity. She didn't need attention focused on her family."

"So I was given up because Alex had a reputation to keep."

Stephan sighed. "I knew this wasn't going to be an easy conversation. But, Macy, please try to understand. Alex feels differently now. Hindsight is twenty-twenty, and I know she would keep the baby if she had to do it all over again. She's an old woman, Macy. She's trying to correct some of the mistakes she's made during her long life."

"Too bad one of those mistakes was a human being." I knew I was being petulant now, but I couldn't help it.

Stephan ignored my tone. "As Alex has gotten older she's become less and less interested in what other people think. She's come to realize the importance of having family. She took it for granted for too long, and now that both Diana and Forrest are gone, she has had to face the consequences of her decision not to raise Diana's baby. She's alone and she regrets that decision."

"It's a little late for her regrets."

"I agree, but I'm not in her position. I think she was beginning to feel desperate."

"So why the elaborate plot to get me to come here under false pretenses? That wasn't fair."

"Well, in Alex's defense, I wouldn't say they were false pretenses. She really did break her hip and she really did need a nurse."

"But why the big plot?" I demanded again.

Stephan rubbed his chin and thought for a moment before answering. "I don't necessarily agree with the method that Alex used to get you here, Macy. But while her intentions may have been selfish, they weren't malicious. You'll have to agree with that." He waited for some sign of agreement from me, but I said nothing.

"I wish I could make you understand how badly Alex needs to feel a connection with someone in her family. How badly she needs to feel a connection with Diana. She suffers a lot of guilt over not having been a more attentive mother to Diana. And now Forrest is gone too, so the rock she used to lean on is no longer there. Sure, she leans on me, but I'm just her friend. I'm not family."

"What about Will?" I asked.

"Alex is fond of Will, but he's not her son. You are Alex's only living blood relative. Oh, Will is her nephew, but he is related on Forrest's side. You are the bridge to Diana that no one else can be."

"How do you know so much about this?"

"I know Alex. I'm her closest confidant and friend. I know that she wanted to tell you all these things herself, but I doubt you would have listened. Am I right?" He smiled for the first time.

"Yes, I suppose you are right," I acknowledged.

"As I started to say earlier, I guess I'm partly responsible for this whole situation. You see, I'm the one who arranged your adoption by Fred and Marianne Stoddard."

"You knew them?"

"No. But the attorney who set up the adoption for the Stoddards was a friend of mine, and I managed to stay in the background of the entire process. At the request of Alex and Forrest, I checked references and did a lot of digging of my own to find out all I could about the Stoddards. They were practically perfect, and Alex and Forrest wanted to be sure that you were going to a wonderful home."

He paused. "Over the years, I've kept tabs on you. The Stoddards never knew anything about it. Nor did Diana. But we knew when you graduated from high school and when you graduated from nursing school. And when your parents passed away. If you look through some of the papers that Alex gave you this morning, you'll find some of the information we kept about you throughout your lifetime. Macy, when you think about it, you had two families looking out for you. Alex has always loved you. Forrest did too. They've been very proud of you."

"So what's next? Am I supposed to stay here?"

"That's entirely up to you. Alex obviously can't make you stay, but I think she'd be thrilled if you did."

"But I don't know what to say to her or how to act around her or anything."

"Well, you're Alex's nurse. I think that for now your primary role has to be one of caregiver. I don't think she can expect more than that from you right now."

I nodded soundlessly.

Stephan got up to leave. "I know this is a lot for you to digest. But take some time to think about the things I've said. I hope you're able to forgive Alex for doing this to you."

He turned to leave, but I had one more question for him.

"Stephan, who else knows about this?"

"Just you and Alex and I. We've always been careful to keep the situation confidential."

After he left, I remained at the leaning tree for a little while longer, reflecting on his words. But eventually my headache became so bad that I needed to go back to my room to lie down. Quietly, so no one would know I was back in the house, I let myself in the front door. On the foyer floor near the door I found an envelope with my name scrawled across it in Alex's spidery handwriting. I didn't really want to open it, but my curiosity got the best of me and I opened it slowly. A short note and a key fell into my palm. Glancing at the note, I read Alex's words:

Macy,
I thought you might like to have the key to your turret room. Please feel free to spend as much time up there as you wish.
Alex

I still needed to lie down. Maybe I could rest up there on the couch. Maybe nobody would find me if I went up there for a while.

I pocketed the key and continued up to my room. I left the papers Alex had given me in the desk, took some aspirin, and let myself out onto the balcony, where the sunshine and sparkling blue sky mocked my sour mood.

Slowly climbing the stairs to the turret, I could already see the bright light that would greet me when I got up there. I remembered thinking that I would never want to close the shades up there. I chuckled wryly. I couldn't wait to get those shades drawn today. I wanted nothing more than to lie down and shut out the sun.

When I got up into the turret, I found a long-handled instrument that I could use to easily pull down the shades. I closed my eyes and tried to rest on the sofa, but not surprisingly, I could not sleep. My mind flitted rapidly from one image to another, all of them unwanted. I saw the picture of Diana that Alex had painted downstairs at Summer-place. Over it were superimposed the images of my parents, whose funerals had taken place so recently. I saw Alex, pacing slowly. I saw Diana swirling in water, fighting for her life. I saw Forrest, lying on the ground at the base of a staircase. I shuddered and my eyes jerked open.

Maybe painting would ease some of my disquiet. I stood up and found that my stomach was less queasy now and my headache was subsiding, but I wasn't ready to face the daylight yet, so I turned on a lamp near the easel. I picked up a canvas out of the basket of blank ones and chose several dark oil paints. My painting would match my mood.

I skipped the sketching this time and just painted what my hands wanted to. Before long I had a rough outline. I didn't recognize it as the leaning tree until I stood back to look at my work. But there it was, reaching out its limbs over the restless water. I thought again of the place that the tree had held in the lives of the family members at Summerplace. My family.

No. My family was from Connecticut. I had a wonderful mother and father who had given me a loving upbringing—an upbringing that I never would have traded for anything.

Why did Alex have to go and ruin everything?

I was lost in my own dejected thoughts when I thought I heard a very faint click. That noise was followed by a heavy scraping sound, then silence. I stood still for a moment, listening, but could hear nothing. I had begun to feel restless, so I decided to clean up my painting supplies and take another walk outside. When I had cleaned my work area and set my painting aside to dry, I went downstairs to let myself out onto the balcony.

The door was locked. I didn't remember locking it behind me, but I must have. I tried the door to my room, but it also wouldn't open. I reached into my pocket for the key, but it wasn't there. An icy trickle of apprehension began to crawl up my spine. I must have left the key in the turret door when I went up earlier. Someone had found the key and locked me in! That must have been the clicking noise I had heard.

I ran back up into the turret and immediately raised all the shades. Nearly blinded by the sudden sunlight flooding into the room, I looked around for someone outdoors whose attention I could attract but saw no one. I tried opening the windows to yell outdoors, but they had been painted shut. Fuming, I sat down on the sofa and tried to relax, but I found that I was too angry. I got up every couple of minutes to check outdoors again for signs of people. No one was there.

Who had done this?

Could it have been Stephan? I didn't think so. If anything, he wanted me to come downstairs sooner so that I could start patching things up with Alex. How about Will? This seemed like just the type of thing he would do in order to get me to leave Hallstead Island, which he had flatly told me was his goal. Vali or Leland? Maybe. Vali certainly wanted me gone too, and either she or Leland could easily have discovered that I'd left the key in the lock and used that knowledge to play a dirty trick like this.

After a little while, the events of the day, combined with my lack of sleep the night before and my raw emotions, got the better of me. I closed my eyes and was finally able to rest.

I don't know how long I slept, but when I woke up the sun was dipping low in the sky. It took just a moment to remember.

Alex was my grandmother.

And I was locked in the turret.

I got up to look outdoors again, and this time I saw Pete walking below. I started banging on the window, and he slowed his pace and looked around. He hadn't seen me, so I banged again, more loudly, and this time he looked up toward the turret. He waved at me and continued walking. I banged the window yet again, hoping I wouldn't break the glass with all my pounding, and finally he stopped and looked up at me. I pointed to the balcony and turned an imaginary key in an exaggerated motion, hoping he would understand.

Either he understood or my skit piqued his curiosity, because he turned around and headed back toward Summerplace. I stayed at the window until I saw him emerge on the balcony, and then I ran down the turret steps and waited for him at the door. Seconds later the door swung open and I smiled at him in relief.

"Thank you so much!" I cried.

He looked at me with confusion. "What's going on?"

"I've been locked up here. That's why I was banging on the glass to get your attention."

"The key was in the lock. Why?"

I took a deep breath. "This has been a rotten day. I must not have been thinking and I left the key in the lock when I went up to the turret earlier."

"But why didn't you just go into your room?" he persisted.

"Because I couldn't open that door, either," I explained.

Pete looked at me incredulously. "What are you talking about?" he asked, exasperated. He leaned across me and tried the door to my room. The doorknob turned, but the door wouldn't budge. He pushed harder but had no luck.

"That's strange," he said, half to himself. "Let's go find out what the problem is."

We went out onto the balcony and let ourselves into my room through the French doors. We both stopped and stared in surprise when we entered the room. The big old desk had been shoved in front of the turret door, blocking the entrance. Now I knew what had caused the scraping sound I had heard earlier. This was even creepier than having the turret door locked—someone had been in my room. I turned to Pete. I had thought about telling him about my day, but now I just wanted to be alone.

"Pete, thanks for rescuing me. If you don't mind, I think I need some time by myself."

He seemed to understand and looked at me with concern. "Let me know if you need anything," he replied.

I nodded and turned back into my room. I would leave the desk where it was for now. I wandered into the bathroom and had a look at myself in the mirror. I looked pretty grim. I needed a shower and a change of clothes, since I had slept in the ones I was wearing.

Once I had showered and put on fresh clothes, I felt a little better. I certainly looked more presentable. I didn't need to glance at my watch to know that it was almost time for dinner. I was starving. I hadn't felt like eating at lunchtime, and all I had had for breakfast was a cup of coffee. Besides, a plan was formulating in my mind and I was looking forward to implementing it.

Stephan and Will were the only people in the dining room. Apparently Alex had decided to take dinner in her sitting room, and for that I could only feel a grateful relief.

Stephan pulled out my chair for me with a questioning look in his eyes, but I didn't meet his gaze. I mumbled a word of thanks and ignored the conversation that continued between the two men.

Presently Vali arrived to serve dinner, which was a delicious salad followed by a pasta dish. I said little throughout the meal, and Stephan and Will talked between themselves. But as Vali came to serve dessert, I cleared my throat and asked a question.

"Would any of you happen to know who locked me in the turret room this afternoon?" My voice sounded loud to me. Will and Vali exchanged glances but said nothing. Stephan looked at me in disbelief.

"Macy, are you serious? Are you sure the door wasn't just stuck?"

"Yes, I'm sure. Because not only was I locked in the turret, but a large piece of furniture was moved in front of the turret door in my room so I couldn't get into my room that way, either. Does anyone know how that happened?" I repeated my question.

There was an uncomfortable silence while I looked around at the others. Vali glared at me and left the room. I wondered how long it would take her to tell Leland what I had said. Will shifted in his seat and carefully inspected his fingernails. Stephan looked at me sadly and finally spoke.

"Macy, I'm so sorry this has happened. It made an already rough day even worse."

Will raised his eyebrows and shot Stephan a look of curiosity but wisely kept his mouth shut. I excused myself and left the room.

I don't think I really expected to get an answer to my question. I merely wanted to show the culprit that I wasn't going to cower in my room in fear because of this silly trick.

Since I had slept during the afternoon, I wasn't tired yet. I stopped in the library for a new book to read, but before going upstairs I took a detour into the living room. It was quiet and dimly lit, and I stood before the painting of Forrest that I had so admired earlier. His eyes and his smile were gentle. I felt again the wish that I had known him when he was alive. My grandfather. Sighing, I turned away from the painting and went upstairs. I built myself a fire, curled up in my armchair, and read my book. Once or twice I felt a twinge of guilt over not having exercised with Alex all day, but I quickly brushed those feelings away. She couldn't possibly expect me to spend any appreciable amount of time with her after her bombshell announcement. I wondered what I would say to her in the morning.

Eventually I got into bed, hoping for a rest uninterrupted by nightmares. I slept soundly all night; apparently my afternoon nap had not interfered greatly with my sleep schedule.

I awoke later than usual and had breakfast alone, bracing for my morning session with Alex. Vali came into the dining room once, took one look at me, and announced, "You look terrible."

"Thanks," I shot back.

When I had fortified myself with eggs, toast, and juice, I went to Alex's rooms.

I knocked softly on the door of the sitting room, but there was no answer, so I went through the sitting room and knocked on the bedroom door, not expecting Alex to answer this time either. When she didn't, I continued through the bedroom and knocked a third time, on her office door. This time she answered.

"Come in."

I pushed the door open tentatively and walked in. Alex was sitting behind her big desk, her hands folded in front of her. She looked exhausted. Forcing myself to remember that my relationship with Alex was first and foremost a professional one, I was determined to treat her as I would any other patient. I took a deep breath.

"Good morning, Alex. How are you feeling?"

She looked at me with a wan expression and waved one of her hands. "All right, I guess," she answered.

"Do you feel strong enough to work on your exercises this morning?" She nodded.

I led the way slowly into her sitting room, where we worked on her exercises for the next hour. She went through the motions of her exercise routine dully, and I did not encourage her to talk. If she wanted or expected a heart-to-heart, she was going to be disappointed today. Maybe the time would come when I would feel ready, but that would have to be on *my* schedule, not hers.

At the end of the hour, I suggested that she take a shower, but she declined. She went back to her office to work, and I went outside for a walk. I met Pete walking up to the house from the docks.

"What happened to you?" he asked me. I must have looked worse than I thought.

"You sound like Vali," I retorted. He didn't reply but waited for me to start talking. I didn't know how to broach the subject of my problems, so I just launched into the short version of what had happened yesterday before he rescued me from the turret.

"Alex told me yesterday that Diana was my biological mother."

Pete stopped short and looked at me in amazement. "You're kidding," he finally said.

Did I look like I was kidding? "Of course I'm not kidding," I answered testily.

"You had no idea?" he asked.

"No. No, I didn't. I once tried to find my biological parents, but I had no luck. I didn't want my mom and dad to feel that I didn't think they were good enough, so I stopped looking."

"So where do you go from here?"

I shrugged. "I honestly don't know. It's a little awkward between Alex and me right now."

Pete nodded and waited for me to go on.

"I always thought that finding my biological family would be *my* decision!" I blurted out.

"Maybe you weren't ready to find your biological family when you went looking. But maybe you're ready now."

His remark caught me off guard. I suppose I had been looking for sympathy, but his comment made me stop and think.

"Maybe," I conceded. "Where are you headed?"

"I've got to go talk to Alex about one of the boats."

"Oh."

"I'm sure I'll see you later. Hang in there." He smiled.

His smile warmed me and I walked away with spirits that had lifted just a little.

I ate lunch alone after my walk and then went looking for Alex again. She informed me that something important had just come up with her work and that she wouldn't be able to walk this afternoon. Part of me was glad that she had canceled our usual afternoon activity, but part of me was a little anxious. She was not going to heal effectively if she skipped her exercises, and she hadn't done any yesterday.

Now I had the afternoon to myself, and I decided to go up to the turret to paint. When I walked into my room to get to the balcony, I was surprised to see that a thin envelope had been pushed under the door. The letter was from New York City, from an administrator friend at my nursing agency. She had written to check in on me and see how things were going. If only she knew! Although it was technically against agency rules, she had written to tell me that another job had become available. If I was interested, she wrote, this would be a great opportunity for me. The patient was a well-known New York City matron who lived in posh surroundings in an old building on the Upper West Side. She needed nursing supervision only twice a day and I would be paid handsomely.

I was torn. Suddenly I had an opportunity to leave this place and forget about Diana and all the heartache she had caused. I could leave Alex to her memories and not be responsible for bridging the gap between her and her family's past. I could start fresh.

But leaving Alex—did I really want to do that? She was still in the process of healing and I had a professional responsibility to her. I didn't know whether I could live with myself if I left her now in the care of a stranger. I looked at the letter again. My friend needed an answer soon. I would have to decide quickly.

I put the letter in my desk and continued on my way to the turret. This time I was sure to pocket the key after I unlocked the turret door. No one was going to lock me up there again! Unlike the day before, I left the shades up and felt a welcome warmth from the sunlight. Looking critically at the painting of the leaning tree that I had started, I acknowledged that it certainly was dark. I had used dark greens and browns and maroon for the tree, a charcoal gray for the water, and a dusky blue for the sky. It actually wasn't bad for a painting that had been completed in just a few hours. Even the water, which was my weak spot, didn't look too bad.

Today I wanted to paint a picture in colors that were a little lighter and brighter. I painted the first thing that came to mind: a small, uninhabited island. I sketched first—the trees, the rocky shoreline, the clouds, the reeds and bushes. After a while, when I was satisfied with my drawings, I took out the paints and painted my island. I used light greens and yellows, a sapphire blue for the water, and a light blue for the sky. When I stood back from it to have a look, I had to admit that I liked this painting better than the one I had completed the day before.

While I worked I was able to completely empty my mind of all unpleasantness, but everything came back in a flood as I was putting the painting supplies away, my thoughts tumbling around in my head. What should I do about Alex, if anything? Should I accept the other position? Should I tell anyone here about my newly discovered identity? I was unsure of how to proceed. As for Alex, her actions had hurt me, and I certainly wasn't ready to accept her as a grandmother.

As for the new position, I was leaning toward accepting the offer from my agency. It might help both Alex and me if we had some space between us, and another nurse would surely treat Alex well.

As for telling anyone my new identity, Alex and Stephan already knew, and now Pete as well. I wasn't ready to tell anyone else just yet. I think I feared being despised even more around Hallstead Island if others knew about my true relationship to Alex. Vali and Leland and even Will disliked me enough already. Why give them another reason?

When I was done cleaning up, I went back to my room and sat down at the desk. I needed to respond to my nursing agency. Though I drafted a letter accepting the position in New York, there was a slight feeling of unease in the back of my mind, a feeling like I was running away from a challenge and a stirring of guilt that I was leaving Alex in someone else's care. But the more I thought about it, the more the positive aspects of the new job outweighed the negatives. I would sleep on it and mail the letter from Cape Cartier in the morning. Pete could take me over in the boat.

I didn't feel like talking with Stephan or Will that evening at dinner, so I went downstairs an hour before dinner and made a sandwich for myself. Dinner for the others was cooking, but luckily Vali was not around to harass me. I left a note for her stating that I would not be downstairs for dinner and I took my sandwich upstairs to eat. On the way I checked quickly in Alex's rooms. She was in a consultation with Stephan and Will and said she would be fine for the rest of the evening.

I spent the rest of the night catching up on some correspondence that I had been neglecting, including letters to two coworkers from my previous job, letting them know that I was coming back and would see them soon.

Feeling tired, I got into bed early. There was a fire burning in the grate and my room was nice and warm. I was just starting to doze off when there was a knock at my door. I threw on a robe and went to the door quietly, unsure of whether I should open it. I stood next to the door and said softly, "Who is it?"

"Pete."

I opened the door and stood back to let him in, but he stayed in the doorway.

"I'm sorry if I woke you up," he said.

"That's okay. I wasn't asleep yet. I just got into bed a little early."

He seemed unsure of what to say next.

"Did you need something?" I prompted.

"Not really. I was just wondering if you wanted to go on a little day-trip with me tomorrow. I'm heading over to Heart Island, where there's a big castle you might like to see. There's an interesting story behind it."

"I'm not sure I should leave Alex for a day."

"Actually, this was Alex's idea. She's good friends with the curator, and he's agreed to let us have the place to ourselves tomorrow. Normally the castle isn't open to the public at this time of year." He paused. "Alex thought you might like a day away from here."

I nodded. I *could* use a day away. And as long as Alex had given her permission, I could go with a clear conscience. Pete's reference to an interesting story behind the castle sounded intriguing. So I smiled at him and said, "I'd love to. What time are you planning to leave?"

"We'll go around midmorning. Come down to the dock around ten thirty and we'll head over."

"Thanks, Pete."

"See you in the morning." And he turned and walked down the stairs.

I went back to bed with a feeling of anticipation. The castle and Heart Island sounded interesting, and I couldn't wait to hear the story. And it might be nice to spend the day with Pete too.

I got back into bed and fell asleep quickly. But it wasn't long before I woke up feeling wide-awake. Maybe going to bed early hadn't been such a good idea after all. The clock on my nightstand read twelve thirty. When I wasn't able to fall asleep again after much tossing and turning, I finally got out of bed. I had finished my book earlier and I was bored. I didn't want to be alone with my thoughts, though, so I put on my robe and slipped into the hallway and down the stairs.

The door to the library was closed. I pushed it open, expecting to find the room in darkness. But to my surprise, several lamps were on and the room was lit warmly. I didn't see anyone at first, but when I looked around the room, I gave a start. Alex was sitting in one of the leather chairs, staring at nothing. She was wearing a nightgown and slippers and her hair was again in a braid.

"Alex! What are you doing in here? It's after midnight!"

She turned her head slowly to look at me, but she didn't appear to have heard my question. I was starting to become alarmed. I went over and put my hand on her shoulder. "Alex," I repeated, "is something wrong?"

She stared up at me blankly. I took her cold hand in mine and felt her pulse. It was a little faint. I pulled another chair next to hers and sat down. "Alex," I began softly, "can you tell me what the problem is? I can't help you if I don't know what's wrong. Are you sick?"

She shook her head almost imperceptibly. I waited for her to speak. This was very unlike the Alex I knew during the day.

"I need your help," she finally whispered.

"How can I help you?" I asked.

"Someone killed Forrest. They're going to kill me, too."

I stared at her in shock. Was she hallucinating? "Alex," I said gently, "Forrest died in an accident several years ago. He wasn't killed."

"Yes, he was," she insisted. "You don't know."

"Don't know what?" I asked. I was becoming very confused.

"You don't know what I know."

"What do you know?" I thought it would be best to humor her until she snapped out of this strange funk.

"It was my fault."

"I'm sure that Forrest's death wasn't your fault."

"It was my fault Forrest died," she repeated, this time with more urgency. Her voice was stronger; she was beginning to sound more like the Alex I knew, and I was becoming disturbed.

"Can you explain to me how it was your fault?"

"I didn't push him, but I could have saved him."

"I don't understand," I told her. She sounded more lucid now, but her words still weren't making much sense to me.

She swallowed and began her chilling story.

CHAPTER 10

"All of this happened several years ago, but I remember it like it was yesterday. I was sitting on the floor up in my studio—your turret room. I was surrounded by cardboard boxes. I had taken a day off from my work and there were so many things in the studio that I needed to sort through and organize. I remember being in a panic thinking that I might not be able to finish it all in one day. It was beautiful outside, and the room was bright with sunshine.

"Forrest came up the stairs looking for me. He had also taken the day off and he was bored. He had already been fishing early that morning and he didn't want to be inside on such a nice day. He asked me if I wanted to go for a walk with him. Or take a break on the balcony."

Alex sighed. "I told him I didn't have time to go walking just then and that I didn't need a break yet. There were so many things I thought I needed to accomplish that day, and I figured we could take a walk or relax later that afternoon. Or the next day.

"So Forrest went out on the balcony for a look around. He did that sometimes. He would walk around the entire balcony on the second floor just to have a bird's-eye view of Hallstead Island. He loved it here," she added wistfully.

"After he left, I kept working. At one point, I heard voices out on the balcony. They were low, and I couldn't hear what was being said. I couldn't even tell who was talking. But it didn't matter. I stayed focused on what I was doing and it wasn't long before I didn't even notice the voices anymore."

Alex paused, then closed her eyes and took a deep breath, as if trying to steel herself against what was coming. Then she continued. "After a while my knees started to hurt. So I decided to take that break. I went in search of Forrest, assuming he was still on the balcony somewhere, probably sitting in the sun. When I didn't see him, I walked around the balcony looking for him. I figured he was on the opposite side of the house. But he wasn't. I had gone three-quarters of the way around the second floor when I saw him." Alex covered her face with her thin hands and shook her head.

"As long as I live, I will never get that sight out of my head! He was lying there on the ground, on the rocks. There was blood everywhere and there was a large gash on his head. His body was broken. I have never been so scared in all my life. Even when Diana died, I was always thankful that I wasn't the one to find her. I couldn't have lived with that memory."

She paused for several moments, then went on more calmly. "He was at the bottom of the staircase leading from the balcony to the ground. I hurried down the stairs, screaming for help. He had already died when I found him." She swallowed hard. "It wasn't long before everyone was gathered around Forrest and me. Vali and Leland were there, and Pete and Will. I couldn't bear to leave Forrest's side, but I was covered in blood and Will pulled me away. Pete had called for a doctor, who got over to the island quickly, bringing the police with him. But it was too late. Before long the coroner came and took Forrest away.

"Do you see, Macy? If I had taken that walk with him, like he asked, he wouldn't have died that day. I could have saved him. I could have prevented what happened, or I could have gone for help sooner and he wouldn't have died."

In spite of myself, my heart went out to Alex all over again. I took her ice-cold hands in mine. "Alex," I began, looking into her eyes, "Forrest's death wasn't your fault. It was a tragic accident. And if the fall hurt him as badly as you say, then you wouldn't have been able to get help in time to save him. He would have died anyway. You can't blame yourself for what happened."

"But it wasn't a tragic accident, Macy. Someone killed him. I know it."

"What makes you so sure?"

"The voices that I heard. Whoever was talking to him killed him. I know because I asked everyone later who had been talking to him before he died, and no one admitted to having been on the balcony with him." She looked at me imploringly. "Who could possibly have wanted to kill my Forrest?"

I wasn't convinced that Alex was remembering the events of that day correctly. "Alex, the police investigated and ruled Forrest's death an accident, didn't they?"

"Yes, they did, but I never told them about the voices that I had heard."

"Why not?"

"Because everyone else believed that he had fallen down those stairs. After all, he was getting on in years and going up or down those balcony stairs could have caused him to fall. Everyone else said that I must have been imagining things when I heard those voices. They said maybe I was hearing the wind in the trees. I started to believe that I was cracking up, that maybe I had actually imagined the voices. And I was afraid for myself. I was afraid that if I did really hear the voices and if I said something to the police whoever killed Forrest would kill me, too."

"So what happened that you weren't able to sleep tonight?"

"Nothing out of the ordinary," Alex acknowledged. "It's just started to bother me again. I think I pushed my fears to the back of my mind when nothing happened to me or anyone else following Forrest's death. But now you're here. And you are part of this family. I've been thinking a lot about my family since your arrival, and I've gone back over the events of that awful day again and again. And I'm sure that Forrest didn't die accidentally. He was killed. And I needed to talk to someone about it. I'm glad you found me in here, Macy. I think Forrest would have wanted you to be the one I talked to."

"What can I do to help you?"

"You need to help me find out who killed Forrest."

I stared at Alex in shock. "Alex, how on earth am I going to do that? I'm a nurse, not a detective."

"That's what makes you the perfect person to help me," Alex urged. "You won't arouse suspicion if you ask questions. Everyone will just think you're curious."

"Alex, I'm already public enemy number one around here. Who's going to answer any questions I may have?"

"I don't know. But we'll think of something."

"Alex, this comes too closely on the heels of your big announcement that Diana was my mother. I don't know how to deal with that yet. I don't even know that I'll be staying here."

Alex looked at me with pleading in her eyes. "Please help me, Macy. I don't know who else to ask."

"How about Stephan? Or Will? Or even Pete?"

"I can't ask Stephan. That would hurt him too much. He was so close to Forrest. I can't ask Will because Will won't believe anything I say about my fears. He will refuse to believe that Forrest was killed. And I don't think it's fair to ask Pete. He's a very private man. He doesn't want to be dragged into all of this."

I didn't want to be dragged into all of this, either.

Confused thoughts raced and tumbled around in my head. Was it even possible that someone had killed Forrest? The very thought was horrifying. Who could have done it? If indeed he had been murdered, the perpetrator must have been someone on the island. Pete? The very idea was unthinkable. I could not imagine Pete having committed such a heinous act. Will? I didn't like Will and I didn't believe he was above using violence, but he wouldn't have killed his own uncle. What about Stephan? He wouldn't have done it—Forrest was his good friend. Vali? Leland? What reason could they possibly have had? Brandt or Giselle? Neither of them had any reason to kill him.

I changed the subject. "I want you to get some sleep. Would you please do that? You might be able to sleep better now that you've gotten all of this off your chest."

She nodded. "I think you're right, Macy. I think I will be able to sleep now."

She snapped off one of the lamps nearby and turned to go. "Thank you," she said quietly.

"Good night, Alex."

After she left the library, I flopped down in the chair where she had been sitting. I didn't know what to do now. My first thought was of the letter I had written but not yet mailed to the nursing agency. Maybe I should stay. Or maybe it would be best for me to leave this place.

But what about the things Alex had told me tonight? I wasn't sure Alex was right, but I couldn't be sure she was wrong, either. What if someone *had* killed Forrest? That meant there was a killer somewhere out there. The very thought of it sent chills down my spine.

I wanted to get up to my room as quickly as I could. I grabbed the first book I saw on the closest shelf and ran lightly upstairs. I doubted I could concentrate on a single word of it, but I knew for sure that I wouldn't be able to go back to sleep.

I was right. On both counts. I wasn't able to concentrate on the book and I didn't sleep a wink the rest of the night. I finally got out of bed at around five o'clock the next morning, tired and wound up like a spring. I forced myself to shower and dress slowly before I went downstairs for breakfast. Vali still wasn't around, so I had the dining room and kitchen to myself.

After breakfast, I wandered into the living room again to look at the portrait of Forrest. Something about that portrait drew me to it.

"What happened to you?" I asked softly. "I wish you could talk to me."

I went to the library to wait until Alex awoke, working halfheartedly on my new cataloging system for the books, then finally went in to see Alex at about six thirty. She was up, dressed in comfortable clothes, and ready to do her exercises.

"How did you sleep last night?" I asked her while we were working.

"Quite well, after I spoke to you. Have you thought any more about what I said?"

"How could I *not* think about what you said?"

"I mean, have you made any decisions yet?"

"No, Alex, I haven't. You've thrown a lot at me the last few days. I need some time to think and to sort it all out."

"Are you going over to Heart Island with Pete today?"

"Yes. And thank you for arranging it."

"You're welcome. I thought you could use the rest of the day off. I won't spoil the story of Heart Island before you get there. It's something you have to experience for yourself."

We worked for longer than usual on Alex's exercises. She seemed eager to move forward and I wanted to see how much she was capable of doing before getting too tired. She did quite well and we were both pleased with her progress.

I left her with a promise to check in on her when I returned from Heart Island and then went upstairs for a warm coat and gloves.

I took my time wandering down to the boathouse. I was still feeling anxious about my conversation last night with Alex and I was jittery about going on the boat this morning, so I thought taking a leisurely walk might help me clear my mind and de-stress.

It was a chilly day, and I was glad I had worn warm clothes, since the boat ride would be even colder. The crisp, clear air was good for my frame of mind as I walked, though, and I arrived at the boathouse by ten thirty calmer than when I had walked out the front door of Summerplace. I looked forward to spending the day with Pete and I hoped to put some of my worries out of my mind, at least for the day. Maybe I could even talk to Pete about the happenings of the past few days. He might have some grounded advice for me.

When I reached the boathouse, Pete was loading a basket into one of the boats. He greeted me with a smile and asked, "Ready?" I nodded and offered to help load the boat.

"We're only taking the lunch basket, and that's already packed. Hop in and we'll get going."

I stepped gingerly into the boat and sat up front. Without a word he handed me a life jacket, for which I was grateful.

"You ever going to learn how to swim?" he asked, grinning.

"Maybe," I replied noncommittally. The thought of me floundering in the water learning how to swim was not how I wanted this excursion to begin. I changed the subject quickly.

"How long does it take to get to Heart Island?"

"We should be there in about fifteen minutes."

"What's so special about it?"

"There are a lot of things that make Heart Island special," Pete said. "I want you to see it first; then I'll tell you all about it."

Now I couldn't wait to get there. Even my apprehension about the boat ride wasn't enough to dampen my excitement about seeing it.

We pulled away from the boathouse and navigated into the channel. Once in deeper water, Pete opened the throttle and we started moving faster. He looked over at me and raised his voice above the rushing wind.

"Do you mind this?"

Gripping the sides of my seat, I sat perfectly still and must have looked pathetic. Pete laughed and slowed the boat down a little. "I'm sorry. I was just anxious to get away from Hallstead Island for a while. I promise to go slower."

"Thank you," I squeaked.

As the boat cut through the waves to our destination, I asked Pete to tell me a little more about the history of the Thousand Islands region. He was happy to oblige, since this appeared to be his favorite topic.

"After the War of 1812, a man by the name of Colonel Elisha Camp acquired the American islands. He then sold the islands to a man named Mr. Walton for the sum of $3,000. Can you believe that? Now just one island can sell for millions."

"You mentioned that some big tycoons had owned islands around here."

"George Pullman, who invented the Pullman sleeper car for railroad travel, built an amazing home that he called Castle Rest. It was an incredible piece of architecture and it's what put the Thousand Islands on the map, so to speak. Pullman was good friends with President Grant, who came up here on a well-publicized trip. The whole area exploded in growth after that."

"Where is Castle Rest?"

"It's not far from here, but the main building was dynamited after World War II for tax reasons. There are a few smaller structures that still remain on the island, but the real showplace is gone." He shook his head. "It's a shame."

We passed by a boat. Two elderly men sat dangling their fishing poles in the water. Pete waved. They looked up at us and waved back, smiling.

"That's part of what I love about this place," he said.

"What?"

"Even perfect strangers become familiar out on the water. Do strangers in the big city wave to you?"

"Not usually," I responded dryly.

"It's just part of the culture here."

"Do you fish?" I asked.

"All self-respecting river rats fish," Pete answered with a wide smile.

"What's a river rat?"

"It's a term used to describe people from the river. It was originally meant to be derogatory and some people think it's offensive, but I'm proud to be one."

"I can see that."

"The fishing-guide business got started in these islands when a *New York Times* reporter came up here and wrote about his fishing excursions. More and more people started coming to fish. Every guide has a secret fishing spot, and you can catch anything from perch to muskie."

I nodded, without the faintest idea of what a muskie was.

"That's a big fish," he said, as if having read my mind. "Usually fishing guides bring their customers out here and they fish all day and then everyone gets treated to a shore dinner at night."

"What's a shore dinner?"

"The traditional shore dinner has three specialties, besides the fish. Boiled coffee, a BLT made with rendered fatback melted over the fire, for deep-frying the fish, and Thousand Islands Guide French toast."

I made a face. "It sounds awful."

"There's nothing better. The French toast is the best part. The guide deep-fries bread real quickly then serves it with heavy cream, maple syrup, and a shot of bourbon. We'll have to make sure you have a shore dinner sometime."

"I'll try anything once."

We rode in silence for several minutes, enjoying the view. It wasn't long before Pete pointed to an island in the distance.

"There's Heart Island," he said proudly.

I sat up a little straighter in my seat and craned my neck to get my first glimpse of the island I'd been waiting all morning to see.

I saw the scarlet-roofed towers first. Several of them stood above the line of trees, regal and lofty. On many of them I could see ornate spires stretching skyward, and as the boat drew closer, I could see turrets and chimneys protruding from the gracefully steep rooflines.

"What am I looking at?" I asked in wonder.

"You're looking at Boldt Castle. That's what we came to see."

Pete slowed the boat considerably as we approached the island. As we rounded the end of Heart Island and slipped out of the channel, I could better see the magnificent form of the imposing castle above me. Surrounded by sloping lawns and manicured formal gardens, the castle, made of stone and standing several stories tall, was the very picture of grandeur. Its many windows glinted in the morning sunlight.

As the boat continued around the island, I took my eyes off the castle long enough to notice that there were several smaller buildings as well. Just like the castle, each one was a work of art, and I couldn't wait to get out of the boat and go exploring.

Pete pulled the boat up to a long dock along one side of the island and hopped out. While he secured the boat, I got out and stood on the dock to wait for him. There was one other boat tied up at the dock, but I didn't see anyone else around.

Pete stood up and nodded toward the other boat. "That's Emery's boat," he stated. "Emery is the caretaker. He should be here to meet us any minute."

"Tell me about this place," I urged him.

He laughed. "I know the basics of the story of this island and the castle, but Emery knows everything. Plus, he's a much better storyteller than I am. I'd wait for him if I were you."

He beckoned me to one end of the dock and pointed across the water to where a huge, beautiful boathouse stood. Its enormous doors were closed. "That boathouse goes with this island. The man who had this castle built kept lots of boats over there."

Just then we heard footsteps behind us. A tall, thin man was walking toward us, smiling. When he reached us, he extended his hand to Pete.

"Good to see you, Pete. How've you been?"

"Great, Emery, thanks. I'd like you to meet Macy Stoddard, Alex's new nurse. Alex wanted me to bring Macy over here today and show her one of the river's greatest treasures."

Emery turned toward me and shook my hand. "Glad you could visit, Macy. I think you'll like Boldt Castle."

I grinned. "I like what I've seen so far," I told him eagerly.

"How's Alex doing?" Emery asked us.

Pete answered first. "She's doing all right. It's slow going, though, after hip surgery." He nodded at me. "Macy is the best person to ask."

I spoke up. "Alex is remarkable. She's recovering nicely, considering her age and the surgery she had. I think she wishes she were getting better even more quickly, but she amazes me with her drive."

"Alex is remarkable, no doubt about that," Emery agreed affably. "Tell her I've been thinking about her and wishing her well."

I smiled at him. "I'll do that."

"Shall we have a look around?" Emery asked.

Pete nodded, smiling, and answered, "I told Macy that you're the storyteller around here, and I think she's anxious to hear about Boldt Castle."

"I am," I agreed.

Along one side of the dock was a low, narrow, rustic building with several doors. Signs indicated what could be found behind each door: an office, a ticket booth, a snack stand, and a gift shop. Emery led the way through the small office, nodding to the ticket booth nearby. "We're closed this time of year, but during the high season we get quite a few folks through here to see the place." We exited the office and walked up a sloping sidewalk toward the immense castle.

"First let me tell you a little about Heart Island," Emery began. "It wasn't always called Heart Island, you know. It used to be known as Hemlock Island until it was sold to a Mr. Hart in 1871. He then renamed it 'H-A-R-T' Island. The island changed hands yet again before being sold to the Boldts, but its name remained the same. When Mr. Boldt became the owner, he brought in materials to change the physical shape of the island to vaguely resemble a heart. He then changed the spelling to 'H-E-A-R-T' Island, a name which obviously has stood the test of time. I'll tell you more about the Boldts very soon.

"When Mr. Hart owned the island, he had a beautiful summer home built here. It still stood on the island when it was sold to the Boldts." Emery turned to me. "What do you think happened to the house?"

"Did it burn down?" I guessed.

"Nope. Believe it or not, in the dead of winter in 1899, when the river was frozen solid, the house was slid across the ice to Wellesley Island, where it was re-designed and used for many years as a golf clubhouse."

"I didn't know that," Pete remarked in amazement.

"True story," Emery said.

"So what happened when the Boldts bought the property?" I asked.

"The story of what happened to this island once the Boldts became her owners is one of the greatest love stories ever told," Emery answered.

"George C. Boldt was a Prussian-born immigrant who worked very hard to eventually become an important figure in New York City around the turn of the twentieth century. He managed the most luxurious hotel of the age, the Waldorf-Astoria. He also managed a grand hotel in Philadelphia, Pennsylvania, and was a trustee of a world-class university, among other accomplishments.

"But none of these accomplishments and achievements was as important to him as was his wife, Louise. And the story of Boldt Castle is the story of his love for her." Emery concluded his introduction of Boldt Castle just as we approached the sweeping stone veranda and climbed its wide, semicircular steps. At the top of the steps, Emery paused and looked back toward the property we had just traversed. Here and there across the lawn were small patches of rich green, undoubtedly the summertime color of the grass on the island. Statuary dotted the gardens, inviting wanderers to enjoy the view that the statues gazed upon always. It was a breathtaking scene, but I was eager to see the inside of the castle.

And I wasn't disappointed. We walked through the large wooden doors inlaid with leaded glass and into a gilded and marble space, which could only be called a great hall, rather than simply a foyer. Portraits hung on the walls in heavy scrollwork frames, and the space was lit by a magnificent glittering chandelier. On each side of us were rooms with exquisite furniture and grand fireplaces, and in front of us was a gorgeous staircase that separated at a landing and led upstairs to the left and the right. I could picture barons and baronesses descending the staircase in their coattails and ball gowns.

Emery preceded us into a large dining room with the biggest table I had ever seen, set with china and crystal and bowls of flowers as though a banquet were to begin at any moment. Wandering over to the large window at one end of the room, I was treated to a sweeping view of the grounds and the river. I returned to Pete and Emery as Emery continued his story.

"As I mentioned before, George Boldt was an immigrant from Prussia. He was born of poor parents and he had little when he came to this country. He started working in a hotel kitchen when he was thirteen and that's how he got started in the hotel industry. He worked his way up. He eventually made lots of money, enough to purchase this island and begin construction on the castle.

"When George bought Hart Island, his idea was to build a Rhineland castle right here on the St. Lawrence River, reminiscent of the castles of his youth. He wanted to build the castle as a testament to the love he felt for his wife, Louise. It was going to be a Valentine's Day gift."

A sigh escaped my lips.

"Construction began on the castle around 1900. It was to have six stories rising from the foundation level, an indoor swimming pool, one hundred and twenty rooms, an elevator, tunnels for the servants, a power house and clock tower, Italian gardens, a drawbridge, a dovecote, and a playhouse for the children and their guests, among other things. It took countless man-hours and unnumbered tons of materials to build the castle of Boldt's imagination. During construction, the Boldt family stayed on the island when they were on vacation from the city. They stayed in Alster Tower, which was to become the playhouse after the castle was completed.

"But in January of 1904, just when construction was nearing

completion, Louise Boldt died suddenly. It is generally accepted that she died of heart trouble. George Boldt had lost the love of his life. He couldn't imagine Louise's castle without her mistress, so he sent a telegram to Heart Island with just three words on it: 'Stop all construction.'

"The three hundred men who had been working put down their tools and left the castle behind. George Boldt never set foot on Heart Island again. In fact, he was so brokenhearted that he made his children promise that they, too, would never again set foot on the island, and they kept that promise. Over the decades following the death of Louise Boldt, the castle and grounds fell into a very sad state of disrepair from weather and vandals. It was only after seventy-three years that the Thousand Islands Bridge Authority acquired the island and its castle and decided to restore it to its former intended glory.

"And that," concluded Emery, "is the story of the castle and its beginnings. Quite a tale, isn't it? Of course, the restoration has taken years, and as you'll see when you head upstairs, it will take many more before it's complete. But the first floor is done, and it's beautiful, isn't it? You'll find displays down here of the Boldts and the Thousand Islands area. Why don't you two spend some time wandering around? Feel free to go upstairs and to look around at the other buildings, too. I've got some paperwork to do back in the office, but I'll find you later."

Emery left us then, and we headed upstairs to see the rest of the castle. I tried to imagine as we walked around what the rooms would have looked like if Louise Boldt had ever had the chance to furnish them. They would have been magnificent! I wondered aloud to Pete if he would be around to see the completed castle.

"I'm not sure how long the restoration is supposed to take," he answered. "But I'd love to see the finished product someday."

We continued walking up the large staircases to visit the rooms on the ascending floors. At the top was a beautiful stained-glass dome skylight comprised of hundreds of pieces of colored glass in a huge oval shape. It was a spectacular, dazzling piece of architecture that suited the castle perfectly.

In one room at the top of the castle was a door leading to a large veranda outside. We stepped out onto the balcony for a bird's-eye view of the island and this part of the castle. What an amazing sight! We could see miles of the majestic river. Close by, we saw a few boats traveling on the chilly water and the islands surrounding Heart Island. Eventually, the wind at this height became so strong that we reluctantly went back indoors.

"I'm starving! Are you ready for lunch?" Pete asked as we descended the stairs to the first floor.

I waited in one of the gardens while Pete headed down to the boat to get the basket with our lunch. When he returned, we ate in the garden on a lovely stone bench that faced several small trees and topiaries. Although there was still a chill in the air, we were both dressed warmly. The lunch was delicious and it was nice to sit outdoors admiring the scenery surrounding the castle. It was *almost* enough to allow me to forget for a while the troubles that I had left behind at Summerplace. But not quite. I sat thinking in silence.

"Anything wrong, or are you just imagining yourself as Louise Boldt?" Pete teased.

I smiled at him. "As amazing as this castle is, I don't think I could live here. It's almost too grand. I guess my tastes run to the simpler things. It's fun to just come here and imagine what it could have been like if the castle had ever been finished and given to Louise. I think that to feel comfortable in opulence like this a person has to be used to it. And I'm certainly not used to it!"

"I know what you mean," Pete agreed. "And as nice as Summerplace is, it's a far cry from being a castle."

"This has been a very memorable morning. Thank you for bringing me here."

"It was Alex's idea, but I'll be happy to take the credit." Pete grinned. He paused, then put his hand lightly on mine. "I'm glad you were able to get away from Hallstead Island for a little while at least. I know how oppressive that place can seem after a while. Everyone needs a break from it now and then."

I nodded, wondering whether I should discuss Alex's fears with him. She had declined to discuss her problems with Pete, but I needed someone to talk to, someone who could look at this problem with fresh eyes and tell me either that I was crazy to take Alex seriously or that I should take careful note of the things she had told me about Forrest. Pete might be able to give me some much-needed advice and perspective. Taking a deep breath, I decided to tell him everything. I hoped Alex wouldn't be upset.

"Pete, there's something I'd like to discuss with you, if you don't mind."

"What is it?"

"I couldn't sleep last night and I went in search of a new book to read. It was after midnight, and Alex was in the library, acting strangely."

Pete's brow furrowed, and I continued. "She was afraid of something." I related to him the story she had told me during the night. He listened, not interrupting, and sat in silence after I finished speaking.

"What do you make of her story?" he finally asked me.

"I don't know what to make of it. I was hoping that you could provide me with some insight."

Pete thought for a long time, looking out over the water. Finally he spoke. "She was absolutely lost when Forrest died. He was a great man; those two were made for each other. It took her a long time to start living again. I do remember that she mentioned once that she had heard voices shortly before Forrest died, but like everyone else I suppose I chalked it up to her state of mind at the time and didn't take her claim too seriously. Maybe I should have."

"Did she ever mention it again?"

"Not to me. And I think if she mentioned it to someone else, I would have heard about it. It concerns me that she still feels this way after four years. And I hate to think of her sitting in her rooms like a prisoner, afraid for her own life."

"So you think there's something to what she says?"

"I honestly don't know, but maybe it's something you should discuss further with her. I would talk to her about it, but she went to you with her concerns, not me. I'm not sure she would even want you discussing this with me. But I'm glad you did," he added.

"I'm glad I did, too. I didn't know where to turn. But there's something else I've been thinking about."

"What's that?"

"I received a letter recently from my nursing agency. They have another position for me—a woman in New York who needs a private nurse. They are wondering if I'd like the job and they need an answer soon."

He nodded and looked again at the water. Without looking at me, he asked, "And are you thinking about it?"

"Yes," I answered truthfully.

"What about your job here?"

I sighed, exasperated. "I feel like I was tricked into coming here! I feel like my job is secondary to the real reason I was asked. I don't know anything anymore! Alex has overwhelmed me these last couple of days, and I think it might be best for me to take that job."

"Well, if that's how you feel . . ." His voice trailed off. He stood up abruptly. "It sounds like you have a decision to make before you start worrying about Alex's problems. Do you want to look around the island anymore?"

I was startled by his sudden change in demeanor. "Uh, yes," I stammered. "Do we have time?"

"I guess so."

"What should we see first?"

"I've seen everything. Why don't you start in that building over there while I take the basket back to the boat?" he suggested, pointing to a building that seemed to rise right out of the water and was joined to the island by a small bridge.

"What is it?" I asked.

"The Power House and Clock Tower," he answered. "There are a lot of exhibits on the walls in there. It should be pretty self-explanatory."

Perplexed by his mood swing, I wandered off toward the Power House while he walked away in the opposite direction. I was intrigued by the building's interior. It was indeed self-explanatory, and I learned that, as its name suggested, its intended use had been to provide electricity for the castle. As I walked back over the small bridge to the main island, I saw Pete striding toward me. I waited for him before making my way to another small building nearby. When he joined me, his attitude seemed to have softened a bit.

"What did you think of the Power House?" he asked.

"It was interesting," I told him lightly.

"Do you want to see Alster Tower next?"

"Alster Tower was the playhouse, right?"

"That's right."

"That sounds fun."

Pete nodded and continued walking. He didn't say anything else until we reached the front of the playhouse, a magnificent structure that any child would be thrilled to have. Then he turned to me suddenly and asked, "What about me?"

"Huh?" I asked, utterly confused. "What do you mean?"

"I mean . . . ," he began, then stopped. More quietly, he began again. "I mean that *I* don't want you to leave Hallstead Island to take the job in New York."

I was at a loss for words. I opened my mouth to speak several times before shaking my head and laughing. "Is this why you've been such a jerk since we finished lunch?"

He threw his head back and started laughing too. "Yes," he admitted, "I'm sorry. Your announcement took me by surprise."

"Apology accepted," I said with a smile. But I didn't know what to say next. It made me happy that Pete didn't want me to leave, but that didn't solve any of my other problems. I still needed time to come to grips with being part of Alex's family, and I needed time to decide what to do about her plea to help find the person who supposedly killed Forrest.

I tried to put my confusion into words. "I don't know what to say," I told Pete. "It's not that I *want* to go back to New York, but I feel confused here. I don't know what to think about being Alex's granddaughter and I certainly don't think I'm in a position to help her find out who killed Forrest. If anyone really did kill him."

Pete sighed and took my hands in his. "I'm sure Alex knows that it will take time for you to accept her as a family member. And as for her request that you help find out who may have killed Forrest, all I can say is that you have my support and her support, and that's something.

"But I can't stop thinking about you." And with that, he pulled me to him and kissed me. He must have known I'd be willing. I got a feeling in my stomach like butter melting as I kissed him back. It had been a long time since I had felt this way, at least since the beginning of my relationship with Alan, and I hadn't felt close to anyone in a long time. Some of my fears about staying on Hallstead Island, wisely or not, began to fall away in Pete's embrace. I looked at him earnestly. "You'll help me if I decide to stay?" I asked.

"You know I will." He grinned.

"Then I'll postpone sending that letter to my nursing agency," I told him. "But I haven't decided for sure. I have to let my head clear a little," I warned.

He reached for my hand and we walked up the steps into Alster Tower together. We were exploring the playhouse when Emery came in.

"I thought I'd find you in here," he remarked. "Pretty interesting place, isn't it? The room we're standing in is called the Shell Room because of the shape of the roof. It was intended for dancing. Did you see over the railing to the basement level? There was a bowling alley planned for down there. How many kids do you know with a bowling alley in their playhouse?" He laughed.

"Upstairs, there were plans for a billiard room, a library, bedrooms, a café, a kitchen, and a grill. Amazing, isn't it?"

Pete and I agreed, nodding.

"I hate to mention it, but it is getting late in the day. Maybe we should start heading back to Summerplace," Pete said.

I agreed and the three of us walked toward the boat. As we were passing the main entrance to the castle, I turned to Pete and Emery. "Do you mind if I just run and look inside one last time? I took pictures, but I want to see it in person again."

They smiled and shook their heads. I ran lightly up to the veranda and let myself in through the great wooden doors. I gazed in awe once again at the chandelier, the beautifully decorated rooms on the main floor, the gleaming wooden railing of the grand staircase, and the fine artwork on the walls. I hated to leave this place and return to the uncertainty and turmoil on Hallstead Island, but at least I was leaving with an ally I could depend on for support and encouragement. I smiled to myself, remembering the feeling of Pete's arms around me, and left the castle behind.

When we got to the boat, Pete and I both thanked Emery for his time and his storytelling. Then we were off, Emery waving from the dock.

"Well, what did you think?" Pete asked, looking at me.

"I loved it. Thanks for bringing me today," I answered.

"I wouldn't have missed it," he replied, reaching out to put his hand on my shoulder.

I held his hand in mine and we stayed like that for the ride back to Hallstead Island. It felt right; I didn't dwell on my fear of the water (though I did wear the life jacket), and for once I was not ready for the boat ride to end when we pulled up to the dock.

I collected the picnic basket and told Pete that I would take it up to the kitchen and put it away. Then I thanked him a second time for taking me to Boldt Castle and he kissed me again, quickly this time, before I left him. I walked to Summerplace with a spring in my step that hadn't been there earlier in the day, and I found that I was actually looking forward to seeing Alex. Pete had done more for me than he suspected.

Once inside, I deposited the basket in the kitchen and went in search of Alex. I didn't have to look for long; I found her in her office, where I supposed she would be.

She noticed the change in me at once.

"Whatever happened today did you good," she said approvingly.

"I think you're right," I agreed. I didn't tell her what had happened to cause this change in me, but I'm sure she knew it all along. She had probably sent Pete and me to Boldt Castle together intending for us to grow closer. It didn't matter to me . . . I was glad she'd done it.

CHAPTER 11

I enjoyed a restful, dreamless sleep that night and woke up the next day feeling hopeful and brighter than I had the previous morning. I still wanted to postpone sending the letter to my agency, though I knew I would have to make a decision soon about staying. After breakfast I went to see Alex. She declined to go for an early morning walk outside and instead announced that she wanted to spend some time today packing up the things in her rooms that would make the trip to her winter home on Pine Island. She assigned me to packing up her clothes. I spent the entire morning going through her voluminous wardrobe and putting her heavy winter things in boxes. Before I was done with the clothes, Alex requested that Vali bring lunch on a tray for us.

After lunch, I spent a short time in the library packing the books she had requested, largely works of fiction and books about the Thousand Islands. I found Alex working again and proposed that she take a break to do some exercises, which she consented to do for about an hour. After that, she needed to do some more work in her office and she suggested that I take a couple of hours to do whatever I wanted. I made my way up to the turret room, where the warmth of the day made it quite comfortable. I got out all the supplies I would need to start a watercolor painting. I knew just what I wanted to paint—Boldt Castle. It had so inspired me yesterday that I wanted to try to do it justice on canvas. I didn't want to paint it up close; I wanted a distant view of it, with other islands and the river surrounding it.

As usual, I sketched first. Using a light touch, I penciled the castle as I envisioned it from my memory. I added islands nearby, including the tiny island I had seen that barely had enough room on it for a small cottage. It took a couple hours of complete focus to get a general idea of the castle forming on the canvas, but the work was good for me. I don't think I looked up once, except to notice the light changing and shadows shifting slowly around me as the afternoon lengthened.

I had just put down my charcoal pencil to stretch my fingers and arms when I thought I heard a scuffling noise on the turret stairs. Not wanting to be stuck up in the turret again for several hours, I ran over to the door to catch any would-be perpetrator before he or she could lock me in. I yanked the door open and stared, shocked, at what I saw.

Alex stood at the top of the turret stairs, her mouth a thin white line of determination and pain. She was breathing heavily and she kept turning around to look behind her. In her hand was a slip of white paper. The paper shook as she held it out to me with trembling hands. I quickly took it from her, shoved it in my pocket, then led her gently over to the sofa, where she sat down heavily and leaned her head back. I helped her lift her feet so she could lie down, but she resisted and kept trying to sit up again. Finally she relented and sank down, bringing her hand to her head.

"Alex, tell me what's wrong. You aren't ready to be climbing stairs. That was dangerous! Thank goodness I heard you."

Her voice was small and scared when she answered me. "Macy, I was right. I've known it all along."

"What are you talking about?"

"The note. Read the note!" Her voice rose to a shrill pitch as she spoke, and I quickly took the crumpled paper from my pocket and spread it on my knees. There were only a few words typed on it, but their message made my blood run cold:

*There are no accidents. First Diana, then Forrest. Who
do you think will be next?*

I must have read the note a dozen times before I looked up at
Alex. She was staring at me with a mixture of fear and anger.

"Someone killed my daughter," she stated dully. "All this time I
thought it was a terrible accident," she whispered as she gazed at the
sky through the tall windows. "Who would have killed her?"

I couldn't answer that. I held her hands in mine as she continued
talking.

"And Forrest. My wonderful Forrest. I knew his death wasn't an
accident. I suppose all this time there's been a part of me that wanted
to believe that I really was hearing things that day, like everyone else
thought. But now I can't indulge that part of myself anymore." Tears
spilled slowly from her eyes, and I got her a clean cloth from the table
nearby. She spoke again.

"This note makes me sad and angry at the same time. Sad because
now I'm mourning Diana all over again and because I'm still mourning Forrest. And angry because how could anyone do this to my family? And why?"

Silence hung in the air. I had no answers for her. Neither of us had
mentioned the last part of the note. What did it mean? As if reading
my mind, Alex wiped her eyes and looked up at me. She struggled to
a sitting position. "And now this—this—person is arranging another
accident! I know I'm going to be next! What should I do?" she asked
me imploringly.

I knew then that I needed to stay on Hallstead Island. I couldn't
leave Alex now. I would have to put aside my confusion and hurt in
order to help her.

"I'm going to stay, Alex. We'll get you through this."

"Will you, Macy? Oh, thank you. I should be thinking of nothing
but my daughter and my husband right now, but the truth is that this
note has me scared to death. I'm scared to be in Summerplace alone.
I don't know who wrote the note, and I'm afraid to die." Alex had
worked herself into a very agitated state. Her voice had risen by an
octave, her face was ashen, and her body was trembling. I needed to
calm her down before we could talk more about the note.

"Alex, let me help you downstairs, and I'm going to give you something to help you relax and rest for a while. Then we can talk about this."

We walked over to the stairs and I went down first, backward, to help her on each step. Going down those stairs was even harder for her than going up had been. She bravely made it down to the balcony and leaned on me only a few times.

I thought it best that Alex lie down in my room for a while rather than trying to walk down another flight of stairs to her own rooms. She agreed and let me help her to recline on my bed. After assuring her I would be back in just a minute, I ran down to her bedroom to get the sedatives her doctor had prescribed for her. When I returned, she insisted that I give her only half a tablet so she wouldn't feel groggy after she rested. Reluctantly, I gave her what she asked for, then settled down in one of the armchairs in front of the fireplace to wait while she slept. I think that my presence helped her to relax a bit, and she was asleep quickly. I spent the next hour, until she woke, wondering again who could have killed Forrest and, apparently, Diana. No one on Hallstead Island seemed to have any reason to kill either of them. Alex rustled the quilt, sitting up slowly.

"Macy, I think I'd like to eat dinner tonight in the dining room. I'm too frightened to eat alone. Would you join me? Stephan and Will will be there too, so there will be plenty of people around to help take my mind off things."

"Of course I will. Alex, how did you find the note in the first place?"

"I had called Vali and asked her to bring some tea to my sitting room. I was getting tired and I needed a little lift. So when she brought it I sat in there for a short time, just drinking my tea on the sofa. When I went back into my office, there was an envelope on my desk. It just said 'Alexandria Hallstead' in typed letters. I don't think it had been there earlier, so someone must have gone into my office from the porch outside. Anyway, when I opened the letter I panicked immediately and didn't know who to talk to or where to go. I couldn't stay in my office. You were the first person I thought of. I called for you downstairs, and when you didn't answer, I managed to get upstairs and I called for you up here too. When you still didn't answer, I took a chance that you were up in the turret rather than outside. So somehow I got myself up those turret stairs. I'm so lucky I found you."

"Have you discussed the note with anyone else?"

"Not yet. I wanted to tell you first. Do you think we should tell people?"

"Yes," I answered. "I hate to say it, but I think you should tell everyone on the island. They might be in danger. I think we should tell the police, too."

Alex nodded grimly. "You're right." She looked at me with haunted eyes. "Why is this happening?"

"I wish I knew."

"How do you think everyone will react?"

"I honestly don't know. What about you?"

"I think Stephan will insist that I move back to New York for my own good. I lived there years ago. But I don't want to do that."

"What about Will?"

She sighed. "I can generally count on Will to do the things a doting nephew should do, like pulling out my chair for me at the table or holding a door for me, but I'm never sure how much he really *cares*. I think he might pay me some lip service and feign concern if I told him about the note, but in his mind he would probably shrug it off as some kind of joke. He tends to be rather mocking sometimes, and I don't care to be on the receiving end of that."

"How about Pete?"

She shook her head. "I hate to drag Pete into these things. He works so hard around here and he's so good to me. It's not fair for me to burden him with the problems of my family."

Now it was my turn to sigh. "I know you don't want to tell Pete, but I think you have to. He's entitled to know since he may be in danger, too. You should know that I have discussed with Pete what you told me about hearing voices right before Forrest died. I just had no idea what to do with that information."

"I understand, Macy. Let's go down to dinner. Stephan and Will should be in the dining room by now, and I have to tell Vali to set a place for me."

Slowly, gingerly, we walked down the stairs together. When we entered the dining room, Alex made a visible effort to appear strong and self-assured, but I could feel her fingers trembling on my arm.

"Alex!" Stephan exclaimed when he saw her. "I'm so glad you've decided to join us tonight!"

She smiled at him as Will asked solicitously, "Aunt Alex, can I get you something to drink?"

"No, thank you, dear," she replied. Vali must have heard us enter the dining room, because it took only a moment for her to bustle in with another place setting for Alex.

It wasn't long before we were all seated around the big, elegant table with Alex at the head and the rest of us seated at her sides. Vali served a delicious meal of trout with rice pilaf and brussels sprouts, followed by a dessert of sliced fruit. Conversation throughout dinner was light, as Stephan and Will entertained Alex with personal reviews of some of the new shows that had opened on Broadway. I listened, curiously uninterested in the talk of New York. At one point Will asked me, "Macy, don't you miss all that?"

"No, I really don't," I answered honestly, surprising myself a little. Will raised an eyebrow at me and grinned slyly. "I can't imagine what's got you so uninterested in New York all of a sudden."

I looked at him blandly and ignored his remark.

As dinner came to an end, Alex looked at me questioningly. I nodded in encouragement and she started to speak.

"I want you both to know that I received a note in my office today that confirmed that Forrest did not die from an accidental fall. He was killed by someone."

"What?" Stephan and Will asked together.

"Let me finish," Alex stated. "The note also said that Diana's drowning was not accidental either, and that someone else will be next."

"What are you talking about?" Stephan asked incredulously. "What note? Who's next?"

"It was an anonymous note that I found on my desk. I showed it to Macy right away, but no one else knew about it until now. And it doesn't say who's next."

"May I see it?" Stephan asked.

The note was still in my pocket. I handed it to Stephan, who read it slowly with a growing look of confusion and surprise. Will held out his hand and Stephan handed it to him. They looked grimly at Alex when they had read it.

"Alex, I think it would be in your best interests to move back to New York," Stephan said gravely.

"I knew you would say that, Stephan. I want to stay here. This is my home," Alex explained.

"Are you sure this isn't some kind of a joke?" asked Will.

"I really don't think so. I don't know of anyone who would play a joke like that."

"You don't know of anyone who goes around killing people, either," Will pointed out.

"I think the best thing for me is to stay here at Hallstead House and make sure that I spend as little time alone as possible. Macy will be a big help with that. No one is going to hurt me with another person in the room."

"Alex, if you're determined to stay here, we'll make it work so you stay safe. But I'd still feel better if you moved back to New York," said Stephan.

"I appreciate that, Stephan, but I would be lost in New York."

"Let us know if there's anything we can do, Aunt Alex," said Will.

"Thank you, dear. I will. I should be fine with Macy." Will shot me a look of scorn; I ignored him. After dinner, Alex and I went back to her sitting room. I asked her if she wished me to continue packing her clothes for the move to Pine Island, but she didn't answer. Her thoughts seemed far away, and I suspected she wasn't interested in packing tonight. I didn't have to ask what was troubling her—I knew she was scared to be alone in her room all night.

"Alex, would you like me to sleep on the sitting room sofa tonight?" I asked gently.

She heaved a sigh of relief. "Would you, Macy? Oh, I would so appreciate that."

I ran upstairs to get my things and was back in a few minutes. Poor Alex. She hadn't moved while I was gone. She really was paralyzed with fear, and my heart broke for her.

She let me help her into bed that night, I think because she was so physically and emotionally exhausted. I told her we would go easy on the exercises the following day since going up and down the stairs today had been such a strenuous activity for her. She readily agreed.

"Still," she said to me, smiling, "I did a good job on those stairs, didn't I?"

"Yes." I laughed. "But please don't do it again without warning me first!"

Alex had asked me to stay in her bedroom until she fell asleep. I wasn't in there long, because she fell asleep so quickly. I wish I could say the same for myself.

I lay down on the sofa in her sitting room and tossed and turned for what seemed like hours. I tried going into the library to find something to read, but for once I wasn't even interested in books. I lay down again and eventually drifted off to sleep, only to find myself swirling in an eddy of roiling water underneath the branches of the leaning tree. The river current was strong and swift. I was drowning. Though I was gasping for air and flailing my arms wildly in an attempt to claw my way onto the shore, I knew my efforts would be in vain. In a twisted reversal of roles, my parents watched me from the shore. They wanted to help but couldn't move. Alex was there too, trying to save me. I swallowed a mouthful of the water, its iciness burning my lungs. As the water closed over my head again and again, my eyes focused with shock and horror on a sight far below me. Diana's grotesque, lifeless body hung suspended in the river, her limp hands reaching toward me.

I think it was the sight of Diana that finally woke me up. I was sweating, panting, and utterly terrified. My blanket was wrapped around my legs and I couldn't remember where I was. I sat up straight and looked around in the darkness, but it was several seconds before I realized that I was in the sitting room. I didn't know if my thrashing had made much noise, so I got up and tiptoed to Alex's bedroom door. No sound. I peeked inside and saw that she was still sleeping soundly. Breathing a sigh of relief, I went back over to the sofa and sat down. My heart was beating too fast and my hands shook a little. I was still scared. The depth and immensity of the water had seemed so real. And I would never forget the terror of seeing my biological mother floating in the water, reaching for me.

Gradually my heart rate slowed and I was able to calm down. I nestled into my blanket once again and tried to go back to sleep. It took quite a while but, surprisingly, I was able to sleep again that night, albeit fitfully.

The next morning I woke up a little late. I could hear Alex dressing in her bedroom, so I knocked on the door to let her know that I would be back after a shower and breakfast.

I ate breakfast with Stephan and Will in the dining room. They were engrossed in a conversation about a transaction that would be closing in the next several days, so they didn't pay much attention to me. I ate in silence, wondering how I would go about helping Alex find out who killed Diana and Forrest. I didn't even know what questions to ask, or to whom I should speak. I needed to talk to Pete, whose levelheadedness I could use right now. He deserved to be warned about the note Alex had received.

When I returned to Alex's rooms, she was working at her desk. She, too, was involved in the transaction that Stephan and Will had been discussing at breakfast, and I was glad to see that she had work to do that would keep her mind busy.

Not that she had forgotten the events of the previous day. I noticed that the door to her private porch entrance remained locked and chained this morning, something that was unusual for her. She generally left that door unlocked to allow Stephan, Will, and any other visitor easy access to her. The intruder who had gotten into her office yesterday with the note must have known that Alex's private entrance was usually left unlocked.

But that didn't help me much. Probably everyone on Hallstead Island and even the people on the neighboring islands knew that her door remained unlocked.

I told Alex I would need to talk to her later, then went into the library to continue packing up some of her books while she met with Stephan and Will in her office.

A couple of hours and two large boxes of books later, I went in to help her with her exercises. I proposed that we take a short walk, in part because it was a beautiful day and in part so that we could speak together alone and away from Summerplace.

I talked to Alex about my concerns once we were outdoors. I

hated to dredge up memories that would undoubtedly be painful for her, but these issues had to be addressed if I was going to make any headway. Strangely, I never worried about danger to myself at the time. I was focused on helping Alex, and my concern was for her.

"What else do you remember about the day Forrest died?"

She was quiet for a long time. I was beginning to think she wasn't going to answer my question when she spoke.

"I don't remember anything other than what I've already told you," she answered, shaking her head. "I'm trying, but I just can't think."

"Do you remember who else was on Hallstead Island that day?"

She thought again. "Well, besides Forrest and me, Pete was here. He's the one who called the doctor. And Will was here. And Vali and Leland. I remember seeing all their faces staring at me."

"Where was Stephan?"

"Stephan? Oh, I suppose he was in New York working. I called him that evening after the police had left and he told me he would be here the next day. I remember that he got here in the morning."

"Anyone else?"

"Not that I can remember."

I was exasperated.

"Alex, can you think of any reason anyone would have had to be angry with Forrest?"

She put her hand on her forehead in a fluttering motion.

"No. No. I just can't remember anything like that." She turned to me and I could see tears glistening in her eyes. "Everyone loved Forrest. He was kind and generous and good. He didn't deserve to die that way." Her voice caught on her last words. I put my hand gently on her arm.

"I should have been with him," she added softly.

"You couldn't have prevented what happened. If you had been there, whoever pushed him would simply have waited for another opportunity. You couldn't protect him all the time."

"I know." She sighed. "I just can't help thinking that he died that day because of me."

"Well, that's not the case," I assured her again. I hesitated a moment before broaching the next subject.

"I know you don't want to drag Pete into this, but it's time he found out about that note. It's only fair that he knows. Plus, he might be able to give us some insight or might remember something from that period that you may have forgotten."

"Poor Pete. The last thing he needs is to have to worry about me."

"I'm afraid you're not giving him his due. He has a genuine and deep respect and admiration for you, and I know he feels very protective of you. I think he would appreciate the chance to be able to help."

Alex continued walking and was silent for several minutes.

"Maybe you're right. I love Pete like a member of my own family, but in my zeal to protect his privacy, perhaps I've overlooked his feelings."

I grinned at her. "I'll go talk to him right after we finish our walk."

"I suspect he won't be sorry to see you," she said with a wink. I blushed.

We finished our walk and Alex asked me to stay with her for lunch. The outer door to her office remained locked, and we spent lunch discussing different tasks that had to be completed before the move to Pine Island. Our conversation enabled Alex to keep her mind off her troubles for a brief time. Stephan joined Alex in her office after lunch and I went in search of Pete. I didn't have far to look. I found him on his knees examining one of the large picture windows along the side of Summerplace. He looked up as I approached and smiled broadly.

"Looking for me?"

"Yes, in fact, I was."

"Then it's my lucky day."

I blushed again, to my great embarrassment, and rolled my eyes.

"Pete, I need to talk to you about something. Could we go for a walk away from the house for a little while?"

He stood up, wiping his hands on his jeans. "This sounds serious."

"I'm afraid it is."

"Then let's go down to the boathouse. I need some caulk and a couple of small tools to repair this window, so I have to head that way."

He led the way around the porch to the front of Summerplace, where Brandt and Giselle were coming up the stone steps. They were holding hands and, as usual, Giselle looked well put together in dress pants and a tight silk top.

They stopped and exchanged small talk with us. They were popping in to see Alex, they said; then they would check in on Vali and Leland.

When we had left them, we walked slowly through the trees down to the boathouse while I related the events that had transpired since I had seen Pete last. He was shocked.

"We could really use your insight," I concluded.

"I'll do anything I can," he replied emphatically.

"I knew you would."

"Where do you think we should start?"

"First I'd like you to take me over to the police station in Cape Cartier. They have to be told about the note. Then we need to figure out exactly what happened on the day Forrest died. Alex doesn't seem to remember anything about that day other than what she has already told me. And she can't recall any reason that anyone would have had to be angry with Forrest."

"Run up to the house and get a warmer coat on, then I'll take you over to the police station. The picture window can wait until later. I'll just leave these tools on the porch."

"Thanks." I smiled. We walked close to each other in silence through the trees. We could see Summerplace through the trees when Pete took my hand in his and turned to me.

"It sounds like you've decided to stay."

"I have, at least until Alex gets everything straightened out."

"I'm glad," he replied, and bent to kiss my lips lightly. I felt that same quivery feeling in my stomach and squeezed his hand gently.

"Me too. I'll be right back."

I met Brandt and Giselle leaving Summerplace as I walked in the front door.

"Leaving so soon?" I asked them.

Giselle let her breath out loudly. "I just got a call. I have to go into work to cover a story in Cape Cartier. Aunt Vali could use my help, but it will have to wait." She looked up at Brandt. "Honey, why don't you come with me?" she suggested.

"I told Alex I'd stay here to help Pete. He's got a lot to do and Leland isn't here to help because he took a load of stuff over to Pine Island."

"Please?" she asked plaintively.

"I can't, Giselle. I'll be back soon. I promise."

"Well, okay." She gave him a dark look, clearly not happy with his answer.

"Pete'll give me a ride back to Cape Cartier. I won't be too long."

"Make sure you're not, sweetheart," Giselle answered, her dark look disappearing. She glanced my way and then stood on her tiptoes to give Brandt a long, lingering kiss before turning and running lightly in the direction of the dock.

He seemed embarrassed. "Bye," he said quickly.

"Love you!" she called over her shoulder.

"Sorry about that," he murmured in my direction.

"No, I'm sorry. I should have left you alone," I apologized.

"I'll go find Pete," he said, then walked around the corner of the porch.

I went upstairs and put on a warm coat, then went to join Pete on the porch. He had given Brandt instructions for fixing the window, so the repairs were in capable hands.

A few minutes later Pete and I were in the boat heading for Cape Cartier. When we docked, he accompanied me to the police station, where he let me do the talking. I spoke to a young policeman who had heard of Alex Hallstead but had not been present at the time of Forrest's death. My conversation with the police officer was thoroughly frustrating. He assured me that he would have a look at the file, but he doubted that the accidental death rulings by the police and coroner would change.

In his opinion, the note was a joke. If Forrest's death had come close on the heels of Diana's drowning there might be cause for concern, he informed us; but as his death had been seven years after hers, it was highly unlikely that the two were related.

I left the police station in a foul mood. I was sure the note was real, and I was angry that the police officer had shrugged it off. Pete and I talked about it all the way back to the island.

"It looks like we're not going to get much help from the police,"

Pete concluded. I nodded grimly. "We'll just have to figure it out ourselves."

Back on the island, Pete accompanied me back to the house. I
went to see if Alex was ready to work on some of her exercises. She
was, and we talked as we worked. I recounted my conversation with
the officer and Alex was understandably disappointed in his reaction
to the note.

"What are we supposed to do if the police won't help?" she asked.

"We'll get through it ourselves," I told her simply.

We had to cut her session short because she had a great deal of
work to do. Before she went back into her office, she remarked,
"Macy, I've been thinking about starting to paint again. I need something to keep my mind and my hands busy when I'm not working, or
I'll go crazy with worry. Would you mind going up to the turret and
starting to pack my painting supplies? Don't pack any of the supplies
you might use; we can pack those later."

"Of course!" I beamed, delighted that Alex was again showing
some interest in her art. "I'll get started right away!"

While Vali kept Alex company, I went up to the turret and spent
the next two hours sorting through books, canvases, paints, chemi-
cals, drawing supplies, and countless other implements Alex had up
there. Since I didn't have any boxes handy, I grouped media supplies
together in piles around the turret.

I wanted to go out for a walk before it started getting dark outside,
so I hurried down to my room, threw a coat over my shoulders, and a
couple of minutes later was treading along the path to the leaning tree.

I was surprised to find Brandt there. He didn't see me or seem to
hear me at first, and I watched as he stared into the water lapping
below the branches of the tree. His face somber, he slowly scanned
the river in both directions.

I made a slight movement so that he would know I was nearby. He
looked back, scanning the trees, then smiled as I emerged and walked
closer.

"I didn't mean to disturb you," I told him.

"You didn't disturb me. I come here once in a while because it's a
good place to think. I like to remember Diana and Forrest."

I nodded. I was thinking. Maybe it was time to tell Brandt about my relationship to Diana. He seemed to be in a reflective mood, and the fact that I had found him alone at the leaning tree seemed a good omen. But I didn't know how to begin. Fortunately, he gave me an opening.

"It's too bad you didn't know my wife, Macy. I think you would have liked her. Diana was fun loving and charismatic. It's a funny thing—your eyes are a lot like hers. She had big violet eyes too."

"Well, it turns out there's a good reason for that." I took a deep breath to brace myself, and he looked at me, puzzled.

"Diana was my mother. I just found out myself a few days ago."

I could see immediately that I had given him a shock. He stared at me, his mouth opening and closing soundlessly. He didn't say anything for several moments.

"Are you sure?" he asked dumbly.

I smiled ruefully. "Yes. Diana gave birth to me when she was only fifteen years old, and the family felt they would be disgraced if their baby was raising a baby of her own."

He nodded slowly. "I didn't meet Diana until several years after that. I wonder why she never mentioned this," he said thoughtfully.

I had no answer for him.

He went on. "You know, we tried to have a baby after we were married, but we never could. We were just starting to see doctors about it when she drowned, so I never followed up." He shook his head again. "This is all so incredible."

"Believe me, I know," I said. "I still haven't come to grips with it myself."

"How did you find out?"

"Alex told me. She and Stephan have kept tabs on me for all these years."

"How does that make you feel?"

I drew in another deep breath. "There isn't really a short answer to that. I've felt waves of lots of different emotions over the past few days. Anger, confusion, exhaustion. I've wondered what to do about my position here."

"Are you going to stay?"

"For now," I answered noncommittally.

Brandt walked over to me and took my hands in his. "Macy, thank you for telling me these things. You've given me a lot to think about. I'm sorry about everything you've gone through and I'm sorry I didn't know you when you were growing up. Our lives would both have been so different if Diana had decided not to give you up. She would have been proud of the person you've become."

"Thank you, Brandt."

"I'm going to see if Pete is ready to take me back to Cape Cartier."

"Before you go, could I ask you a favor? I'd like to keep this between us for now."

"Absolutely." He patted my shoulder sympathetically and walked away through the trees.

Now that I was alone, I sat down on the ground at the base of the leaning tree, leaned my head back against the rough bark, and closed my eyes. I needed this respite, this time away from Summerplace, away from the people on Hallstead Island. I needed time to myself to face everything that had been happening. I needed to think about Pete as well, but that would come later. I knew he would wait until I had straightened out the rest of my topsy-turvy life. I smiled at the thought of him.

With my eyes closed, I could focus on the sounds of the river. The wind rustled the trees gently, whistling its peaceful song, and the water slapped quietly against the rocks. I could hear birds passing overhead somewhere nearby. I hoped they were heading south before the cold settled in to stay. I opened my eyes, drinking in the tranquility around me, and I felt that some of my strength had been restored to me. I fancied that Diana and Forrest were both looking out for me, watching me at this tree that had represented both life and death for them. They could rest peacefully if only I could help Alex find out who had taken their lives from them.

I walked slowly back to Summerplace, lost in thought. It was almost time for dinner, and I had just enough time to check on Alex and get out of my jeans and into clean clothes. When I found Alex in her office, she announced that she would be having dinner in the dining room again tonight.

After I changed, I went to get Alex and we walked to the dining room together. We were joined by Will and Stephan a few minutes later, and we all sat down to another of Vali's delicious meals. I complimented Vali as she brought in dessert. I should have known better; she glowered at me and said nothing.

Over dessert, Alex mentioned that she was feeling well enough to attend church the next morning. I think her trip to the turret had given a boost to her confidence, and I encouraged her, pleased that she was showing an interest in taking on other physical challenges.

"I think that's a great idea," I told her.

"I was hoping you would go too, Macy," she replied. "I belong to a church in Cape Cartier, but if you go I'll see if Pete will take us to another church here on the river. It's an enchanting old place on Dark Island."

"Of course I'll go," I answered enthusiastically. I noticed Will looking at me intently, his eyes narrowed, and I met his gaze silently.

"It's settled, then. As long as Pete can take us." She addressed Stephan and Will next. "You two gentlemen are welcome to join us."

"Thank you, Alex, but I need to finish up some of the closing documents. I should probably stay here to do that," Stephan answered.

"Me too," added Will, still looking at me.

"All right," Alex said. "I'll talk to Pete this evening and see if he can take us, Macy."

After dinner I walked back to Alex's sitting room with her. "Would you like me to stay in here tonight?" I asked.

Alex shook her head. "I asked Leland to put chain locks on my sitting room and bedroom doors today," she explained. "I'll just lock them tonight and I'll be fine."

I was hesitant about Alex locking herself into her rooms at night. If she needed help, how would anyone get in to assist her? I voiced my concerns, but she answered, "I'll be fine, Macy. I really need to do this. . . . I need to be able to stay by myself without panicking. Please don't worry about me."

So, reluctantly, I bid her good night. She mentioned that Pete was coming up to the house so she could ask him to take us to church, but I didn't need to stay with her for that.

I went up to my room and built a cheerful fire. As the room warmed, I got into pajamas and settled down in front of the fire to read.

About an hour later, there was a knock at my door. Startled, I went over and asked, "Who is it?"

"Pete," came the answer.

Relieved, I opened the door and invited him in.

"I guess you weren't expecting company," he grinned, nodding at my pajamas.

I laughed. "No, I expected a nice, quiet evening."

"Alex wanted me to come up to Summerplace so she could ask if I'd take you two over to Dark Island tomorrow. I told her I'd be happy to."

"I knew she was planning to ask you. I'm glad you can take us."

"I remembered something that I wanted to tell you. I remembered it when Brandt was here this afternoon. Have you asked Brandt about his relationship with Forrest?"

"No," I answered, puzzled. "Why?"

"It's probably nothing, but I remember hearing something about a discussion he had with Forrest not long before Forrest died. Forrest was the one who mentioned it to me. But all he said was that he had broached an 'unpleasant subject' with Brandt."

"He didn't say what the subject was?"

"No."

"Well, I'm not sure where that leads us, but it's a start."

Pete turned to go. "I left some stuff unfinished above the boathouse. I need to get that done. I'll see you in the morning." He leaned forward and I kissed him good night. Smiling, he closed the door and left. I sighed happily as I listened to him descend the stairs.

I made a mental note to ask Brandt about Forrest the next time I saw him. When we had discussed Diana and my adoption earlier, it had never occurred to me to ask him about Forrest.

I fell asleep hoping my rest would be free of nightmares. It was.

CHAPTER 12

The morning dawned bright and crisp. I was looking forward to spending the morning with Alex and Pete, while at the same time harboring some apprehension about going in the boat again. For someone living on an island in the middle of a river, I had been very lucky not to have had to do much boating thus far. I supposed I would eventually learn to get used to it, but I didn't have to like it.

I ate breakfast quite late, after showering and taking my time dressing. I had brought only one dressy outfit, but it didn't seem suitable for church. Instead, I found a casual skirt and sweater that would do.

When I found Alex, she was dressed beautifully in a long, swirling skirt with a matching jacket. Around her neck she wore a long silk scarf.

"Alex, you look beautiful!"

"Thank you, Macy." She beamed.

We waited for Pete to come up from the boathouse. Alex had asked him to accompany us to the boat so she wouldn't slip on the rocks. He appeared and looked at us approvingly as I helped Alex with her coat.

"Alex, that's a gorgeous bracelet you're wearing," I told her. A dainty gold chain studded with small garnets encircled her wrist.

"Forrest gave me that for Christmas one year," she answered proudly. "It's one of my favorites."

Pete and I each held one of Alex's elbows, and we picked our way carefully through the woods down to the dock, being sure to help her over the uneven spots. She did remarkably well, though I could feel her stiffen slightly when we reached the rocks we had to cross to reach the dock. No wonder, since it was a slip on these rocks that had caused her initial hip injury.

Pete had a slightly difficult time helping her into the boat, but she was determined to get in and go to Dark Island. After trying a couple of different ways to get Alex into the boat with as little discomfort as possible, we finally got her seated. I think she was feeling a little fatigued by the time Pete pulled the boat away from the dock, but she assured me that she was fine. The trip to Dark Island would take a little while, she reasoned, so she would be able to rest a bit.

"Tell me a little about Dark Island before we get there," I suggested to Alex once we were under way.

"This is an incredible area of the river," Alex began. "You've already seen how beautiful Boldt Castle is. We'll be passing by that very soon. Between Heart Island and Dark Island is an area known as Millionaires' Row. When you see the magnificent homes on many of the islands that make up that stretch of the river, you'll see why it earned that name.

"But you asked about Dark Island, so I'll tell you about that. The church service we'll be attending is held in Singer Castle, the home on Dark Island. Singer Castle was originally called the Towers and was owned by Frederick G. Bourne, who was the fourth president of the Singer Sewing Machine Company.

"Frederick Bourne bought Dark Island as a surprise for his wife, Emma, and their children. Singer Castle has four stories, twenty-eight rooms, and a five-story clock tower. Inside there are grand stone spiral staircases, secret passageways, and even a dungeon."

"It sounds amazing," I noted.

"It is. You'll enjoy looking around. Singer Castle was one of the only castles to be built, fully furnished, and lived in around the turn of the twentieth century. Frederick Bourne actually commissioned his architect to design a hunting lodge on Dark Island. At the time, the architect had just finished reading Sir Walter Scott's novel *Woodstock*, so he took his inspiration from the castle in that book."

"I've never heard of that novel," I mused.

"We have a very old copy of it in the library at Summerplace," Alex told me. "It's not in the best condition, but you might be interested in reading it sometime."

"I would love to," I replied.

We were almost halfway to Dark Island, Pete informed me. Alex leaned her head back against her seat and closed her eyes. Her tale had interested me enough to make me less anxious about being in the boat, but when she stopped talking, all my fears rushed back. I tried to push them to the back of my mind by concentrating on the lovely islands and homes we were passing, and though Pete was going more quickly than I would have liked, I knew we had to reach Dark Island in plenty of time to help Alex ashore before the church service began. He must have known I was feeling nervous, because he began to point out different islands as we sped along, telling me their fanciful, often descriptive names. I especially liked the name Lazy Days Isle.

After a while, Pete pointed up ahead and said, "There's Dark Island." Alex opened her eyes.

"Macy, wait until you see the clock tower," she said. "There are four faces, each with a twelve-foot clock. The Westminster chimes still ring—I'm sure we'll hear them from the boat. Local legend says that the clock faces were made from solid gold!"

I smiled. Alex was clearly enjoying herself, and the role of local guide suited her. I was glad she had suggested this excursion.

The castle's granite façade grew as we approached, and, as I had with Boldt Castle, I felt a thrill to be getting an up-close glimpse of the splendid structure. Dark Island rose out of the water like a fortress, its Spanish-style tiled roofs glowing crimson in the sunlight. The multipaned windows lining the towers and the many wings of the castle reflected the bright morning light back to us.

"It reminds me a little of Boldt Castle," I said to Pete.

"It is a little like Boldt Castle," he conceded. "But there are some major differences. For one thing, there are a lot more rooms in Boldt

Castle. And Singer Castle was actually finished. They're both beautiful, though. They were both built around the same time, by the same builders, as a matter of fact, and they both used lots of local materials in their construction."

We pulled up slowly to the dock, each of us drinking in the view of this structure modeled after a seventeenth-century castle. When we had docked, Pete and I helped Alex out of the boat. Though she was loath to use it, she had brought a cane with her, and it provided her with some stability as we made our way up the gently sloping grounds to the chapel.

The chapel was breathtaking. Set in a long room ringed with tall, leaded-glass cathedral windows, it was simpler than I had expected. Rows of wooden chairs gleamed in the bright sunlight streaming into the room. At the front was a makeshift pulpit with a piano to one side and exposed stone walls rising above. The whole effect was calming. I didn't feel overwhelmed by formality in this room, and the glory of the river and the castle's surroundings were inspiring sights visible to every congregant.

The church service, which Alex informed me took place now only on certain Sundays, was simplicity itself. The message was delivered by a local pastor, and we closed with an old hymn, "God Be with You till We Meet Again." Alex told me that services at Singer Castle had always closed with the same song.

After the service, we took a brief tour of the castle. Parts of it were almost medieval, like the suits of armor that stood sentinel in some rooms, and the crossed swords that graced several of the fireplaces. Other parts of the castle bore witness to its original intent as a hunting lodge. Several deer heads hung from stone walls, and one room was presided over by a chandelier made of antlers. Pete entertained me with stories of the castle's hidden rooms and secret passageways. The castle was designed like that, Pete said, so that servants could monitor guests' needs without being obtrusive.

"I think I'd prefer an obtrusive servant to someone watching me from a secret hiding place," I stated.

"My thoughts exactly," Pete agreed.

I was sorry that we couldn't spend more time wandering Singer

Castle and the grounds of Dark Island, but I didn't want Alex to become too tired and I knew she had a lot of work to do back at Summerplace. We reluctantly headed back to the boat.

We were quiet for most of the ride home, with my thoughts occupied chiefly by wishing that we could be off the boat sooner. When
we were in sight of Hallstead Island, Alex made an announcement.

"The HSH Oil deal that I have been working on with Stephan and
Will is supposed to close in a couple of days. I would like to have a
nice dinner party at Summerplace to celebrate. We'll invite Brandt
and Giselle. Maybe we can even look into having it catered so that
Vali and Leland can join us. What do you think?"

Pete and I exchanged glances, and I eyed Alex warily. "Are you
sure, Alex?" I asked her. "I don't know if that's a good idea."

"Why?"

"For several reasons. First, you've been working very hard mentally on this closing. Second, you've also been working very hard
physically over the past few days. Don't you think you should give
yourself a little bit of time after the closing to rest, both physically
and mentally, before you throw a party? And third, although I hate to
say it, the person who killed Forrest and Diana is likely to be there.
Are you sure you want that person in a room filled with all those
people?"

"That's just it, Macy. We don't know who killed Forrest and
Diana. Whoever it is, I've undoubtedly been in the same room with
them many times since Forrest and Diana passed away. Now that they
have given me that chilling note, it's evident that they have plans.
Maybe putting that person in a room filled with everyone else will
force or scare them out of hiding."

I was very skeptical. I was afraid for Alex, and I truly did believe
that she should allow herself some time to rest before having a dinner
party to celebrate the closing of their transaction.

She seemed to read my thoughts. "I know you disagree with me,
but I've been giving this a lot of thought. I can't hide forever because
of the person who left that note for me. I'm an old lady. I want to
show them that I intend to go on living my life despite their threats. I
refuse to let them turn me into a recluse. This trip to Singer Castle

has only strengthened my resolve. Besides," she added with a coy smile, "it's about time this gloomy old place had a party in it."

I couldn't argue anymore in the face of her determination. I shrugged and smiled. "Okay. If that's how you feel, I'll support you."

"Good girl!" She turned to Pete. "And you?"

"I'll be there."

"I'm going to start making the arrangements right now." By this time we had docked at Hallstead Island and Pete was helping Alex out of the boat. Together, the three of us made our way slowly up to the house. When we got to the front door, Alex insisted on going into her office without our help. Pete went back to the boathouse to change and get to work on packing up some of the items above the boathouse.

I was on my way upstairs to change my clothes as well when Will emerged from Alex's rooms. He saw me and scowled.

"Macy, Alex just told me about this party she's planning. Personally, I think the whole idea is ridiculous. It'll be the same people who are always here."

"It's Alex's decision, not mine," I replied, and continued up the stairs. He followed me, and at the top he caught my elbow in a vise-like grip. His face was very close to mine. I could see tiny creases around the corners of his eyes.

"I've asked you before to leave this island. Nothing good will come of you being here," he snarled quietly. He turned on his heel and went to his room, slamming the door shut behind him.

I went into my own room with trembling legs. I walked as far as my bed and sat down.

Will was dangerous; I knew that now. I could not ignore the threat in his eyes, his words, and his grip.

I didn't care to spend the afternoon in the turret by myself. Instead, I headed downstairs to the library. It took some searching, but I found the novel *Woodstock* by Sir Walter Scott. Alex had been right; the book was somewhat tattered and very fragile, its pages yellowed and cracked with age, so I set it down carefully on a table to have a look at it. I read the first few pages, but the words were written in such archaic language that I closed the book after several minutes. As much as I wanted to read it, I didn't have enough time to devote to it right now. I needed to work some more on packing the books Alex wanted to take with her to Pine Island. They took quite a long time to pack, since there was so little organization in the library. I worked on my categorization system as I packed, and the afternoon passed quickly.

Brandt and Giselle appeared shortly before I finished the day's packing. Brandt poked his head into the library, and Giselle stood behind him. "Alex tells us there's going to be a party," he greeted me.

"It looks that way," I told him, standing up from my spot on the floor. "Hi, Giselle."

"Hi, Macy."

"She seems excited about it," he noted.

"She does indeed."

"Do you think she's up to it?"

"Well, I asked her that very same question, and she assures me that she's ready for it. She's been working very hard lately and she says she wants to celebrate. I asked her to hold off and have the party after she's had a few days to relax, but Alex isn't much of a relaxer."

Brandt laughed. "It didn't take you this long to figure that out, did it?" I laughed too.

Giselle broke in. "Macy, Brandt tells me you're planning to stay on Hallstead Island for a while."

I stole a quick look at Brandt. I hoped he hadn't told Giselle about our conversation. "Yes, I am. Alex is doing better, but she still needs someone to help her physically. There are a lot of exercises that I can help her with, but she's not quite ready for them yet. She's a work in progress."

"Oh, I forgot to mention something to Alex about moving to Solstice. I'll be right back," Brandt told us.

Giselle walked into the room and sat down at one of the tables, then picked up a book and idly leafed through its pages. "Brandt was awfully quiet when he came home the other day," she mused. "Did anything happen after I went back to Cape Cartier?"

"No, not that I know of."

"Oh. I thought you might know the reason for his funk."

"I'm sorry I can't help."

She sighed. "That's okay. I'll go find him. We need to head back to the mainland. See you at the party." She waved her hand at me as she walked out of the library.

I had hoped to find a few minutes to talk to Brandt alone about the discussion he had with Forrest before he died. But that would have to wait for another time. It was difficult to find him alone since Giselle always stuck so closely to him.

I changed for dinner and joined Alex, and we entered the dining room together. Will and Stephan were already there; Stephan bowed slightly when he saw us.

Alex went to him immediately and engaged him in a conversation about business. Will leaned against the wet bar and swirled his glass of scotch on the rocks. He glanced my way once but ignored me otherwise. He was quiet throughout dinner, speaking only when Alex or Stephan spoke to him.

After dinner, I accompanied Alex back to her sitting room. She looked tired, so I suggested that she take a long, hot shower and go straight to bed. She sighed. "I wish I could figure out what drives Will," she said sadly. "He can be such a charming young man, but he broods so much. I don't know how to get him out of his shell. Of course, it's possible that he just doesn't like it here. I know he has HSH Oil work to do, of course, but when he's done with that, there's nothing for him to do here. He probably can't wait to get back home to New York. He must miss the excitement of being in the city. Are you homesick for New York, Macy?"

"No, I'm really not. I like the peace and quiet here."

Alex started to make her way to the bedroom. "Of course, it could be that Will's memories haunt him when he's here."

"Memories of what?"

"Unhappy times. The deaths of his parents, Forrest's brother and sister-in-law. Forrest and I took him in, you know, after his parents died in a plane crash. And then, of course, the deaths of his cousin and his uncle. Especially Diana. Those two were inseparable when they were young. I'll never forget the argument he had with Diana the week before she died. They fought like cats over heaven only knows what, and they still weren't speaking the day she drowned. He never got to say good-bye to her. None of us did. But in his case, I think it was harder because their last words to each other had been so hateful. They never got a chance to make amends."

I looked at Alex sharply. "Diana and Will fought a week before she died?"

"Yes."

"Why didn't you mention this before?"

Alex seemed puzzled. "Because it didn't seem important. They fought sometimes, but it never meant anything. They were like sister and brother."

"You have no idea what they argued about?"

"No idea whatsoever. If they had wanted me to know, they would have said something. But they didn't, so I left them alone to work it out for themselves."

"That could be very important, Alex."

"Why? Surely you don't think Will drowned his own cousin? They were the best of friends. He wasn't capable of such an act."

"But you just said they argued furiously shortly before she died. How do you know he's not capable of violence?"

"Macy, Will may not be the most agreeable man in the world, but he's not a killer. I know that."

Alex seemed to be getting agitated with our discussion and I didn't want to rile her up before bed, so I dropped the subject. It was one I would reopen, however, the next time I saw Will.

"Do you need my help with anything, Alex?"

"I could use your help getting my bracelet off," she replied, pulling her sleeve up.

The bracelet was gone.

Alex looked stricken. "Oh, no! It must have fallen off! Forrest gave me that bracelet!"

"Let's have a look around. Maybe it just fell on the floor in here or in your office."

We looked for the bracelet for quite some time but were not able to find it. Alex was becoming distraught. "You don't suppose it fell off at Singer Castle, do you? Or what if it fell off in the water? Then I'll never find it!" Her voice rose as she spoke.

"Alex," I said soothingly, "why don't you wait here while I go look in the boat? Maybe it fell off there this morning." The words came out before I could stop myself. The last thing I wanted was to be walking around Hallstead Island in the dark by myself.

"I don't know, Macy," she said skeptically. "Do you think you should go down to the boat alone?" She had voiced my concern exactly, but I didn't want her to feel my fear. So I lied. "I'll be fine. I'll be right back."

I ran upstairs, grabbed a coat and a flashlight, and let myself out the front door. I dashed into the darkened woods, knowing by now the path toward the boathouse. It took only a couple of minutes to reach the stony outcroppings near the dock. I saw the lights on in Pete's rooms, and for a moment I considered asking him for help, but I didn't want to appear needy and incapable.

It was creepy down by the dock at night. I had never noticed it before now, but a single lamp glowed dimly in the darkness, hanging about eight or nine feet above the dock at its far end. The crescent moon was reflected in the waves that sloshed gently against the dock, and the boat bobbed rhythmically. I slowed my pace and stepped onto the wooden dock, holding the flashlight in front of me.

I had gone only about ten steps when the lamp went out. My heart skipped a beat, I stopped dead in my tracks, and I was suddenly trembling so much that I dropped the flashlight into the black water. My mind raced as I tried to decide what to do next. I couldn't go back to Alex and tell her that I was too afraid to be down here alone after dark, but I couldn't make my feet move any closer to the boat. I thought quickly. I needed to go to the boathouse and ask Pete for another flashlight and some help.

Before I could turn around, I heard a noise behind me. Instinctively, I put my arms over my head to protect myself. Rough hands reached out of the inky blackness and shoved me to one side. I lost my balance, teetered for a second, and fell helplessly off the dock and into the water.

The next few moments happened so quickly that I have little recollection of them. I do remember screaming and hearing footsteps running away into the night. I thrashed around in the water and grabbed onto a piling, the first solid object I touched. Terrified, I yelled Pete's name several times and finally heard more footsteps dashing toward me on the dock. Now I was even more terrified—

what if the person had come back? I stopped yelling and hung on to the piling with all my might.

Suddenly a flashlight's beam cut through the darkness and strong arms were pulling me from the water. Before I knew it, I was lying faceup on the dock with the flashlight shining into my eyes. A voice exclaimed, "Macy! What are you doing down here? What happened to you?"

I pushed the flashlight away so that I wouldn't be blinded. I was staring into Will's face. He was still gripping my arm.

I shook my arm free and sat up straight, backing up as I did so. "I was pushed into the water," I answered breathlessly. More footsteps were running toward us now, and the light at the end of the dock sputtered on again. It was Pete.

"What's going on? I heard someone screaming!" he shouted as he ran up to us.

"It's Macy," Will replied. "She says someone pushed her in the water. I happened to be out for a walk and I heard her yelling. I pulled her out."

Pete turned to me. "Are you all right?" Without waiting for an answer, he asked incredulously, "What on earth were you doing down here?"

I was slowly catching my breath. I answered crossly, "Alex lost her bracelet. She was upset, so I told her I would come down here to see if it was in the boat. What difference does it make why I was down here? What matters is that someone pushed me in the water!"

"Who was it?" Will asked.

"I don't know," I told him, a little more quietly now. "The light went out at the end of the dock and then I dropped my flashlight into the water and a few seconds later someone pushed me from behind. Thank goodness I was able to grab on to the piling." I shuddered thinking of what might have happened if it hadn't been within reach.

"It was a good thing I happened to be walking nearby," Will said.

"You were lucky he came along, Macy," Pete agreed.

"I know. Thank you, Will," I told him.

"No problem."

Pete reached down to offer me his hand. His forehead was creased with worry.

"This is serious," he said grimly between clenched teeth. "Will, you didn't see who pushed her?"

"I didn't see anything or anyone. It was just by chance that I was walking nearby."

I was afraid. The full meaning of what had happened was just beginning to dawn on me. I rose shakily to my feet with Pete supporting me on one side and Will on the other. My teeth were chattering uncontrollably, and not merely from the cold. As we made our way toward the boathouse, Pete ran ahead and up to his rooms. I didn't want to be left alone with Will, but if he was the one who had pushed me, I knew he wouldn't try to harm me when Pete would be returning so quickly. Will didn't say anything while Pete was gone, and it was only a minute before Pete came clattering back down the boathouse steps. He was at my side again right away with a soft blanket and a heavy coat. He and Will wrapped them around my shoulders and we set off through the trees back to Summerplace. When we reached the front door, I thanked them for seeing me back to the house and told them I would get up to my room by myself.

"I just need to dry off and lie down," I said wearily.

"Be careful—lock yourself in," Pete warned me.

"Yeah, you should," Will chimed in. I looked at him intently, then turned and went inside. I heard him come in behind me, but I didn't look back. His footsteps faded away toward the kitchen.

When I got to my room, the first thing I did was to slide an armchair in front of each door. The desk was still in front of the turret door, so that would stay where it was. Next I changed out of my wet clothes, built a roaring fire, and crawled into bed, physically and emotionally spent.

I don't think I moved all night long, and I don't remember having any nightmares. But when I woke up the following morning, my body felt battered, like I had run a marathon in my sleep. And my mind was still exhausted, like it usually was after one of my nightmares. I saw the sun streaming in my balcony doors, normally a welcome sight, but I groaned and turned away from the blinding brightness. I didn't know what time it was and I didn't care.

There was a knock at my door. I heard myself mumble loudly, "Who's there?" A voice answered, "Pete."

Moaning, I somehow managed to slink out of bed and shuffle toward the door, though every muscle in my body screamed at me in protest. I tugged at the armchair until there was just enough room to open the door. I opened it and turned immediately back toward my bed.

Pete followed me. When I had pulled the covers back up to my chin and closed my eyes, he sat down next to me on the bed and asked solicitously, "How are you feeling this morning?"

I opened my eyes and peered at him. "I've been better," I managed.

"I spoke to Alex this morning. I told her you fell last night down near the dock and that you're probably pretty sore today. She is very concerned about you and she feels terrible that she let you go down there. I didn't think you'd want me to tell her what really happened." He paused for a moment, then continued, "I don't know what it is about you, but you seem to have brought things to a head around here since you arrived."

"I don't know what it is about me, either. I don't even want to think about that right now. But thank you for telling Alex that I just fell. Oh my gosh, I forgot all about the bracelet!"

"I found it and gave it to Alex. I went down to the dock first thing this morning and looked in the boat. It was lying on the floor right next to her seat."

"I'm so glad," I breathed.

"I'm not staying. I want you to get some more sleep. Is there anything I can get you?"

"Could you go in my bathroom and get me some aspirin?"

"Sure." He left and was back a minute later with two aspirin and a glass of water. "Take these and I'll be back to check on you in a couple of hours. Maybe you'll feel a little better by then."

I nodded, and I think I was asleep before he even let himself out the door. I slept soundly until he returned, this time carrying a tray. When I asked him what time it was he informed me that I had slept through lunch.

"I came back a while ago and knocked, but you didn't answer. I peeked in and you were in a deep sleep, so I left. You must be feeling a little better because you at least woke up this time."

"I do feel better," I said drowsily. It was true. The extra sleep and aspirin had done the trick. My muscles didn't seem to ache nearly as much as they had earlier when he had come up to see me, and my mind felt much more lucid. "How's Alex?"

"She's fine. And she wants you to take as much time off as you need until you feel a hundred percent."

"That's nice of her."

"Can you sit up and eat something? I brought you some lunch."

I sat up and he placed the tray on the bed next to me. He had brought soup, a buttered roll, and iced tea. It tasted wonderful. "I wish I could say that I made this, but it's from Vali. She makes great soup."

"She's a wonderful cook," I agreed.

"When you're done, do you want to try walking around a bit?" he asked.

"Yes, absolutely. My muscles are only going to get stiffer if I lie here much longer," I replied.

"I'll walk with you," he offered.

After I finished my lunch, I showered and dressed while Pete waited for me in the library. I felt much better once I was up and moving around. My arms and legs still ached, but the pain was tolerable.

We walked around outside for a little while; then he went back to the boathouse and I went in to check on Alex. I found her in her office. She was surprised to see me.

"Macy! How are you feeling? I'm so sorry I sent you down to that dock last night for my bracelet. It was all my fault. Thank goodness Will was down there and could help you!" Her words tumbled from her mouth in a rush.

I chuckled. "Alex, I'm fine. I just went for a short walk and I'm feeling much better. And please don't blame yourself for any of this. I was just sorry that I wasn't able to bring your bracelet back to you."

"Of course I want you to take all the time you need to feel better before you start worrying about me," Alex said.

"By tomorrow my muscles should have recovered enough to be able to work with you on your exercises and take you out for a walk."

"Just don't rush yourself," she cautioned me.

"I'll be fine," I assured her. "By the way, has Will been in here this morning? I wanted to thank him again."

"No. He and Stephan left for New York very early this morning. Our deal is closing tomorrow and they had a lot of work to do in the New York office."

I thanked her and left. I heard her lock her door behind me. I had wanted to talk to Will this morning to ask him some questions I had about last night. Like how he happened to be out walking exactly when and where I was pushed into the water. And what he and Diana had fought about in the days before she died. Now those questions would have to wait until he and Stephan returned from New York.

I wandered into the large living room and stood before the painting of Forrest that hung above the mantel. I heard a noise behind me and turned to see Vali walk into the room. When she saw me, she turned around quickly to return to the dining room, but I called her back.

"Vali, I want to ask you something. Do you know who pushed me off the dock last night?"

She fixed me with a blank stare for several seconds. "*I* didn't do it," she finally growled, and walked back into the dining room.

I sighed. I wasn't going to get anywhere with Vali. Perhaps Leland would be more willing to talk. I went in search of him, but I wasn't able to find him in the house or around the grounds. I thought briefly of stopping by the cottage he shared with Vali but decided against it. I didn't want to be alone with him.

I was walking around the porch to the front of the house when Pete walked out of the woods.

"Feeling better?" he greeted me.

"Much."

"I have to go over to Heather Island to my mother's house. I thought you might like to go with me."

"How far away is it?"

"It's not that far." As if reading my mind, he continued, "It's a quick trip in the boat."

"Okay, I'll go along," I agreed. He had told me a little about Heather Island, and I was interested to see the place where he had grown up. He waited for me on the porch while I went upstairs to get a heavier coat, and we walked together through the trees and down to the dock.

I wasn't prepared for the fear that swept over me like a tidal wave when I stepped onto the dock. Suddenly the events of the night before were rushing at me again. It was dark, an unseen pursuer had pushed me from behind, and I was fighting to keep my balance on the dock.

I closed my eyes and started to sway, my breath quickening, when Pete put his arm tightly around my shoulders. It steadied me a bit.

"Macy, you're okay now. Try to think of something else. Come on, I want to introduce you to Heather Island."

His words helped to focus me, and I walked determinedly down the dock to where the boat sat waiting. After I got in, the first thing I did was to put on a life jacket. My experience the previous night had affirmed my resolve never to be without one on the water.

Before long we were bumping lightly over the waves of the St. Lawrence River toward Heather Island. Much of the scenery that we passed was new to me; I hadn't been very far on the river in this direction yet. The character of the waterway and its islands changed somewhat as we headed north. The river widened and there were more watery passageways to discover among smaller islands. Pete took us on a detour through one such hidden waterway.

"We're in what's known as the Lost Channel right now," he explained as he slowed the boat a little. "During the French and Indian War, a British ship got lost among these islands, called Ivy Lea, searching for French ships. The British sailors started calling this area of the river the Lost Channel, and the name stuck." Shadows darkened the water between the islands in the Lost Channel, and the effect was Edenic. Dark evergreens swayed together in the slight breeze, and here and there bright leaves from maple and birch trees loosened their hold and drifted slowly down into the water. There wasn't another soul in sight. I imagined that the scene had changed little since the time of the French and Indian War. I also imagined that one could very easily get lost among these islands.

When we were back on our way to Heather Island, Pete told me a little about his family.

"My mother was originally from Québec. Her family moved to the island while she was still a young girl. My father moved there when they were married. Only about fifteen families live on the island year-round, so it can get pretty isolated in the winter. My sister goes to school in Ontario, but she gets home quite often to see my mother. My father passed away when I was a teenager," he concluded.

"I'm sorry to hear that," I responded sympathetically.

"Dad was great. He's the one who taught me how to fix anything. He had a great love of the river. He had met Forrest at a museum in Canada. They shared an interest in Native American history and artifacts, and eventually they became good friends. That's how I came to work for Alex after my dad died. Forrest and Alex kind of took me under their wing, much like they had done with Will after his parents died.

"That's also why I'll do anything I can to help Alex. I owe her a debt for all the help she gave me years ago."

We were approaching Heather Island. It looked immense to me, rising out of the water.

"My sister is going to meet us at the public dock. She'll drive us to Mom's house."

I wrestled out of my life jacket while Pete secured the boat to the dock. He helped me out of the boat and we walked to a park-like area near the dock. He waved to a younger woman sitting in a parked car nearby and she got out and walked toward us. She was petite, with long red hair. She shared her brother's lively green eyes. I recognized her as the young woman in one of the photos in Pete's living room.

Pete walked up to her and kissed her cheek. She stood on tiptoes and put her arms around his neck and squeezed. I stood several feet away.

Pete turned to me and said to his sister, "Colette, this is Macy Stoddard. She's Alex's new nurse."

Colette smiled broadly and shook my hand. "So you're Macy! Pete has told us about you." I blushed.

"How do you like Hallstead Island?" she asked.

"It's beautiful. In fact, this whole area is just breathtaking."

She nodded. "That's why we love it, isn't it, Pete?"

"You bet."

"Let's go home," Colette suggested. "Mom's anxious to see you."

We drove for several minutes along a bumpy road until we came to a charming home set back from the road amid a grove of birch trees. The gabled cottage was white with dark green shutters and a dark green front door. A white picket fence surrounded it, and fall flowers grew in profusion in front of the quaint porch. American and Canadian flags flew from two porch posts. The entire scene could have been lifted from the pages of a picture book.

We mounted the front steps and Colette opened the big green door into a small hallway. "Mom, we're back!" she shouted.

Another petite woman with close-cropped, stylish gray hair came into the hall wiping her hands on a dish towel. She looked chic in slacks and a Fair Isle sweater.

She kissed Pete on the cheek and held out her hands to me. "You must be Macy." She beamed. "It's so nice to meet you. I'm Pete's mother. Call me Hélène." She spoke and pronounced her name with a slight French accent.

I liked Hélène and Colette immediately. Within just a few minutes I was laughing and talking with them as if we'd been friends for years. After a short time, Pete suggested that we all have a look around Heather Island. Hélène said she had work to finish and dinner to make, and Colette declined too, saying she had to study. So, seated in his mother's four-by-four, Pete and I set off by ourselves on a tour of the island.

Heather Island, I learned, was one of the largest of the Thousand Islands. It was covered with forests, wetlands, grasslands, working farms, and large and unspoiled wildlife habitats. We passed an old one-room schoolhouse ("that schoolhouse was open as recently as 1985," Pete told me proudly), an abandoned cheese factory, and an ancient cemetery. But most impressive were the views of the water, both inland and on the river. I could see islands belonging to both Canada and the United States, bays surrounded by trees that were mirrored in the calm, dark water, and endless cattail marshes. It was a delightful tour and I was sorry when it ended.

It was late in the afternoon when we arrived back at Hélène's house. She insisted that we stay for dinner, and we were treated to a simple, delicious meal of grilled chicken, couscous, and roasted cauliflower. The lively, noisy dinner with Pete's family was so different from the staid, formal meals at Summerplace. I enjoyed myself immensely and too soon it was time to return. Hélène and Colette made me promise to come back soon, and it was a promise I made happily.

I was once again clad in my puffy orange life jacket when we shoved off from the public dock and made our way back to Hallstead Island. We took no detours along the way and arrived quickly. It was becoming dusk, and I was getting chilly. My arms and legs were starting to ache again, though they hadn't bothered me at all during our trip to Heather Island. Pete invited me to come up to his rooms over the boathouse for a little while, but as much as I wanted to accept, I was getting very tired and felt I should get some sleep if I were to be of any use to Alex the next day. Pete understood and walked me back to Summerplace, then kissed me good night. I went indoors and checked on Alex, then went straight to my room, where I fell asleep early after taking a nice, long bath.

That night I had a nightmare again, the one in which I was drowning under the branches of the leaning tree. Again I was thrashing in the water and couldn't save myself. As was usual when I had a nightmare, I woke up in the middle of the night trembling and drenched in sweat. The dream was even more frightening since I had been in a similar situation the night before, wildly grasping a piling with all of my strength. Thankfully I was able to fall asleep again, although it took a couple of hours.

When I woke up in the morning, my body felt better but my mind was still tired, no doubt from the stress of my experience at the dock but also from the exhaustion I usually felt after one of my nightmares.

After breakfast, which I ate alone in the dining room, I went to see Alex. As usual, she was already up and dressed.

"Would you like to do some early morning exercises today?" I asked her.

"That's a good idea," she replied. "I'm expecting Will and Stephan back from New York later this morning, and Stephan and I need to meet to discuss some things."

Alex and I worked in her sitting room for more than an hour before she went back to work. After she returned to her office, I went to the library to continue with the packing, and soon I heard Stephan and Will arrive. Shortly after their arrival they went into Alex's office.

My concentration eventually started to wander, and I was becoming tired, so I went into the kitchen to make myself some tea. Sitting in the dining room while I waited for the water to boil, I was staring out the window at nothing in particular when Will walked in. He was startled to see me but smoothly recovered himself.

"How are you feeling?" he asked.

"Much better. Thank you again for helping me the other night."

"No problem," he mumbled. He walked to the sideboard and poured himself a cup of coffee.

No time like the present, I thought. I launched into the conversation I had been waiting to have. "Will, I'm glad you're here. I wanted to ask you about something."

He raised one eyebrow and looked at me suspiciously. "About what?"

I hadn't really thought this through carefully because I hadn't expected to run into Will yet, so I had to think quickly.

"Oh," I answered breezily, "nothing much. Alex was telling me about her family, and she mentioned that you were good friends with your cousin, Diana, before her death. She thought that you two had argued before Diana died and she couldn't remember what you argued about. It's just stuck in her craw; that's all," I finished lamely. I groaned inwardly. I sounded ridiculous. Will looked at me evenly over the rim of his coffee mug.

"Alex can't remember why Diana and I fought and now she wants *you* to find out?" he asked doubtfully.

"Yeah." I laughed. "You know how some people are when they get older. It's just something that she's wondering about."

"Well," Will said slowly, leaning back in the chair he now occupied across from me, "I don't think that's any of Alex's business. Or yours."

I tried again. "It was so long ago," I stated. "Can you even remember?"

"Oh, yes. I remember it quite well. Diana could be a real bitch sometimes."

I was a little surprised by his choice of words. "Alex would like to remember; that's all. I think it would give her some peace of mind."

Will set down his coffee cup with a thud, and some of the coffee sloshed over the side. "Let me put it this way, Macy. The argument I had with Diana was between me and Diana. I'm not going to tell Alex, and I'm certainly not going to discuss it with some stranger she's hired to play nursemaid." He glared at me, his eyes flashing hatred.

I could feel my cheeks growing hot. "I was just trying to give Alex some peace of mind," I answered quietly.

He pushed back his chair and stalked out of the room. I sat where I was for a few moments, though the teapot was whistling. Will wasn't about to give me any information. Not only that, but I would have to be more careful about being alone with him in the future. He had already made it clear that he wanted me away from Hallstead Island, and his malevolence toward me seemed to be growing.

After I fixed my tea, I returned to the library. I needed to talk to Alex, but that would have to wait until her meeting with Stephan was over.

It wasn't long before I saw Stephan walk past the library doors, and I hastened into Alex's office.

"Alex, I hate to bother you, but I think there's something we need to discuss."

"Of course, Macy. What is it?"

"I've just spoken to Will about the argument he had with Diana before her death. He says he remembers the argument quite well, but he refused to share the details with me. What was their relationship like?"

Alex folded her hands thoughtfully. "Will and Diana were like brother and sister much of the time. They fought like cats once in a while, but truth be told, they were best friends.

"Will came to live with us as a boy after his parents were killed, as I've told you. We always tried to treat him as one of us. We wanted him to feel welcome and nurtured. But as I've told you before, Forrest and I spoiled Diana. We probably let her get away with too much.

I've never spoken to Will about this, but there were probably times that Diana made him feel like an outsider in our family. I'm sure there were times that he was jealous of her. Forrest and I never treated him like an outsider, but Diana sometimes spoke of him like a visiting relative rather than a member of the family. We tried to discuss it with her a couple of times, but there was no changing her, so we never pursued it." Alex sighed. "We should have."

There was nothing I could say to that, so I asked her the question I had been turning over in my mind.

"Alex, do you think Will could have hurt Diana?"

She looked startled. "Oh, no. They really did love each other, despite their arguments."

I wasn't so sure. It must have shown in my face, because Alex insisted again, "They really did love each other."

I nodded. "Okay." I changed the subject. "What packing would you like me to work on today?"

"How about the painting supplies in the turret? I'll ask Pete to bring you some storage boxes from the boathouse and you can start filling them."

"Good idea," I agreed and I left her, reminding her to lock the door behind me.

I worked through lunch and well into the afternoon packing supplies into boxes that Pete brought for me.

The evening passed uneventfully. Alex retired early, and Pete came up from the boathouse to visit me for a while. It would have been entirely pleasant except for the cloud of tension that hung over the house. Will had glowered at me all through dinner, and Alex had seemed distant, despite her announcement that the dinner party would be the next evening. Stephan, who was normally jovial, had been rather moody and quiet. Even he seemed to think that the dinner party should wait for another time.

Once Pete left, I got into bed. I slept well, but I woke up the next morning with a slight sense of apprehension about Alex's dinner party. After breakfast I went in to see Alex, who was very keyed up. Her hands fluttered when she spoke and she seemed unfocused. Her demeanor surprised me, since she was normally so calm and in control. I suggested some therapy exercises just to help her get centered for the day ahead, but she refused. She wanted to work, she said, so I told her I would return later. I spent the morning in the boathouse with Pete, organizing tools and supplies and helping to pack them for the winter move to Pine Island.

I went to see Alex again early in the afternoon. Her lunch sat on a tray on her desk, untouched.

"I just wasn't hungry," she said when I asked why she hadn't eaten.

"Why not?"

"I have other things on my mind. Macy, I'm starting to think that the dinner party tonight isn't such a good idea."

"It's not too late to call it off," I said pointedly.

"I know, but how would that look?" she lamented.

"Who cares how it would look? You can just tell everybody that you've decided to rest a bit and have the party a little later."

She thought for a moment. "No," she said firmly. "I don't want to appear weak. The person who sent me that note has to be shown that I'm as strong as ever and I refuse to be bullied."

"Okay. I can understand your feelings," I said. "As I told you before, I'll support you in whatever you decide."

She smiled grimly. "Thank you, Macy. I'm going to have the party. Maybe we'll learn something tonight."

I wasn't so sure I wanted to learn anything more at her dinner party, but I gave her hand a quick squeeze. "I'll come down early to help you dress," I promised.

Later that afternoon, I was working in the library when Alex appeared in the doorway. "Would you mind going for a walk with me?"

"I'd love to," I answered enthusiastically. It wasn't often that Alex took the initiative in getting outdoors, and I was pleased to oblige her.

When we were out in the sunshine in front of Summerplace, Alex said, "I'd like to go to the leaning tree. Is that all right with you?"

I was a little surprised that she wanted to veer from our usual, comfortable path, which was relatively flat and which Pete kept free of branches, leaves, and other debris. But I told her that I thought a walk to the leaning tree would be fine as long as we walked slowly and carefully. She seemed pleased.

We walked to the leaning tree in relative silence, since all our focus was on the ground before us. The path was worn, but it was still bumpy and tangled with roots, fallen leaves, and small rocks. When we reached the leaning tree, Alex leaned against it, breathing a little heavier than usual. When she had rested for a few minutes, she wandered aimlessly around the small area surrounding the leaning tree, scanning the river slowly. I noticed that she avoided looking directly into the water below the branches of her special tree. Perhaps she was afraid of seeing Diana's face in her mind's eye. Perhaps she didn't want to look at the place where the ashes of her long-lost daughter and beloved husband had been scattered.

Alex did want to talk about Diana, though. "After she gave you up for adoption, she changed. I think she finally began to realize that some actions have lifelong consequences. That her life wasn't going to be one long party in which she was only accountable to herself.

"Forrest and I were so happy when Diana met Brandt. He was a responsible young man with a good head on his shoulders. He still is. He was able to get her to calm down in a way that Forrest and I were never able to do. Diana respected him and they came to love each other very much. I'm glad he came along when he did. He gave Diana the gift of serenity, which she had needed for a long time. He made her see herself the way he saw her, as a good person, and she needed that." Alex sighed. "I'll always be grateful to Brandt for rescuing Diana from herself." She laughed wryly. "Even Will got along with Brandt, and he didn't like any of Diana's boyfriends."

I felt a sudden pity for Alex and for her daughter, the mother I had never known. I tried articulating my feelings to Alex. "Even though I couldn't have asked for a better or more loving mother than the one I had, I do wish I had been able to meet Diana before she died. I'm glad that she was able to find a peaceful happiness with Brandt," I said honestly.

Alex placed her thin, white hand on the trunk of the leaning tree. She found the spot where she and Forrest had so long ago carved their initials into the rough bark. She traced her delicate fingers over the letters with a wistful look. "Forrest liked Brandt, too. He was very proud when Brandt became a member of our family." She turned around and looked at me, her eyes moist. "I wish Forrest could be here tonight," she said softly.

"I know."

Alex seemed to shake off her melancholy then, and said, "We should be getting back to Summerplace. We need to start getting ready." We walked back as we had come—slowly, carefully, and in silence, both of us lost in our own thoughts.

When we got back to the house, Alex went into her bedroom to rest for a short time while I worked for just a bit longer in the library. Late in the afternoon I went upstairs to shower and dress. I took my time getting ready for the dinner party. I styled my hair so that it framed my face softly and I dressed in the only fancy outfit I had brought with me from New York, a classic little black dress. The last time I had worn this dress had been at a museum fund-raiser in New York with Alan. It seemed a lifetime ago. Funny; it had been a while since I had thought of him. I was surprised that I felt nothing now when he came to mind: no sorrow, no anger, no loss. It was as if all that had happened to me on Hallstead Island had eased my hurt feelings and I could remember our relationship with a welcome detachment.

The dress flattered my figure, but it needed something. I looked at myself in the mirror and thought for a moment. Then it came to me— I knew just the thing.

I rummaged in my armoire looking for my jewelry case. I slid it out and opened the clasp, and inside, nestled among tubes of velvet, lay a pair of pearl earrings that my mother had given me when I graduated from nursing school. I stared at them with a stab of grief and loss. They had belonged to her and I had loved them from the time I was a little girl. Each perfectly round pearl dropped delicately from a small diamond stud. They glittered in my hand as I examined them under the light. They would be perfect with this dress.

After I had given myself a last look in the mirror, I went downstairs to help Alex get ready for the dinner party. She was having some trouble pinning her long white curls to the top of her head, so I helped her with that. Then I helped her into a lovely navy blue suit of brocade and matching low-heeled pumps. She was the very picture of elegance and refinement.

She stood back and admired my outfit. "You look wonderful, Macy," she said. "Those earrings are very pretty with that dress."

"Thank you." I beamed. "They were a gift from my mother."

She tilted her head to one side. "The neckline of that dress is just crying out for something to jazz it up, though," she mused. "Do you mind if I lend you a necklace?"

"That would be lovely," I answered. *That's nice of her*, I thought.

She disappeared and returned a moment later dangling a stunning necklace from her fingers. It was a long, luscious strand of pearls, and hanging from it was a large, gleaming diamond pendant in the shape of a teardrop. It looked somehow familiar.

"Alex," I breathed, "that is absolutely beautiful!"

"I'm glad you like it," she replied as she fastened the clasp at the nape of my neck. "It was Diana's. I hope you don't mind. It just seems fitting that you wear it this evening."

Now I realized why the necklace looked familiar. I recalled the portrait of Diana in the living room; she was wearing the necklace. I wasn't sure how I felt about wearing a necklace that had belonged to her, but I didn't want to upset Alex right before the dinner party, so I decided not to voice my feelings.

"I'll be happy to wear it," I told her.

She smiled broadly. "Forrest and I gave that necklace to Diana for her eighteenth birthday. She just loved it. It's been sitting in my jewelry box all these years. Shall we go into the dining room?"

As we left her sitting room, we met Will coming downstairs. He looked exquisite in a tailored dark gray suit, and his dark hair shone as he bent to kiss Alex's cheek. He offered her his arm and they continued toward the dining room, with me behind them. He turned around once to fix me with a sardonic look, and as he did so, his eyes drifted to the necklace I wore. His veneer cracked visibly as his eyes widened and his lips set themselves in a thin white line. I fancied I saw his jaw tighten.

". . . lovely night," Alex was saying.

Will took his eyes off me and grinned smoothly at Alex, once more the solicitous and gentlemanly nephew.

"You picked a fine evening, Aunt Alex," he said.

When we entered the dining room, Stephan, Brandt, and Giselle were already there. My eyes (and Will's too, I noticed) were drawn immediately to Giselle. Her outfit, a one-piece black pantsuit, showed off her figure to magnificent effect, and its proportions were not lost on any man in the room. The tops of her ample breasts shone with a translucent, glittery powder, and her pant legs flared generously, giving her the illusion of floating as she moved. With her hair pulled back in a chignon, a few blond wisps carefully falling around her face, her appearance was electrifying. She was pouring herself a glass of wine as we came through the door, and when she finished she drifted over to where Brandt was standing, talking to Stephan.

Stephan and Brandt, like Will, were dressed in suits. The conservative image Brandt portrayed contrasted starkly with Giselle's very sexy appearance.

Will poured a small glass of wine for Alex, then a scotch on the rocks for himself, leaving me to pour my own wine from the decanter on the bar. Alex walked to Stephan's side and stood listening to his conversation with Brandt. They were discussing a river preservation project and Alex seemed very interested in the topic. I listened quietly, somewhat outside of the group. Giselle, who had placed her hand on Brandt's arm, was talking and laughing quietly with Will, who was openly flirting with her. I imagined that a woman with Giselle's obvious physical charms would be very attractive to a man like Will, and I found myself wondering what Brandt saw in Giselle, besides the obvious.

It wasn't long before Pete joined us. He arrived looking decidedly uncomfortable in crisp tan slacks and a sport coat. Bypassing the bar, he walked over to where I was standing, fingering the knot of his tie nervously. He noticed my necklace immediately and raised his eyebrows in surprise.

"I recognize that," he said by way of greeting, gesturing at the necklace. "Forrest and Alex gave that to Diana years ago."

"Yes. Alex wanted me to wear it tonight." I chuckled. "I guess my neck must have looked naked without it."

Pete and I stood a little way off while the conversation about the river project grew more animated. I suspected that Pete had an opinion about it but didn't care to share it with this group. Will had joined in, and Giselle was not speaking but was nodding in agreement whenever anyone spoke.

Vali and Leland came in then, each bearing a beautiful silver tray of hors d'oeuvres. Alex had apparently decided not to have this dinner catered. Vali actually looked nice; she was dressed in a long, flowing, dark-gray skirt and a soft, light-gray silk blouse. Her limp hair was drawn up on the sides in tortoiseshell combs.

Pete was explaining to me the controversy over the project that everyone else was discussing when Giselle walked by us to refill her wineglass. Her eyes drifted over my dress and settled for a second on my necklace. It was clear that she recognized it instantly. Her eyes met mine for a brief instant, flashing disbelief and malice.

What was it about this necklace? Had Alex known that everyone would recognize it?

Giselle poured her wine with an obviously unsteady hand, then started to place the crystal decanter back on the bar. As she did so, she knocked the side of the decanter against the bar's marble top. A split second later, the decanter shattered into a thousand pieces on the floor and the wine sloshed down the side of the bar. Giselle jumped back in time to avoid getting any wine on her outfit.

Brandt ran over to her immediately. "Are you all right?" he asked with concern.

She looked at him with doe-like eyes and replied, "Yes, darling. I'm fine."

Brandt gently took Giselle by the elbow and held her to him for a second, whispering as he did so, "I think you'd better lay off the wine for a while, honey." No one else was standing close enough to hear them, and I pretended not to hear, either.

Giselle glanced at him, then turned to Alex, saying, "Alex, I'm so sorry."

"That's perfectly all right, Giselle," she answered kindly. She walked to the door of the kitchen and called for Vali, who appeared just a moment later. Alex explained quietly what was needed, Vali fetched a cloth and dustpan, and the glass and wine were wiped up in a matter of seconds.

It wasn't long before Vali announced that dinner would be served. As she turned to go back to the kitchen, she also noticed my necklace. She did a double take, making her interest obvious, but I ignored her and I didn't know whether anyone else saw her. I was becoming uncomfortable wearing such a conspicuous piece of jewelry. If I had known how people were going to react to its presence around my neck, I would have refused Alex's suggestion to wear it. I began to wonder whether she had asked me to wear the necklace purposely to get a reaction out of a particular partygoer, but if that was her intention, it didn't seem to work. Everyone had recognized it and everyone had shown some sort of reaction to it. Everyone, that is, except for Stephan, who hadn't noticed it yet. I could tell that he noticed it later during dinner but, true to his character, he gave no indication that he had seen it at all.

Dinner was lively and Vali produced a masterpiece. Her leek soup had a delicate earthy flavor and was followed by a grapefruit sorbet. After that, she brought in a crown roast of pork, which was a work of art. I truly envied her ability to cook and wondered how a person with such a shockingly gruff manner could produce such excellent cuisine.

During dinner Alex proposed a toast to Stephan and Will for closing the transaction that the three of them had worked so hard to complete. They both saluted her with their glasses and she accepted gracefully. Brandt raised his glass as well, and I noticed that Giselle raised a glass of water in salute, rolling her eyes as she did so. I also noticed that she never let go of Brandt's hand throughout the entire meal. The two of them were like teenagers experiencing puppy love.

Alex had requested that dessert be held for a short time. While we waited, the talk around the table ranged from the oil business to the weather to the move to Pine Island to local politics. Vali came in at one point to refill everyone's wineglasses. With the wine flowing and people talking all at once, it seemed almost festive in the dining room. One could almost forget that Alex had an ulterior motive in bringing the members of this group together. And when Vali brought out a *dacquoise* for dessert, all talk turned immediately to her fine culinary skills. Vali was clearly proud of herself, and she rightly deserved all the praise she received. She moved quietly among the guests, filling coffee cups and topping them off with brandy or liqueur. Dinner and dessert lasted well into the evening. Alex seemed to enjoy herself, though nothing else of note had happened. It was getting late when she finally excused herself from the table, bidding us a good evening. She was tired, she said, and ready to go to bed.

Pete and I accompanied her to her sitting room, where she bid us good night again. Before we left her, I unclasped the necklace and gave it back to her with a sense of relief. I was glad to have it off my neck. Then I walked with Pete to the front door. He kissed me tenderly.

"You are beautiful," he told me, his lips against my hair. But there was something else he wanted to say. "Listen, ignore all the looks you got about the necklace," he advised, reaching for my hand. "Everyone in there knew that it belonged to Diana, and they hadn't seen it since before she drowned. That's why they were all so surprised."

I thanked him for the explanation, though I still wondered why Alex had lent me that particular necklace. She had to have known it would elicit some kind of reaction.

I said good night to Pete, who was dying to get out of his stuffy and uncomfortable clothes, and went upstairs to my room. I could hear Stephan, Will, Brandt, and Giselle still talking in the dining room, but I had no desire to join them. I doubted that Brandt and Giselle would be taking a boat back to Cape Cartier tonight; they were probably staying in Summerplace or over at Vali and Leland's cottage.

I slept soundly that night but woke up very early the next morning. It was too early to check in on Alex, so I did something that I had wanted to do since the previous night. After I showered and dressed, I went downstairs to the living room. Faint light was just beginning to creep into the sky, and the room was still quite dark. I switched on a small lamp and turned toward the object I had come to see.

CHAPTER 13

It took a moment to sink in. I stood staring, astonished, at the grisly portrait before me. It was the portrait that Alex had painted of Diana on her eighteenth birthday, the one in which she wore the necklace that I'd worn the night before. But this was not the same portrait I had seen my first day here. There was no face in this picture. It had been cut out, a jagged gash where Diana's smiling countenance had once been.

And suddenly I was afraid.

There was a disturbing violence underlying the damage to the picture. At the party I had assumed that the necklace had affected everyone the same way; they were merely surprised. But now I knew differently. Now I knew with chilling certainty that someone had been compelled to commit this macabre act as a result of seeing Diana's necklace encircling my throat.

I fairly flew out of the living room now, taking the portrait with me. I didn't want to run into anyone while I was alone, so I went up to my room until I heard people moving about downstairs. I left the portrait inside my armoire; I didn't want Alex to see it.

When I went downstairs, I found Brandt eating breakfast and reading a newspaper in the dining room. Stephan and Will had already left for New York for a few days, he said, and Giselle had gotten a ride with them to Cape Cartier so she wouldn't be late for work.

"Do you work today?" I asked him.

"Yes, but I don't go in for a little while," he answered.

I went into the kitchen to fix myself something to eat. Vali was in there, and her relatively good mood of the previous night had disappeared, at least toward me. She didn't acknowledge me as I fixed a bowl of cereal, tea, and a grapefruit. I carried my food back into the dining room and sat down opposite Brandt.

"Did you enjoy the dinner party?" he asked.

I nodded. "Yes, I did. I was a little worried that Alex wasn't up for it, but she seemed to hold up very well. The role of hostess agrees with her."

"You're right." He paused. "I noticed the necklace you were wearing last night. It used to belong to Diana."

"You weren't the only one who noticed it," I said ruefully. "Everyone seemed surprised to see it on me."

"Did Alex give it to you?"

"No. She lent it to me to give some flair to my outfit. I wouldn't have worn it if I had known it would cause such a stir."

"What kind of stir?"

"Well, I saw more than surprise on some faces last night. I saw shock. I wasn't prepared for it."

Brandt frowned but politely did not ask who had exhibited such a reaction to the necklace, and I did not volunteer the information. Instead, I changed the subject. I needed to ask him about the conversation he had had with Forrest before Forrest's death.

"Brandt, Pete tells me that you and Forrest had a rather unpleasant conversation shortly before Forrest died."

Brandt thought for a moment before answering. "Yes, actually, we did—"

Alex appeared in the doorway to the dining room just then, looking as though she had just awoken. Her hair still hung down her back, and she was dressed in a nightgown and robe. Her eyes were moist from crying. I rose quickly and went to her.

"Alex, what's the matter?" I asked in alarm.

"The necklace . . . it's . . . it's . . . gone," she stammered.

"What?!" Brandt and I cried out simultaneously.

She nodded. "It's gone. I've looked everywhere. I put it on top of my bureau last night. I was so tired, and I figured I would replace it in my jewel case this morning. But when I woke up, it wasn't where I left it." Tears rolled down her soft, wrinkled cheeks.

Instinctively, I knew that Alex was right. The necklace was gone. But instead I said, "Maybe the necklace fell under the bureau. Would you like me to come look?"

"You can look again, but I tried to look under it and I didn't see anything. What do you think happened to it?"

Brandt and I exchanged looks. "I don't know," I answered.

"Would you like me to help?" he offered.

"Thanks, Brandt. I'll help her. That way you can get home and get ready for work," I replied.

I followed Alex through the living room and into her suite. Thankfully, she was so focused on the loss of the necklace that she didn't seem to notice that her daughter's portrait was missing from the living room. It helped that the room was still rather dark during the early morning.

She led me into her bedroom and walked directly to the bureau.

"This is where I put it when I went to sleep last night," she stated. I got down on my hands and knees and peered under the dresser. Nothing. I slid my arm underneath it and felt around and back against the wall. Nothing. I stood up slowly.

"Alex, you were exhausted when you went to bed last night. Is it possible that you put it somewhere else and just don't remember?"

She shook her head. "I know I put it right there on that bureau," she insisted. "But we can look around if you think that would help."

"Why don't we?" I suggested. "Maybe it'll turn up. I'll start looking while you dress and eat breakfast, if you'd like."

She shook her head again. "I can't eat right now. I'm too upset. I'll get dressed, though."

While Alex dressed, I looked for the necklace in her sitting room. Though I searched the entire room, under cushions and behind furniture and inside drawers, I didn't find the necklace. After Alex was dressed, I did a methodical search of her bedroom while she started looking in her office. Neither of us had any luck. Finally, as I helped her look through her office, I asked, "Did you lock your doors from the inside after I left you last night?"

I knew the answer before I asked the question.

"No. I forgot. I was so tired . . ." Her voice trailed off; then she looked at me intently, her eyes wide. "Do you think it's been stolen?"

I nodded grimly. "I'm afraid it's starting to look that way."

"But why would someone do that?"

I had no answer for that. But I had another question.

"Alex, what did you hope to learn from my wearing that necklace last night?"

She sighed and sat down slowly at her desk. "You know why I had that dinner party, Macy. Of course I told everyone I wanted to celebrate the closing of our transaction, but that wasn't the real reason. I wanted to flush out the person or people who killed Diana and Forrest."

She paused for a moment. "I thought that if you wore that necklace, it just might spook someone into revealing something."

"The only reaction was surprise, and *everybody* showed that," I told her.

She nodded ruefully. "I know. I feel like we're back to square one. How are we going to figure out what happened to my husband and daughter?"

"I honestly don't know. But we'll think of something."

She looked like she had aged overnight, and I knew she was tired and scared. I changed the subject. "Let's concentrate on something else for now. First of all, we have to work on your exercises this morning. Second, it won't be long before you move this household to Pine Island. Would you like me to do some more packing today?"

Alex thought for a moment. "Why don't you go down to the boathouse and find Pete? He and Leland can start taking my clothes and books and art supplies over today. They know where everything goes at Solstice. If you accompany them, they can tell you where to start putting things. That would be a big help. And we'll exercise after you've found Pete."

"Okay." I smiled.

Minutes later, I was making my way through the trees to the

boathouse. The brisk walk helped to clear my mind, and I wished that Alex could travel this path more easily, because she could use the same rejuvenation. I breathed deeply of the clean, crisp air perfumed by pine needles. I could hear the insistent honking of the ever-present geese, though they were invisible above the trees. Closer to me, there were birds chirping loudly in the woods. I hoped they would pack up and move soon too.

When I got to the boathouse, Pete was already outside. He heard me coming and turned to wave to me.

"What are you doing down here so early?"

"Hi. Alex asked me to find you. She wants you and Leland to start taking some of her personal things over to Solstice today."

"Sounds good to me. It's about time she started to move her things over there. It won't be long before everyone has to move. Does she want me to come up to the house?"

"Yes."

"Coffee first?"

"No, thanks. I've already had my caffeine this morning. But I'll sit with you while you have yours."

We climbed the stairs to his kitchen, where there was a small pot of coffee already brewed. He poured himself a big mug. "I'm going to need this after that dinner last night. I'm not good at staying out that late." He winked. "How's Alex this morning?"

"Not good. Diana's necklace is gone."

He looked at me with surprise. "But you gave it to her when she went to bed last night."

"I know. But it was missing this morning. We've turned her rooms upside down looking for it, but it's vanished."

"It has to be around somewhere."

"I'm not so sure. She didn't lock her doors last night when she went to sleep. Anyone could have gone into her bedroom and taken it."

"Do you think that's what happened?"

"I'm sure of it. She was exhausted last night. If someone had gone in there in the middle of the night looking for the necklace, she would have slept right through it. The problem is that everyone was around last night, so it could have been anybody. Thank goodness she wasn't harmed."

Pete shook his head. "Poor Alex. What else can go wrong?"

"There is something else," I said.

He looked at me in surprise. "What?"

"This morning I woke up earlier than usual. I got to thinking about that necklace and where I had seen it before. Diana was wearing it in a portrait that was in the living room."

"Yes. I've seen that portrait."

"I wanted to have a look at it, so I went down to the living room. No one else was around yet. When I found the portrait, someone had slashed out Diana's face. It's absolutely grotesque."

He let out a low whistle. "Has Alex seen it?"

"No. I took the portrait back to my room and hid it in the armoire. I didn't want her to find it."

"Good thinking. I wonder if the same person who took the necklace also slashed the picture."

"I wish I knew."

"Things seem to be building up around here."

"What do you mean?"

"Before you got here, the house was basically quiet most of the time. Now all these bizarre things are going on. It all started when you arrived on Hallstead Island—you've been the catalyst."

"I can't understand it."

"I can't either, but it's not necessarily a bad thing. Maybe this island needed some shaking up. Maybe some old questions will be answered because of you."

"I hope so, for Alex's sake." I sighed.

"I'll go see her," Pete replied as he stood up to rinse out his mug.

We walked together through the woods up to Summerplace. The sun was climbing higher and the day promised to be beautiful. It would be a good day to transport some of Alex's belongings to Solstice.

I worked on packing the last of her summer clothes. Pete retrieved a handcart from the boathouse, and we made several trips down to the dock with boxes of clothes. It wasn't until I helped Pete load the boat with the clothes that I realized the extent of Alex's wardrobe. Just the summer clothes would require two trips to Pine Island.

"Why doesn't Alex leave these clothes here over the winter?" I asked Pete as we set off for Pine Island with the second load of clothes.

"It isn't unusual for her to take off for the tropics for a while when it gets really cold," he explained. "It saves a lot of time and effort if no one has to come back to Summerplace to get them. If she goes this year, maybe she'll take you along."

I grinned. "Sounds like a nice perk."

My time over the next couple of days was spent going back and forth between Summerplace and Solstice, taking Alex's belongings from her fair-weather home and depositing and organizing them in her winter home. Alex asked me at one point to make sure that Diana's portrait was packed. I hated being deceptive, but I told her I had already taken care of it.

I was getting a little more used to riding in the boat by now. I wasn't exactly comfortable out on the water, but I wasn't in a white-knuckled panic each time I stepped into the boat either. I was able to appreciate more of the sights that Pete pointed out on our trips and I was finding myself increasingly awed by the majesty and moods of the river. Depending on the day, the water could be placid and glassy, angry with whitecaps, or jubilant with sparkling, lilting waves. I was becoming adept at guessing the mood of the river each morning before I saw the water, just by looking at the sky and feeling the wind on my face. Pete was noticing my growing cognizance of the river's many temperaments, and he was pleased.

Once the bulk of Alex's clothes, books, and art supplies were at Solstice, organized and put away, the household began a period of controlled busyness, during which every room, every surface, was cleaned from top to bottom. In my infrequent spare time I worked in the library on my categorization system.

During this time, a rather restrained atmosphere settled over Summerplace. It was as if we were marking time, waiting for something to happen.

If I had known what that something would be, I would have insisted that Alex and I move to Solstice immediately.

CHAPTER 14

Over the next couple of weeks, we didn't see much of Stephan or Will. They came up to Hallstead Island from New York a few times, but their stays were brief, usually just overnight. Interestingly, I was not bothered by any pranks during this time. Brandt would come to visit Alex once in a while, and it was always pleasant to see him. Alex enjoyed his visits. As usual, Giselle came with him when he visited the island. Generally, she would pay her respects to Alex for a short time and then go to see her aunt and uncle in their cottage.

One day when Brandt was visiting, Alex invited him on our morning walk. He cheerfully agreed and the three of us donned coats and descended the steps to the flagstone path in the brilliant sunshine. We walked around Summerplace several times, and Brandt and Alex spoke together of past long winters and times spent at Solstice. I said little, content to be listening to their light and fascinating conversation and thoroughly enjoying my education in winter life on the river. How exciting winter must be for the children living on the river! They could enjoy everything from skating to sledding to ice fishing.

As the three of us walked slowly around the flagstone path for the third time, my eyes were drawn to Vali and Leland's quaint cottage. It was dark brown, just like Summerplace, and it also had a weather-vane on top. It was a lovely home and I wondered whether the inside was as pleasant as the outside. Sheer white curtains hung in the windows on each side of the front door. As I looked, the curtains moved gently and parted. Not much; just enough to afford a clear view of the three of us from inside the cottage. I couldn't see the person behind the curtain but I knew someone was standing there. After a couple of seconds, the curtains slipped back into place again and the watcher was gone. By the end of our third trip around the house Alex was ready to go inside and get back to work. Brandt left us to go down to the boathouse to talk to Pete.

By now, most of Alex's belongings were gone from Summerplace, transported to Solstice and awaiting her imminent arrival. I had fervently hoped that we would find Diana's necklace while we were packing her remaining belongings, but it never turned up. I was firmly convinced that the necklace had been stolen, and though Alex didn't talk about it, I was sure that she was convinced as well. I could only hope that the necklace would be returned to her at some point, even if we never found the person who stole it.

Though no pranks were played on me during this time of packing, of cleaning, of waiting for something, my nightmares unfortunately did not abate. I was dreaming less frequently of my parents and their burning car, but I was dreaming more often of the leaning tree, of being caught in a swirling vortex of angry water beneath its branches. My biological mother was often in those dreams, at the bottom of the river. It was terrifying, and often I was unable to go back to sleep once the dream had interrupted my rest.

One morning Alex suggested that after our walk I go down to the boathouse to see if Pete needed any help readying the boats for winter storage. I was done with the packing inside Summerplace and I was looking for somewhere to be of assistance. Alex was working in her office and knew that I was bored. So I went looking for Pete.

When I found him upstairs in the boathouse, he was surprised to see me.

"I haven't seen you in a few days! Where have you been?"

"Helping Alex. She still had some packing to do. I did my own packing too, but that didn't take too long."

"Are you here to help me?" he asked with a grin.

"Put me to work," I instructed him. "Alex mentioned that you might need some help getting the boats ready for winter storage."

"Actually, I will need help with that, but first I have to take a trip over to the storage facility. It's in Cape Cartier. Why don't you help me here for a while; then later on this afternoon we'll head over. Maybe we could grab an early dinner over there too."

"Sounds great. Where should I start?"

"Come with me." He led the way upstairs and put me to work cleaning and packing small tools in various wooden boxes. It was dirty, greasy work but I enjoyed it. I worked until lunchtime, then told Pete I would return later. I went back to Summerplace and joined Alex for lunch in the dining room again. It was nice to see her taking her meals in the dining room, taking pleasure in using her own home rather than remaining locked and imprisoned in her private rooms. She seemed to enjoy coming out for meals too. It was a nice break for her in the middle of the day and, quite simply, it was healthy for her to get out of her office once in a while. We took a short walk after lunch before she encouraged me with a coy smile to go back down to the boathouse to see Pete again.

"Alex, I know what you're up to."

"Isn't Pete handsome?"

I laughed. "He is. You're right."

"Then what are you doing up here with me?"

"I'm your nurse, remember?"

"You get down there," she scolded.

I left her in her sitting room and went in search of Pete again. I found him down on the dock.

"Are you ready to go over to Cape Cartier?" he asked.

"Yes. Need help loading anything onto the boat?"

"Yes, thanks. We can take a quick trip over to Solstice and then stop at the marina in Cape Cartier. You can get one of those small boxes over there," he told me, pointing to the pile of wooden boxes I had stacked for him earlier.

Our trip to Pine Island was quick. I was bundled up in my life jacket, which did double duty by granting me peace of mind and keeping me warm against the cold wind that cut across the river as we sped along. We quickly unloaded the boat at Solstice, put the tools away in the basement of the old house, and left again for Cape Cartier.

We drew up to the marina, which wasn't far from the main street. Pete found the man he was looking for and turned to me. "Why don't you go look around for a while? I won't be too long, and Main Street is just over there," he suggested, pointing. "I'll come find you when I'm done."

I hadn't had any time to explore the picturesque little town on the day I arrived in the Thousand Islands, so I left him at the marina and headed toward the main street. There were more pedestrians than I expected, probably enjoying this beautiful day before the onset of winter weather, which everyone promised would be here soon. The town was charming, just what I would have expected, with small bungalow-like shops and restaurants nestled side by side down the block. I browsed in several shops, enjoying the local art, books, and photography. In a tiny bookshop that smelled deliciously like pine and mulled cider, I bought a book on Thousand Island recipes and the islanders who had invented them. I wasn't the greatest cook, but it would be an interesting read.

I continued along the street, looking into shops now and then, when I saw a small crowd gathered ahead on the sidewalk. A van with a small antenna on top was parked in the street next to the group. I approached the group intending to walk around them, and I was surprised to see Giselle in the center of the gathering as I came closer. Apparently she was on assignment for her job with the local television station. She was interviewing pedestrians about their plans for the beautiful fall day and their predictions for the winter ahead. She was good at her job and was able to get many in the assembled crowd to talk to her on camera. She didn't see me at first, so I looked on, fascinated, while she worked the crowd. As usual, she looked marvelous. As I watched, though, I noticed how tired she looked. She must have been exhausted if she had been at work since four o'clock that morning. Her makeup seemed heavier than usual, but that was probably because I was seeing her in the bright sunlight for a change. I usually saw her indoors at Summerplace or outdoors in the shade.

When she finally saw me, she smiled and gave a little wave. She made her way to me and put the microphone near my face.

"How about you, miss? Any predictions for the upcoming season? Do you think it will be a bad winter?"

"I . . . I'm . . . I really don't know," I stammered, surprised that she would ask me.

Giselle laughed. "Did I catch you off guard, Macy? Don't worry, we won't put that on the air. Let's pack it up, Joe," she said to the cameraman. "What are you doing in Cape Cartier?" she asked me as she handed the cameraman her microphone.

"Just looking around. Pete is at the marina and I'm waiting for him."

"Oh." She nodded. "Gotta run. See you later, Macy." Then she turned and started talking to Joe. I walked quietly away and into a perfume shop, and when I came out the television van and crew were gone.

I had gone as far as I could on the main street, which ended at a quiet bay. I sat down on a bench for a while and watched the water and the infrequent boat traffic. The sounds of the shops and pedestrians behind me drifted by in a peaceful hush. After a while, I started walking down the other side of the street. It wasn't long before I saw Pete walking toward me, his stride long and purposeful. He reached me in a few moments.

"I'm done at the marina. What do you think of Cape Cartier? Of course there's more to it than this, but Main Street is a good introduction."

"It's lovely," I said. "I bought a local cookbook."

"Isn't that bookstore great? I go in there every chance I get," Pete answered. He looked up and down the block. "How does dinner sound? Did you look at the menus of any of these places?"

"No," I replied. "I was too busy looking in the shops."

He smiled. "There are lots of those to keep you busy. I know a place, if you're interested."

"Sounds good."

We walked down to the other end of the block to a tiny pub I hadn't seen earlier. It was the last establishment on the block, a small building painted black with gold trim, and I liked it right away. The inside was rustic and dark, and wooden decoys painted like loons and other waterfowl adorned the inside of the pub. Pete ordered a traditional Irish stew and I had the shepherd's pie, which was delicious. We sat in the booth for quite a while, lingering over our meals, talking of nothing in particular.

"I almost forgot to mention that I saw Giselle out on the street earlier," I told him.

"What was she doing?"

"She was interviewing people about the upcoming winter."

"Did she interview you?" he asked with a smile.

"She tried, but I loused it up pretty well. She assured me it wouldn't be on television." I laughed.

"Giselle hasn't been looking like herself lately," Pete mused.

"I thought it looked like she was wearing more makeup than usual," I noted.

"Not that it's any of my business," he said, "but do you want to know what I think?"

"What?"

"I think she's been drinking."

I suddenly remembered Brandt speaking to her at Alex's party after she broke the wine decanter.

"You may be right," I told him. "That would explain her tired look and the extra makeup."

"If that's the case, it's too bad." Pete shook his head. "She could really go places in her profession."

"Would she leave Brandt?"

"Not in a million years. You've seen the way she hangs on him. She'd be lost without him."

"I'm ashamed of us, talking about her like this," I said. "Are you ready to get back to Hallstead Island before it gets dark?"

I paid the check this time and we left the pub. The sun had indeed started to go down, and it was decidedly colder than when we had gone into the restaurant. Pete reached for my hand and we hurried back to the marina. It wasn't long before we were back on Hallstead Island. I checked on Alex and she was thrilled to learn that I had spent some time in Cape Cartier and that Pete and I had had dinner together.

"I know the place." She beamed. "Cozy and romantic."

I laughed. "Well, I don't know about romantic, but it was dark and the food was great."

"Any old place can be romantic if the right people are there." She smiled knowingly.

"Alex, you're relentless!"

She smiled again. "I just know what I see. And you and Pete are perfect for each other."

"Good night, Alex." I rolled my eyes at her.

"Good night, Macy."

When I went downstairs the next morning, Stephan and Will were there. Alex hadn't mentioned they were coming, so I was surprised to see them. Stephan stood up immediately and came to kiss me on the cheek.

"How are you, Macy?" he inquired in his gentlemanly way. "Getting ready for the big move?"

Will snorted, but Stephan and I ignored him. I helped myself to a cup of coffee from the sideboard and went into the kitchen to make myself a bowl of oatmeal. When I returned, only Will remained. He scowled at me, his eyes dark.

"Don't expect me to be as glad to see you as Stephan was," he began.

I hadn't expected Will to be thrilled with my presence, but his remark still took me aback.

"As I've told you before," I explained coolly, "my job is here. As long as Alex wants me to be her nurse, I intend to stay."

"And as I've told you before," he hissed softly, rising and coming over to my chair, then leaning down close to my face, "I'm going to see to it that you leave this island."

He turned on his heel and left quickly. I sat bewildered, my oatmeal getting cold, wondering why Will had such animosity toward me. I ate the cold oatmeal and went into Alex's room.

"Big news, Macy," she greeted me. "We're moving to Solstice tomorrow!"

I was surprised. I had assumed she would give the household more notice. "How did you decide on that?" I asked.

"Brandt came to visit yesterday while you and Pete were out, and he told me there's a big storm coming. He says the Coast Guard is taking this one very seriously. I thought about it overnight and I think this is a good time to move. If the storm is bad and the temperature drops too low overnight tomorrow, we could have a lot of snow. I want to move before it hits."

"What do you want me to do?"

"We're going to have to pack up my office today. You can help me with that."

We spent the entire day packing the things in Alex's office. Alex directed, and Vali and Leland and I packed the boxes. Special boxes had to be brought from storage and filled in a very specific manner. By late afternoon the office was packed and the boxes stood ready to be transported to Solstice.

Alex and I joined Stephan and Will in the dining room for dinner. All talk centered on the move to Solstice and the work that would have to be done there in order to get Alex's office up and running as soon as possible. Stephan and Will both had small offices in their rooms upstairs in Summerplace, and they left the dining room early so they could spend the evening packing their belongings. I helped Alex do a few brief exercises after dinner, and as I was leaving, Brandt and Giselle appeared.

"We came to help," Brandt greeted us. "Giselle is going to help Vali and Leland with their cottage tonight, so if there's anything you need me to do in Summerplace, just say the word."

"That's very kind of you both," Alex replied. "Actually, things are pretty well under control here. But maybe Pete could use some help down in the boathouse. Why don't you go ask him?"

Brandt and Giselle left then, and Alex went to bed early. She wanted to be well rested because, she said, tomorrow would be a long day.

My room was all packed; I had even taken the rock that had been thrown through my French doors and put it outdoors, where it belonged. I carefully packed the slashed portrait of Diana and hid it with my possessions. I planned to take it to a studio in Cape Cartier to see if it could be repaired.

I finished a mystery book I had borrowed from among those remaining in the library downstairs, but I still wasn't tired, so I went downstairs looking for another book and to get a cup of tea. The kitchen was dark, but I could see light from the dining room spilling under the kitchen door. I intended to make my tea and hurry back upstairs when I heard people talking. I recognized the voices of Will and Giselle, speaking together in low tones. I heard the word "Diana."

Suddenly I forgot all about my tea. I crept to the door to hear what they were saying.

"Another glass of pinot?" Will asked, his words slurring a bit.

"Of course," Giselle answered.

I heard a chair being pushed back and footsteps moving to the cabinet where the wine was kept. A few seconds of silence, then footsteps again.

"Thanks," Giselle said.

"Cheers," came Will's reply.

"Anyway," Will was saying, "it's true. I had a huge crush on you. And since you were always here visiting Diana or Vali and Leland, I got to see you all the time."

"You had a crush on me?" Giselle giggled.

"Yeah, but that was around the time that I was supposed to leave for New York to start work for HSH, and Diana convinced me that my career came first."

"It would never have worked out. Your life was moving in another direction, and my only option at the time was to stay in Cape Cartier."

"What do you think would have happened between us if I had stayed?"

"I think it would have been good," Giselle answered evasively. "But our lives have gone different ways. And now I have Brandt."

"I wish I'd stayed. You and I would have been great together."

I didn't stay to hear any more. Will and Giselle kept talking, but I crept quietly out of the kitchen and back up to my room. *This* was unexpected. I had assumed that Will's attraction to Giselle was purely physical. I had no idea he'd actually had feelings for her. It sounded like he still did.

And if Diana had convinced him to put his career first, if Diana had kept them apart, that might give Will a reason to fight with her. To hate her. To kill her.

I tried reading, but the ramifications of what I had just heard in the dining room kept echoing through my mind. I couldn't concentrate, couldn't sleep. Should I tell Alex? Should I tell Pete? No, I decided, they both had a lot on their minds with the move to Solstice. But I would tell them as soon as the move was complete.

I wish I hadn't waited.

CHAPTER 15

Moving day dawned gray and windy. The boughs on the trees outside my balcony doors dipped and tossed; the wind whistled a low rushing sound through the pine needles.

When I went in to see her, Alex was up and dressed and already directing the moving of her office boxes. In fact, the office was almost empty of Alex's belongings by the time I got there. A crew of moving men was helping with the move, men who, I learned, performed this work for Alex every year and were trusted to move the remainder of the household efficiently and within a single day. Pete was in and out of the office as well, helping the movers.

I spent the day helping Pete and Alex, making several trips to Pine Island with Pete and helping unload the boat each time we docked. There were movers at Solstice too, who helped unload the boat and put things in the house. The system worked like a well-oiled machine, and it was fascinating to see this annual move pared down to a science.

The weather worsened throughout the day, and Alex said more than once that she was glad we were all leaving Summerplace before the storm came. Bone-chilling rain spattered several times during the day as the sky darkened and became more forbidding.

At last, the movers were gone. They had taken the very last load from Summerplace over to Solstice. They would complete their work in Alex's winter home and be gone by the time the rest of the household arrived. We were all going to Solstice in Alex's two boats before the storm worsened. Pete was to pilot one and Stephan would pilot the other. Pete was down at the boathouse, Vali and Leland were checking their cottage to make sure nothing had been missed, Stephan and Will were upstairs, and Giselle was helping her aunt and uncle. Brandt had been called in to work due to the storm and had left several hours earlier. Alex and I were in her office, double-checking that we had sent everything over to Solstice. Outside I could hear the rain falling steadily, and several times I saw trees bending almost horizontally in the fierce wind. I wondered, not for the first time, how safe it would be to leave the island under such conditions.

As if reading my mind, Alex said worriedly, "I'm not so sure we should go to Solstice tonight. This storm has gotten bad more quickly than it was forecast to. I think maybe we should stay here until tomorrow."

"Do you want me to tell everyone?" I asked.

"Wait for just a little bit."

Just then the door to the office crashed open.

Alex and I turned with a gasp to see Giselle standing in the doorway, wet, wild-eyed, and breathing heavily. She was wearing a big yellow raincoat buttoned up to her chin.

"Alex! Macy!" she cried. "I just got a radio transmission from Pete! He's in trouble!"

"What? How? What happened?" Alex and I asked in a jumble of words.

"I don't know. I don't know. He's out in the boat and he needs help. I can't find Stephan or Will or Leland. Macy, can you come?"

"Of course! But I thought he was at the boathouse!"

"He said he had to run over to Cape Cartier to get some special computer cable for Alex's office at Solstice. What does it matter? Hurry!"

"Oh, he never should have left in this weather," Alex worried, her voice high. "Macy, what can I do?"

"You stay here in case Pete calls on the radio. If he calls, tell him we're on our way. I'll let you know as soon as we find him," I replied grimly.

"Okay. Go!" she ordered.

I grabbed a coat that was lying on a bench in the foyer, and Giselle and I ran out the front door. As soon as we got outside, we were hit by the full force of the storm. The icy rain stung my face and ran in rivulets down the front of my coat. The late afternoon was dark and had become noticeably colder.

We ran down the stone front steps and around the side of Summerplace to Vali and Leland's cottage, then veered onto the worn path through the woods. In my state of mind, it didn't occur to me at the time to wonder why we were running away from the boathouse. I just kept running, following Giselle, and before long I heard another noise in the woods. A crashing sound, footsteps pounding. Another person was running behind us. Chasing us.

A man's voice called out of the black torrent.

"Macy! Wait!" It was Will. And he was getting closer. I was afraid.

I ran faster, blindly, tripping over small roots and twigs on the ground. The needles made the path slippery, but still I continued, determined not to let Will catch me. Giselle was ahead of me, running faster, looking back now and then to make sure that I was still behind her. I stumbled once, falling and catching myself on the heels of my hands. Will was just behind me. I could hear him breathing hard. I could see his eyes, bright and terrifying.

"Macy, wait! Get back here," he commanded.

"No!" I shouted. I scrambled back to my feet, but he reached out of the darkness and grabbed the back of my coat.

"Let me go!" I screamed, panicking now, jerking the wet coat out of his hands.

I ran then with a strength I didn't know I had, leaving Will behind. I looked back once and saw him bending over with his hands on his knees, still breathing heavily. Suddenly he stood up and went running back in the direction of Summerplace. I turned; up ahead, Giselle was at the leaning tree, untying a small boat that was tethered there.

"Come on!" she shouted, holding the rope in her hands.

I jumped into the boat and sat down. I didn't have time to worry that I didn't have a life jacket. I was so anxious about Pete that I could think of nothing else.

Giselle jumped in behind me, throwing the rope onto the floor of the boat. She gunned the engine and swung out in a wide arc away from Hallstead Island. I looked back but didn't see Will. The rain continued to pound us relentlessly; this boat had no canopy under which to find refuge.

Giselle was saying something, but the wind was shrieking and I couldn't hear her. She was highly agitated. She looked around wildly in all directions as we sped across the water. Pete was nowhere to be seen, and the weather was worsening. I was becoming more worried as every moment passed. Our small boat undulated with the roaring waves for several minutes.

As my eyes scanned the black, churning river water in search of Pete, I hardly noticed that the boat was slowing down.

"Do you see something?" I asked Giselle.

"I do see something," she replied.

"Do you see him? Where is he?" I demanded, my voice getting louder, more urgent.

She had slowed the boat down considerably now, and I couldn't see Pete anywhere. I was in a panic. But she got my attention by speaking again, quietly, so that I had to strain to hear her.

"You can stop pretending now. I know who you are," she said, her eyes bright with malice, her manner entirely calm now, in contrast to the storm raging around us. A chill went up my spine, prickling the hairs on the back of my neck.

"What are you talking about?" I asked her slowly, watching her movements warily now.

"I said I know who you are, Diana," she replied, her teeth clenched.

And then I knew.

The danger had not been from Will. It had been from Giselle all along. She unbuttoned the top two buttons of her raincoat, despite the downpour issuing from the skies, and leaned forward to finger the rope that still lay on the floor of the boat. As she did so, her necklace slipped out from its protection under the coat. With a start I realized that she was wearing Diana's necklace, the one that had been stolen from Alex's room.

"So you've come back, my dear friend," she said with a sneer.

"Giselle, what are you talking about? I'm Macy. You know that."

"Shut up. You're lying. Did you think I wouldn't recognize you the minute I saw you? Did you think I wouldn't know why you've come back?"

"Giselle, please, you're not thinking straight. You know me. I'm Alex's nurse, not her daughter."

"Stop it!" she screeched, squeezing her eyes shut. I was afraid. I needed to get her to change the subject.

"Do you know where Pete is?" I asked.

"I don't know. Probably at the boathouse," she answered nonchalantly. Tentacles of icy fear began fingering my scalp. Pete hadn't gone anywhere. Of course not. He was too smart to go out in a storm like this. Why hadn't that occurred to me before I went with Giselle?

Our small boat was being tossed about in the dark waves, and as I grasped the side of the boat tightly, I looked around for something that could help me. There was nothing. I saw an island nearby, but it was too far away, especially for someone who couldn't swim. Giselle maneuvered the boat slowly around the island until we were out of the main channel. Through the ebony squall I could see a dark hole in the rock foundation of the island. I couldn't see it well because of the increasingly cold rain assaulting my face, but I knew it was there.

It was toward this hole that Giselle seemed to be steering the boat. A wave of panic rose in my throat, as if my subconscious knew what awaited me.

"This is Devil's Oven, Diana," Giselle said in a silky voice that didn't sound like hers. I had heard that name before. My mind seemed to be working in slow motion. Why did it sound familiar?

Giselle seemed to read my mind. "You remember Devil's Oven. Will told you the story not long ago. A man was forced to live in here for months because he did something bad. Just like you."

That was it! That pirate—Bill Johnston. Now the memory of Will's chilling version of the tale thrust itself into my memory like a knife.

"Giselle, I haven't done anything bad."

"Oh, yes, you have." She rolled her eyes. "Are you really going to pretend you haven't?"

"What did I do?"

"Do I have to spell it out for you? It was Brandt. You took Brandt from me. He would have married me if it weren't for you. Brandt and I have always belonged together. But he thought he was in love with you, so that's why I had to get rid of you. So he and I could be together. Don't you understand?" She was talking as though I were an imbecile.

"Killing you was so easy." She laughed softly. "Since you couldn't swim, all I had to do was push you into the water far enough from the leaning tree so that you couldn't reach it."

She was really convinced that I was Diana. Her calm rationale scared me more than anything else. I had to keep her talking.

"So you were the one who left the note for Alex. You killed Forrest, too."

"I had to. You see, he had spoken to Brandt about me. I heard the whole conversation, but neither of them knew it. Forrest was concerned that I was too controlling. Too demanding. He was afraid that I would insert myself into every aspect of Brandt's life. As if Brandt doesn't want me in every part of his life." She laughed bitterly. "Brandt stood up for me, though. He said I merely needed affirmation. He's such a wonderful man."

So that was the topic of the "unpleasant" conversation that Brandt and Forrest had before Forrest's death.

She paused, looking at me intently, then continued. "But I knew then and there that Forrest could impede our happiness, just like you did. So I had to get rid of him, too."

I gasped softly. She chuckled, then said, "It was easy to kill him. I knew that all I would have to do was push him down those balcony stairs. One day when I was visiting Aunt Vali, I saw Forrest on the balcony. I ran up the stairs very quietly and confronted him. He tried to tell me that he was just looking out for Brandt's and my happiness, but I knew better. He was trying to get Brandt to leave me. I told him that I had heard their conversation. Then I pushed him and ran away. No one ever figured it out."

"Forrest was telling you the truth. He wasn't trying to get Brandt to leave you."

She ignored me. "And now—*now*—I find out that you stole Will from me too! And you've come back to rob me of my happiness again. Well, I won't let it happen. This is where I'm going to give you your first swimming lesson. Remember? I told you I would teach you to swim." She laughed eerily and terror gripped my throat.

She steered the boat skillfully into the mouth of Devil's Oven. Inside the island cave it was dark and the waves rolled and pitched. It was relatively quiet, but I could still hear the wind howling outside. I searched my mind frantically for anything that would keep her talking.

"What about all the things that have been happening on Hallstead Island? What about the photo album and the slashed portrait and pushing me down on the dock? What about the rock being thrown into my room?"

"All good tactics to scare you, no doubt. But they weren't all mine. It's true; I did slash the portrait. It looks much better now, if you ask me. And I was the one who pushed you on the dock. You probably thought Will did it, didn't you? And I know what you're doing now, you bitch. You think that if you keep me talking, you'll get away from me somehow. But you're wrong."

And before I knew what was happening, Giselle reached over and slapped my cheek hard. I leaped up from pure reflex and she grabbed my shoulders and shoved with all her might. There was no room for me to step back when she pushed me. I lost my footing and stumbled backward. I heard a blood-curdling scream escape my throat as my body tumbled into the frigid water. My arm hit the side of the boat as I fell, and a searing pain shot through my shoulder. Immediately a wave lunged at me, completely submerging me in an underwater abyss of disorientation. Then, as the wave receded for a moment, my head broke through the surface of the water and I filled my lungs with air. I opened my eyes and saw Giselle as she disappeared in the boat around the outside of the cave that was to become my tomb.

I was thrashing my legs and my unhurt arm, fighting for control over the bitterly cold water. Waves cascaded over my head every few seconds, sending me into spasms of terror and confusion. I was choking on all the water I swallowed, its iciness burning my lungs every time the waves crashed over me.

The darkness in Devil's Oven was complete. I could see nothing. The waves finally gave me a respite of several seconds and by kicking my legs violently and paddling my good arm, I was able to keep my chin just above the surface of the water. I thrashed forward and suddenly felt a breathtaking pain in my foot.

I had kicked something. My mind, though moving very slowly, somehow understood that I had reached a wall inside the cave. I needed to find a handhold or a foothold. I kicked my other foot gingerly as I reached out with my good arm to hug the wall. Finding a wall would do me no good if I couldn't find a ledge or a rocky protrusion on which I could rest. It wasn't long before my fingers moved back into a large crevice in the rock. Here was a place I could cling to for a moment to catch my breath.

I gripped the crevice as best I could with both hands and let my legs dangle for a moment in the water. My foot touched a small ledge under the water and I tried to stand on it briefly.

The pain in my foot was almost overwhelming. I couldn't set it down on the underwater ledge. Waves continued to pound against the rock walls of the cave. Several times the force of the water slammed the rest of my body against the rock, leaving long, searing gashes where my skin was torn away.

I had to calm myself somehow. I had to center myself and try to think clearly about how I might get out of Devil's Oven. But calm was not to be had. Not yet. Panic swept over me like one of the thundering waves when I realized that my joints were starting to stiffen and my foot didn't hurt as much as it had. My body was starting to slow down. I didn't know how long I had been in the water, but I knew the water was winning the struggle. I couldn't survive much longer in this cavern, in the freezing river.

I started to remember things I had done as a child. An image of me learning to ride a bike, my father's strong hands letting go of the bike seat as I tried riding on my own for the first time. An image of my high school graduation. An image of me playing with a cat we used to have, Buttercup.

And then the images stopped. I was filled with a weariness that I couldn't seem to overcome. My fingers began to loosen their grip on the crevice in the wall. My feet floated free. I could hear the violent waves colliding with the walls inside my cave, but it wasn't a frightening sound anymore. It seemed to be more of a raw, strangely natural, background noise.

How easy and peaceful it would be to let go of the rock, to let go of the pain, to welcome an end to the cold, the watery darkness. The waves continued to drive my body into the wall, but I stopped caring. This would soon be over.

Then another image intruded on my fuzzy mind. It was Diana, the Diana from my nightmare, her upturned face staring at me with empty eyes from under the water, her hair billowing about her head in a tangled whorl.

And somewhere in my slowing mind, something clicked. I didn't want to die like Diana had. I didn't want her legacy to me to be one of drowning and terror. I wanted to do everything in my power to live the legacy left for me by my real mother, Marianne. I wanted to live a life of loving and learning.

But as much as I wanted to live, I couldn't swim.

Forcing myself to think calmly, I gripped the rocky crevice with a renewed strength and kicked my good leg gently until it touched the underwater ledge again.

That's when I saw the light. At first I thought I had imagined it, but then I saw it again. Reflected light, bobbing up and down erratically on the walls inside Devil's Oven. Then I heard voices. Men's voices, yelling my name. I tried feebly to yell back, but my exhaustion made it difficult to raise my voice. The light became stronger and the voices got louder, and soon I saw a boat in the mouth of Devil's Oven.

I was not going to die in the water.

The next few minutes were a blur. I remember Pete jumping out of the boat and swimming to me with a life belt. He hooked it around my waist, and someone else, someone on the boat, started dragging me through the water. Pete was behind me, firmly steering me over the waves that still rushed into the cave.

Seconds later strong hands reached down to pull me from the water. They gripped me under my arms, my shoulder protesting, and pulled me out of the water and onto the floor of the boat. I looked up into Will's face.

Will! I didn't know whether to laugh or cry. He had a stack of blankets next to him, and he wrapped them carefully around me one by one while Pete took the wheel of the boat.

After Pete had steered us away from Devil's Oven, the two men switched places. Will drove the boat back into the channel, still through the relentless storm, while Pete, as cold and wet as he was, sat on the boat's floor, his arms around me to try to warm me.

I tried to say something, but Pete hushed me. "Don't say a word. You can tell us everything later."

I was content to say nothing, to be on the floor in his arms. We were going back to Summerplace.

Once at Hallstead Island, Pete and Will fashioned a hammock out of blankets and carried me swiftly and gently up to the house. Alex was waiting for us by the door.

"Macy!" she cried. "I'm so glad you're all right!" The tears rolled down her face, and when I saw her tears, my own started. Pete and Will laid me on the sofa in Alex's sitting room while I tried to compose myself. Alex helped me into one of her robes while Will ran to get a change of his own clothes for Pete.

After a while, the story became clear. After Giselle and I left Alex, she had tried contacting Pete's boat radio unsuccessfully. Before long, Pete had appeared in Alex's sitting room to tell her that they would have to postpone the trip to Pine Island until the morning, since the storm was so ferocious. In answer to her puzzled questions, Pete explained that he knew better than to go out in such weather and had been in the boathouse for hours.

That was why Alex hadn't been able to reach him in the boat. She told Pete what Giselle had said, and they quickly realized that she meant to harm me. At that point Will arrived, running, saying that I was in trouble and that Giselle was taking me somewhere. Brandt came on the scene just then, having used a Coast Guard cutter to get to the island. They all explained to him what had transpired, and Brandt knew immediately where to look. He instructed Pete and Will to go to Devil's Oven to look for me while he contacted the Coast Guard and used a boat to go out searching for Giselle.

Alex had called for a doctor after Pete and Will left, but he could not get to Summerplace until the storm subsided.

I had so many questions. And my body hurt so much. As the others took turns sitting with me, I drifted in and out of sleep while we waited for the doctor. When he arrived a couple of hours later, he saw me alone in Alex's sitting room. Besides bruises and cuts, I had a dislocated shoulder, a broken foot, and a facial laceration requiring stitches. The doctor was able to pop my shoulder back into place, put a soft cast on my foot, and stitch the deep wound. He ordered me to get some rest and, under the circumstances, said a hard cast on my foot would have to wait until the following day.

"You're lucky you didn't go into shock, Miss Stoddard," he told me gravely as he was leaving. "If those fellows hadn't arrived when they did, there's no telling how much longer you would have survived."

After the doctor left, Will came in.

"I asked Alex and Pete to give me a few minutes alone with you," he began. "I won't stay long because I know you need to rest, but I think you deserve an explanation from me. And an apology."

"What do you mean?"

"I mean everything I've done to you. The threats and the scare tactics to try to get you to leave Hallstead Island."

I said nothing, unsure where this conversation was going.

"I know you're Diana's daughter," he stated simply.

I was stunned. "But . . . how did . . . how did you know?"

"A long time ago, I had to go into Stephan's desk in his New York office to retrieve something. I looked in the wrong drawer and I found copies of the adoption papers and documents all about you. I saw the pictures of you. I never told anyone what I found."

He took a deep breath. "Anyway, when I found out that you were coming here, I assumed immediately that Alex was looking for a blood relative—an heir. I could envision her giving you my inheritance and I wanted you gone."

"I never would have taken your money, Will."

"I know that now. Will you accept my apology?"

"Yes." I smiled. "Of course. I have a question for you, though. How did you know that Giselle meant to hurt me?"

Will went on to explain that he and Giselle had had several glasses of wine the previous night in the dining room. I admitted that I had heard part of their conversation.

"You should have stayed longer." He smiled wryly. "Then you could have avoided going with Giselle altogether."

He said that Giselle knew who I was. She had noticed immediately that I shared Diana's violet eyes.

"She spoke cryptically," Will explained. "She said Diana had stolen something from her years before and she wasn't going to give you a chance to come and steal it again.

"I didn't know exactly what she meant. She seemed to be confusing you with Diana," Will said. "But the threat was implied. That's why I ran after you earlier tonight when I saw that she was leading you somewhere."

"Thank you," I said, bowing my head. "I'm sorry I suspected you."

"That's all right. I deserved it. Now, try to get some sleep." He turned to go, but I called him back.

"Will," I asked, "what were the scare tactics you mentioned?"

He looked ashamed. "I threw that rock through your balcony door and I locked you in the turret that day." I lowered my eyes. "I'm really sorry," he said again. I nodded and he left then. Pete came in briefly.

"We haven't heard from the police or the Coast Guard yet," Pete explained. "You rest now, and we'll let you know if there are any developments."

"Pete, there are things that Giselle told me tonight. Horrible things. She killed Diana and Forrest."

He looked at me in shock.

"She pushed Diana into the water because she thought Diana had stolen Brandt from her. She also pushed Forrest down those balcony steps because she thought he was trying to get Brandt to leave her. It was all because of Brandt."

He shook his head in amazement. "At least we know now. We don't have to wonder anymore." He leaned in close and looked in my eyes.

"Pete," I said, "someone needs to tell Alex the things Giselle said."

"That can wait," he replied. He paused. "I don't know what I would have done if I'd lost you tonight," he said softly. "I'm glad you came back to me." He wiped a wisp of hair from my forehead and kissed my lips before leaving.

Alex was the last person to come in. She leaned over and kissed my cheek. "Rest, dear. I'm glad you're going to be all right."

"Alex," I began.

"Yes?"

I hesitated. "Never mind. We can talk in the morning."

She nodded and closed the door softly behind her as she left.

Alone in the sitting room with the fire crackling in the grate, I felt a warm sense of relief flood over me, despite the pain from my injuries. I fell into a dreamless sleep under the soft blankets.

I was awakened just a short time later by voices in the foyer. I called out for Pete and he came to the sitting room door.

"Brandt's here," he told me. "Giselle's dead. Her boat crashed into a bridge support. Brandt was on a Coast Guard cutter and saw the wreckage. Giselle was still alive when he found her, clinging to a piece of the boat."

Brandt and Stephan came into the sitting room then. Brandt wore a pained expression on his face.

"I pulled Giselle out of the water," Brandt said. "Before she died, she told me all that she had done. She told me about killing Diana and Forrest too. I'm sorry, Macy, for what she put you through tonight."

Stephan sat down at the end of the sofa. "Macy, Pete told me that Giselle was responsible for the deaths of Diana and Forrest. We haven't told Alex yet. Do you want one of us to tell her?

"I'll tell her," I answered quietly.

Alex came in then, and Stephan got up to let her sit on the sofa.

"Alex, there are some things that you need to know," Stephan began. He looked at me. "Macy can explain."

Alex looked at me, puzzled. "Macy's not well enough to—"

I interrupted her.

"Don't worry about me right now. This is important. Giselle told me some things tonight that you need to hear." I took a deep breath. "Giselle was responsible for the deaths of both Forrest and Diana."

Time seemed to stop as she swallowed hard and clasped her hands together tightly. "Tell me everything."

"Giselle was the one who pushed Forrest down the balcony stairs. She thought he was trying to break up her relationship with Brandt."

"What?" Alex cried. "Forrest would never have done such a thing!"

"Of course not," said Brandt. He looked at her sadly. "He was concerned that Giselle was a little insecure, and he spoke to me about it once. Giselle must have overheard our conversation."

"She did," I confirmed.

"And what about Diana?" Alex asked.

"She pushed Diana into the water because she was jealous of her. She was jealous that Diana was the one Brandt married. She wanted Brandt for herself."

"But Giselle was such a good friend of Diana's! How could she have done such a thing?" Alex closed her eyes and sat very still. Several long moments went by in silence.

Finally Brandt spoke, a slight catch in his voice. "I can't tell you all how sorry I am about everything."

Alex took his hand. "You have nothing to be sorry about. How could you have known what Giselle did? She hid her secrets from all of us. I'm sorry that you've lost someone you cared about."

Brandt blinked his eyes several times. "I think I need to lie down."

"Use my room," suggested Stephan.

We watched him go. There was nothing more to say after that. There would be time for talking in the days to come. Alex went into her room and closed the door. I lay awake listening to the muffled sounds of her sobs, wishing I could help but knowing that Alex needed to face this pain alone.

I awoke the next morning to Alex sitting on the sofa with me.

"I'm going to be okay," she stated.

I smiled. We would all be okay. No more fear, no more threats, no more danger. Healing lay ahead.

EPILOGUE

Many years have passed since that night, and though I try not to, I think about it often.

The leaning tree was toppled in the storm. Alex had mixed feelings when she learned it was gone. So many memories—some joyful, some painful.

I recovered from my physical injuries quickly; the emotional ones would last much longer. I stayed on as Alex's nurse, and she eventually regained the abilities she'd had before her fall. She started painting again, and her old talent is still there. Though she is still tough and spry, she has slowed down a bit. But she still takes walks and loves to tell stories of her childhood. She no longer runs HSH Oil; however, she keeps a close eye on the business.

Vali and Leland never made the move to Pine Island that autumn. They decided abruptly to retire to the Midwest; their belongings were already packed, so they left quickly and quietly. But not before I confronted them about their actions toward me. As it turned out, I finally solved the mystery of my missing photo album. Vali had been the one who took it. Out of curiosity, she said, but I knew better. She had taken the album to intimidate me. And it had been Leland who was spying on me on the balcony on my first day on Hallstead Island.

Their decision to move back to the Midwest was best for everyone. They had been loyal to Alex for many years, but the time had come for them to go. Alex found a wonderful local couple to help her manage her homes.

Stephan continued working closely with Alex, but Will took a job with a different company. At Stephan's urging, he decided that it was time for him to get some experience away from the family business. He eventually came back to take Stephan's job upon his retirement. We still see Stephan and Will from time to time here on the river.

Brandt eventually came to the realization that his relationship with Giselle had not been healthy for either of them. He had been concerned about her behavior for quite some time, but he had been reluctant to discuss it with her. Several years after Giselle's death, he married a wonderful woman, and they visit frequently.

As for Pete and me, he is by my side, helping me to dispel the nightmares that crop up occasionally. We live in Summerplace, but I prefer to call it Hallstead House. I gradually conquered my fear of boats, learned to swim, and have become a proud river rat.

Not long after the attack, Pete showed me an amazing sight. I was enjoying a cup of coffee early one morning when he came in and grabbed my hand, pulling me along as we walked quickly toward the boathouse. When we emerged from the woods, the sun was rising and the surface of the water was covered with a thick layer of mist. It was as if I could step off the island onto a blanket of swirling opaque softness. Pete called it sea smoke; it is a rare treat, he said, a thick fog that forms over the water, usually in the fall. It was a hauntingly beautiful scene, smudging the outlines of the islands and the trees around it like a watercolor. We watched, hand in hand, until the sea smoke gradually lifted and we could see the river clearly again.

Photo by John A. Reade, Jr.

Amy M. Reade grew up in northern New York, just south of the Canadian border, and spent her weekends and summers on the Saint Lawrence River. She attended Cornell University and then went on to law school at Indiana University in Bloomington. She practiced law in New York City before moving to southern New Jersey, where, in addition to writing, she is a wife, a full-time mom, and a volunteer in school, church, and community groups. She lives just a stone's throw from the Atlantic Ocean with her husband and three children as well as a dog, two cats, and a fish. She loves cooking and all things Hawaii and is currently at work on her next novel. Visit her on the web at http://www.amymreade.com and http://amreade.wordpress.com.

3 Loons flying
there's something on your arm

CPSIA information can be obtained at www.ICGtesting.com
Printed in the USA
BVOW08s1814030316

438968BV00001B/8/P

9 781601 833006